Twin-Sun River
An American POW in China

Shouhua Qi

WingsAsClouds Press

Published in the United States of America by

WingsAsClouds Press
An Imprint of the Muse International Press
museinternational01@gmail.com

Library of Congress Control Number: 2011935554
ISBN: 978-0-9838753-0-7

1. Korean War 2. Prisoners of War 4. Cultural Revolution
5. Modern Chinese History 6. US-China Relations

This novel is inspired by real historical events. Twenty-one young American POWs refused repatriation when the armistice was signed to end the Korean War (1950-53), which scandalized America at the time and for years to come. Of the 21 "Turncoat GIs" all but one eventually returned to their homeland. Among the American POWs still unaccounted for, some are believed to be alive today.

Empty hills, no one in sight,
only the sound of someone talking;
last sunlight enters the deep woods,
shining over the green moss again.

Wang Wei (circa 701-761)

Part I
Spring 2001—

1

He hadn't noticed the old couple in the back of the half-filled lecture hall until much later. He was giving a talk about Chinese landscape painting as part of a continuing education program offered by his college to the local community.

"The essence of Chinese landscape painting, in a nutshell," he recapped, after taking a quick glance at his watch, "is the togetherness of humans and the natural world. As you've seen, in almost every one of the slides I've shown you today, either an old man fishing on a moonlit river, or a lone traveler in a misty mountain, the human figure is always tiny, unassuming, in perfect harmony with. . . ."

"Dr. Ding," a young man with shoulder-length hair at the far end of the first row raised his hand when Ding asked the audience if they had any questions. "Chinese art seems deep, mystifying, like Zen itself."

It was Rob, one of Ding's students, who had driven all the way to Seattle to protest the three-day WTO summit a couple of semesters ago. When he came back weeks later, the thin, pale-skinned young man bragged about being forced face down to the cement ground by fully armored riot police. Ding decided to let Rob pass the course even though he had missed the final exam.

"But I've noticed something," Rob continued, arms folded across chest. "If the Chinese are so much into humans and nature being one and stuff, why do we have so many personal seals on almost every one of the slides you've shown today? Isn't there some kind of inconsistency, or contradiction, see what I mean, doc?"

The assistant professor of humanities himself had wondered about that, too. Classic Chinese landscape painting is an art of poetry, calligraphy, painting, and seal engraving, all four in one, its various parts complementing, enriching one another. Somehow, though, Ding suspected that most of the classic artists and nature poets let themselves disappear into their "Peach Orchard outside the World," or Walden, so to speak, only after they had failed to pursue their dreams in whatever human society they happened to be living in. It was more an act of defeat, surrender, and resignation than of voluntary choice. In the heart of their hearts there could be no real peace.

"Rob, good question," the professor said, pacing closer and looking the student in the eye. "But I don't have as great an answer. . . except that no one can live up to the true spirit of Zen. The desire to act, to own, to possess, to leave some kind of mark behind, is as old as humanity. Zen can never be complete, thorough, or absolute, because to be so would mean negation of self, and indeed, negation of life itself, too."

Rob nodded thoughtfully.

The professor smiled, pleased with his ability to think on his feet in a language he didn't start to learn until well past adolescence. He walked back to the lectern and took a few more questions about Chinese art, poetry, Li Bai, Tao Yuanming, Wang Wei, and the monetary value of classic landscape paintings on today's art market.

Then it was over. The audience began to leave. He sighed with relief, turned off the projector, and began to organize the slides when he heard someone from way back in the lecture hall.

"Dr. Ding?" It was an old man lumped in a seat in the last row. His voice suggested nicotine addiction and chronic bronchitis. "Do you think you, the Chinese, will go to war with us, again, ever? I mean, given the spy plane incident, and all?"

Ding was taken aback by the question. For a moment he didn't know what to say. He was conscious of the eyes of several audience members who had stopped to see what was going on. He stuck the slide between his fingers into a random slot in the tray and paced up to the back of the lecture hall.

"I hope not," Ding said as he neared the last row. The old man was half bald. His face was wrinkled with flecks but still had a healthy glow. "I mean why? For what? Hasn't the captain—Lt. Osborne?—and his crew all returned, safe and sound?"

"Sure, but their aircraft remains in the custody of the Chinese, right?"

"The last time I checked, it's on its way home, too."

"Not before it'd been disemboweled and snuffled inside out, though!" interjected a middle-aged man who had been watching from another aisle.

"Don't worry," Ding snapped, smiling. "It'll be dry-cleaned thoroughly, stitched together, and put back to work again."

He heard people chuckle. The middle-aged man shrugged and moved on.

"I don't know," the old man straightened in his seat and said, almost bashfully. "No offence, Dr. Ding. I was only curious." He paused and hesitated. "By the way, I read your op-ed. Good stuff. What's that line, hon?" he turned to the old woman sitting next to him, who murmured something, then to Ding again. "Oh, yeah, something about U.S. and China being entangled in a geopolitical tango, making it impossible not to step on each other's toes. Makes sense. What's the other line, hon? 'A single spark from an unexpected spot may start a hellish, a hellish—"

"—fire, from which neither could escape unscorched." Ding finished the sentence in his head. A reader has just quoted me almost verbatim! Ding was ecstatic. He had written the op-ed on the spur of the moment, though, when the war-talking hoopla after the U.S. reconnaissance plane was forced to land on an island inside China had crescendoed to a dangerous frenzy. He knew that nobody would pay an iota of attention to an op-ed in a small-town paper penned by an unknown humanities professor. Nonetheless, he stared at the ceiling of his bedroom deep into the night the day after he faxed the piece to the Princetown Patriot. What if he was misunderstood? What if someone started a file on him and his words would come back to bite him five, ten years down the road?

When he picked up the paper the next morning, Ding knew it was too late to call the editor's office again.

The lecture hall became self-consciously quiet. Ding could feel the old man's laborious breathing and the intense gaze of his eyes, one of which showing a hint of cataract. Before he could say anything, Rob cried out from somewhere behind.

"If young Americans have to go to war again and get killed in a hellish fire, we damn sure know who to send the thank-you cards to!"

"Hey, what do you know about going to war, young man?" The old man rose suddenly—the plastic seat flipped and hit its back— his hands shaking nervously. His wife pulled the sleeves of his shirt.

"Rob, folks," the professor intervened, "it's getting late. Perhaps another session on this topic later. It's quite a leap from deep mountains, rivers, Zen, to the white-hot zone of war, isn't it? Why don't we leave it on a more peaceful note?"

After a long swing down the hill the narrow road suddenly forked into two directions.   Ding stepped on the brakes and grabbed the sheet on the passenger seat for the tenth time and strained to read the instructions.

Streaked sunbeams had already quit their dance through the penumbra of tall trees and bushes in this part of a county known as the only one in America without a single traffic light. Dusk was thickening fast. More than 40 minutes had passed since he left home, and he was still nowhere within sight of his destination. Now he wondered if he should have said no to the invitation despite the earnestness in the old man's misty eyes, in his voice.

"Fabulous! We'll leave the light on for you!" The old man had grasped his hand warmly when he promised to visit.

The engine of his beat-up Honda Accord station wagon whined onerously as the road wound up into the tall pines of a steep hill. Ding turned on the high beams: watercolor shapes and shadows morphed into realistic landscape instantly. As he reached the top of the hill, an old, white wood-framed house revealed itself under the cloud-accented sky. Its porch light was on.

2

Ding, Tom, and his wife Dora had been eating and chatting and sipping dark beer around the dinner table for more than an hour now. Ding had relished two bowls of chili, a salad, and a large turkey sandwich. The chili tasted almost as good as his favorite spicy Three Delights seafood soup.

The dining room was not big but could sit a family of eight or ten comfortably. The electric range, the black oven, and the cherry cabinets looked passé, but clean. The décor in the living room was minimal. The wood-burning fireplace, wicker chairs, antique-looking lamps, and faded wallpaper gave the place a cozy, safe kind of feel. On the wall along the stairway leading upstairs were mounted several framed black and white family portraits. The entire place had an odor of tobacco that had not completely vaporized, of memories, flimsy, ineffable, of people who had sat at this same dinner table recently and a long, long time ago.

Whenever there was a pause in the small talk, Ding could feel the whole house buzz urgently, incessantly.

"It's the wind, Jie," Tom chuckled. "At this height, it never quits, and it can get real nasty sometimes, I assure you."

A "Wuthering Heights of American make!" comment was on the tip of his tongue. Ding washed it down with another sip from the bottle.

"Jie, sounds exactly like Jay, but it's J-i-e, right?" Dora smiled. The pair of large teardrop earrings with crystal beads glinted as she reached over to clear away the empty plates. Dora's hair had gone silver, but still had a few streaks of iron gray.

Ding nodded. "I like to keep it that way. Somehow."

Tom gave his wife a "What did I tell you, uh?" look. "I respect that," he said.

Tom's parents had built the house with their own hands soon after they got married. It was their dream house. They brought up their three sons and a daughter here. Tom, the first-born of the siblings, bought the house from his parents when they moved, reluctantly, to a nursing home over ten years ago, where the old man died of a stroke not long after and his wife followed soon. Tom's children, all grown up and married with children, were scattered all over the country, east coast and west coast.

"None of them even pretends to be interested in this old house," Dora interjected with a sigh when she came back from the kitchen.

Ding told them a bit about his family, too, his parents, his sister, his wife and his daughter.

"I'm really sorry about your father," Dora said, misty-eyed.

Ding lowered his gaze. A dull pain swept over him again. "At least I had a chance to show him around when he and my mother came to visit in 1998. Believe it or not, he even had a picture taken with Bill Clinton."

"He did not?" Tom exclaimed incredulously. "Bill Clinton! You'll have to excuse me for saying it, but I wouldn't shake the hand of that draft-dodger, intern f—, you know what, even if he'd let me sleep in the Lincoln Bedroom for free!"

"Shame on you, Tommy," protested Dora. "What's wrong with Bill Clinton? Cut the man some slacks, will you?"

"Not Clinton in person," Ding smiled. He felt embarrassed by how passionate people could still get about the former president more than a year after he had vacated the office. "It's only one of those cardboards—you must have seen one of those?—on the top level of the World Trade Center in New York. My father really liked the photo, though."

"Oh," the old man enthused. "If we had known you then, we could have asked Harry, our grandson, to give your folks a guided tour. He works for an investment management company there. Hired before he even graduated from Wharton."

Ding nodded. He was impressed. He thought of Rob, the tall, pale-faced young man, his torn baggy pants, shoulder-length wavy hair, and smiled.

There was a long pause, as if they each were pursuing a private thought of their own.

"Want another beer?" the old man said, looking up.

Ding eyed the half-empty bottle in hand. "No. . . thanks. I'm the only designated driver tonight, you know."

Tom and Dora chuckled.

"Let me show you something, then, Jie," Tom stood up and said.

"You sure, hon?" Dora looked up from her chair, searched in the face of her husband—who shrugged—and turned to Ding with a resigned look in her eyes.

Tom breathed audibly as he led the way down the long staircase winding to the basement. The light was dim, the air dank, musty.

Ding wondered what Tom had to show him as he followed the old man navigating through old sofas, dressers, tables, chairs, bikes, boxes, lawn tools, and a thousand other things randomly piled on top of each other, almost touching the ceiling of loosely fit fiberglass-batts.

"When you've lived to my age," Tom coughed, "between inheriting and emptying your wallet senselessly, you'll be buried in just as much junk, if not more."

"I know," Ding offered his sympathy. *Who in America can I inherit from anyway?*

Tom pulled a string hanging from the ceiling at the far corner of the basement. A bright light came on.

In the well-lit corner was an area the size of a small office, which featured a table, two chairs, a small TV set with a VCR, an IBM computer, a fax machine, and an old-fashioned rotary phone. On the L-shaped brick walls were posted browned newspaper clippings. A third wall was made of two bookshelves loaded with folders and bags and a pile of overstuffed computer paper boxes.

An oasis of order in a world of apparent chaos and neglect. A mini-command center for some secret operations? Ding was intrigued.

On the brick wall of the "command center" was a big photo of a uniformed young man on the front page of a newspaper whose name was only too familiar. The headline read:

Native Son Yet to Return Home

"My kid brother," the old man said. "Isn't he handsome?"

The young man in the picture looked no more than 20 years old. He grinned happily to whoever was taking the picture. Ding sensed something else in the young man's deep-set eyes, something he couldn't put his finger on. A kind of intensity. A glimmer of some ardent emotion that could still burst to flames despite the best effort to extinguish it. Anger, perhaps.

Other headlines from the local paper and the New York Times, Washington Post, and Wall Street Journal caught Ding's eye, too:

American Boys Refuse To Come Home
21 Turncoats
Diabolic Brainwashing Suspected

All of the clippings, browned by the smoldering fire of time, looked so brittle that at the mere touch of a finger they would all peel off and drift down in ashen pieces. Next to the fax machine on the table were a few folders; the one on the top, the thinnest, had Ding's name on it. *Somebody has indeed started a file on me!* Ding was surprised.

"Oh, that," Tom lowered his voice, confidentially, "is classified information." Noticing the look in Ding's face, he laughed. "Just kidding. Nothing but a clipping of your masterpiece."

"For a moment I thought—"

The old man picked up a faded burgundy photo album and opened it.

"See?" He pointed at a large family portrait on the first page. Despite the encroaching dirty yellow all around its edges the picture still looked sharp enough. "That's my parents, my two brothers, me, and my sister."

As Tom turned the pages of the album, the story of his family, and of his kid brother, unfolded slowly.

Dora lumbered down once with coffee and tea, but both the narrator and his audience were so engrossed in the story that neither touched his cup on the table.

By the time they finished, sort of, and started to climb back to the first floor, it was already past midnight.

Ding was still dazed as he drove back home. When he finally pulled into the garage, Ding shut the engine and sat in the car for a few long seconds before picking up a super-sized manila envelope from the passenger seat.

He didn't turn on the light. He knew where everything was at home. His eyes having adjusted, he found his way upstairs. Passing Emily's room, he noticed light coming from under her door. The muffled sound of drums and pieces of heavy metal colliding into each other in a maddening rhythm slithered through. He knocked on the door gently and walked on. Kids nowadays. Why don't they listen to music?

The door of his study was half open. He walked in and dropped the manila envelope on the writing desk. He stood there, as if undecided, then pulled open a bottom drawer, and stuffed the envelope in.

In the dimness of night, he could make out the shape of his wife under the quilt. It stirred and became motionless again. He undressed slowly, lifted his side of the quilt, and slipped in quietly.

Julie turned in her sleep and placed her smooth, warm naked leg across his thighs. He let it stay there without moving, until Julie withdrew the leg and turned to her side of the bed again.

3

Ding had difficulty focusing during the week that had just passed.
He had missed the exit to his college three days in a row and
had to drive on till the next exit in heavy morning traffic before he
could turn around. Am I getting old? He would wonder, infuriated
with himself, as he stepped on the gas.

He had celebrated his 40th birthday only two years ago, a
surprise party organized by Julie. Age 40. That should mark the
beginning of the proverbial state of no confusion, if the sagacious
Confucius really knew what he was talking about. Ding thought he
had entered the Land of No Confusion a long time before that. He
hadn't exactly searched or negotiated for it. He had crashed onto
its hard ground and had kicked and cried and almost died trying to
get out at the time but to no avail.

Okay, he would be the first one to admit that he wasn't the best
at directions. But the exit to his own college that he had used daily
for the last six years?

And he was still prone to impulse and rushing to action now
and then, as in the case of faxing the op-eds to the Princetown
Patriot without having weighed all the pros and cons and possible
consequences. But he was never confused, and he was always able
to focus. At least he had thought so.

How many times during the past week had Ding caught his
mind drifting into incoherent, disjointed thoughts as he was
driving from home to school and back home, as he was showing
slides of Saint Peter's Basilica, the Great Wall, and Maya temples
in dimmed classrooms, as he was staring at hosts of late spring
daffodils, tulips, and a whole lot of other perennials and evergreen
shrubs quivering under mid-day sun in the quaint little garden

outside his office window?

And he couldn't focus in bed, either.

That was nothing new. He had been resigned to this debilitation for three or four years by now. He couldn't remember when exactly it had started. He didn't think it had anything to do with him approaching the mystic 40th landmark at the time, either. Physically he was fine. He wasn't a health freak or an athletic type but could still jump and deliver a kick on the chin of a taller, formidable adversary if the threat of bodily harm was imminent, one of the *kungfu* moves he had learnt when a teenager.

It was, rather, the accumulative effect of numerous little things: faint half-flushes when talking to people or being talked to, calling up the "spot of joy" on her cheeks with a frequency and non-exclusiveness that he didn't feel comfortable with, giggling and chattering on the phone as if there were no tomorrow, going on week-long new technology training programs with loud business associates of hers, Jerry, Deborah, Ronnie, Shawn, and what-is-his-name, sometimes a whole bunch of them together, sometimes in the intimate space of the same vehicle with only one or two from the bunch, and . . . and her hand resting on her partner's shoulder, her eyes locking him in such a warm gaze while waltzing on the floor, the slicks of her *qipao* revealing a sizable segment of her long, slender leg. Occasionally, though, he would surprise, no, shock, both Julie and himself and attack with savage ferocity, when lying next to her warm body and imagining hotel room scenes of her and her male associates set his own body ablaze with desire. Julie would hold his back and pull him down like someone drowning, her face being twisted beyond recognition, and Ding had to cover her mouth with his hand so their daughter would not hear them from her room. Afterwards he would roll out of bed and go take a shower, feeling both proud and ashamed. When he returned, Julie, not covered by anything yet would still be staring at the ceiling with such a look in her eyes, her cheeks still rosy with a sort of afterglow, as if she were clinging to a dream that was fading away, and fading away for sure without leaving behind a signal when it would return.

One early evening Julie had caught him staring outside the window of his study at home when she stepped in to retrieve the investment folders from one of the cabinets and update their gains and losses according to the day's Dow Jones and NASDAQ figures.

"What?" She mumbled in Chinese, flipping through the files in a folder. "Being touched to tears by sunset? It'll rise again tomorrow, I bet you a thousand dollars."

He kept his gaze outside the window.

"So, *Da-jiao-shou*, Big Prof, of Princetown College above sharing with his uneducated wife now, that it?" Julie switched to a hybrid of Chinese and English, a speech she'd adopt whenever she needed to be more expressive, to show her excitement, or displeasure. "I got news for you, *Da-jiao-shou*: Princetown? No Princeton. Need not put on airs!"

"What are you talking—" Ding murmured in protest, crawling back from whatever labyrinth of dreams he had lost himself in, but Julie was already stomping out of the study with the folders.

Julie had a temper and a tongue that could lash and sting when provoked. When did that start? Ding couldn't recall, either. The long brewing of little things, too?

In the stream of disjointed thoughts, though, there had been one consistent, coherent theme that would assert and reassert itself:

The look in the eyes of Tom's father. Like a pair of candles that had burnt close to the end, they flickered, streaked with large, messy teardrops, struggling to hold on to something still burning deep inside, a lingering, sputtering ray of hope, knowing only too well that the end was coming, and coming fast.

And his faltering voice as he hunched in the ancient wicker chair in the living room of discolored wallpaper and fumbled through a speech of welcome just in case one day his long-lost son would return and he wouldn't be there to give the son a bear hug and pat him on the cheek.

Between sniffles and tears and handkerchief, the old man's wife of 50 years, frosty hair, her small, wrinkled body barely filling the wicker chair, couldn't get out one complete sentence.

The videotape had apparently aged. The picture and sound quality couldn't compare to what people could get with digital technology that had just become a rage among consumers. Ding was shaken. He thought of his own parents' farewell speech he had recorded with a new Sony digital camcorder the night before they were to return to China. His father had said that he would love to come and visit again.

Could he have said no to Tom?

"I'm not ready to tape something like this yet," Tom had said, lighting the first and only cigarette of the evening, his hands shaking visibly ("You mind?"). Ding was conscious of the old man's gaze on his face, of a ray of light shining through the cloudy surface of his eyes as he spoke. "I'm not ready to quit. Not yet, at least not without giving it one last try. When I'm gone, who else in my family will carry it on? It'll be forgotten soon enough, I assure you. Like this country has forgotten it since a long time ago, as if it had never happened. I mean nobody really cares. Young people nowadays, you know how they are, Dr. Ding, I mean Jie, probably have never even heard of that ugly war. I can't go and see my pop and mother without something definitive about my kid brother, either way, can I?"

Ding shook his head and turned his eyes to the young man grinning happily in the big, browned picture on the wall. Now he knew what it was that burned beneath that pair of deep-set eyes. Sort of. He wouldn't really know until he had a chance to meet the kid brother (who must be in his early 70s by now!) face to face. Even then he might never really know. Most probably he would never have such a chance. He was not delusional. When he turned his head back, the old man's eyes were still on his face. Could he have said no? Yet if the US government, the Army, the Defense Department, and numerous Congressional delegations, powerful agencies, and advocacy organizations, had all failed to give Tom's family, and the families of hundreds of other Korean War POWs still unaccounted for, any hope toward a definitive answer all these last forty, fifty some years, what could he, an assistant professor of a small liberal arts college in the middle of nowhere, do? Besides, whatever trail there once was of Tom's brother, it must have been cold by now. Buried deep in the dust of time. And, Ding all but blurted out the thought, why me? What can I do, really?

And he had, nonetheless, nodded and promised to do whatever he could before realizing what he had committed himself to. A vague sense of the weight of his promise, though, came over him when the old man placed the big manila envelope in his hands.

"Jie, honestly, sometimes I feel hopeless, ready to give it all up and move on." Tom said when they finally rose from their chairs in the basement. "Other times, I still see hope, a ray of hope, like when I came across your op-ed. I don't really know why. Perhaps I was hoping that you might be able to reach people in China who know people that know something. Don't feel obligated, though. Just give that hope of a desperate old man whatever it is worth, a last shot. No more."

And no less, Ding had promised himself.

4

The family of three sat at a table inside Royal Garden, the only decent Chinese restaurant in Princetown, to celebrate. Celebrating what? Ding wondered. His daughter's talent, of course, and her burgeoning womanhood, flaunted at her high school's "Talent Show" only an hour ago? Emily and a few other girls, scantily clothed in glossy black miniskirts and tight, sleeveless low-cuts, twisting their young bodies on the stage cheered on by oceanic waves of dark, satanic music and beastly screams from a few males in the packed auditorium? Ding shook his head again in disbelief.

"What is it, Dad?" Emily looked up from her egg drop.

"Nothing," Ding said while shaking more dark pepper into his Three Delights seafood soup.

"As if I don't know what you're thinking!"

"Don't mind him," Julie grunted from across the table. "He been acting weird lately."

"Dad's always been weird, right, Dad? Admit it."

"Sure, I'm the family's closet weirdo who's just had a big coming out—" Ding said with an exaggerated confessional tone.

"Dad!"

Nobody said anything again during the rest of the meal. The entire restaurant had only a few other customers still eating and chatting, mostly in subdued tones. At a table not far from the Dings' sat two young women who had already finished but hadn't paid yet. One of them, a bit on the heavy side, large eyes, pale skin, hunched toward her friend across from her and talked animatedly, an exact copy of the repackaged Monica Lewinsky being interviewed by Barbara Walters in a not-too-distant past. Servers and bus-persons were more than halfway through cleaning and setting up tables for the following day.

Ding was the first one to finish. As always. He sipped more tea even though it tasted so flat, leftoverish, and watched Julie and Emily nibbling the food in their plates.

"May I have your attention please, ladies," Ding said suddenly; the smile in his voice was only a partial success. "I need to tell you something."

Julie and Emily looked up at the same time.

"I think. . . I need to visit China again."

"What?" Julie's eyes opened as big as the bronze-accented light hanging above their table. "When? You visited China last summer!"

"Yeah, didn't you, Dad?"

Ding had caught himself by surprise, too. *Why have I chosen this moment to tell them?*

"For how long?" Julie asked.

"I don't know," Ding faltered, "a couple of months, perhaps. Or a bit longer."

"What? Whole summer? You crazy?" Julie's eyeballs looked ready to jump out of their sockets. Little honey waiting for you in China?"

"Mom!" Emily said as she eyed the table neighboring theirs ("Monica Lewinsky" was deciding how much tip to leave on the table, having checked her confession session with a semi colon) and servers and bus-persons were watching blankly in their direction. "Lower your voice!"

"I need to see my mother again." Ding lied, but it wasn't a complete lie.

"Grandma fine," Julie said. "What you worry about? Uh? She living in a brand new apartment and only five bus-stops from your sister lives!"

Julie hadn't objected to Ding's idea of buying his mother the apartment after his father had died. To balance things somewhat, Julie suggested, which Ding supported whole-heartedly, sponsoring a fully funded three-week SMT (Singapore-Malaysia-Thailand) vacation for her father and mother armed with a new digital camera and camcorder and whatever they needed to make it a memorable experience. It was a sort of retirement gift for Professor Zhu although the old man still supervised about ten graduate students any given semester.

"Yeah, Dad, the whole summer?" Emily's eyes were still on his face. Ding had never been away from his daughter for longer than a month since she and her mother came to join him in 1990. "That's quite a long time, right?"

"Can't believe this!" Julie glared at him. "Whole summer. I thought you going to teach this summer. How many classes? Three? Three thousand dollars per class, right? Ten grand altogether. One full year college tuition for Emily!'"

"Mom!" Emily begged. "Don't exaggerate. And please lower your voice."

Even though Emily hadn't made up her mind about a major, there was no doubt that she'd go for the Ivy League schools. Given their two-income situation and the college financial aid formulas they had tried online, the Dings couldn't hope for anything more than ten thousand dollars' worth of loans and scholarships combined. That would cover less than a third of the tuition and fees any of those schools would charge.

"Be a proud Princetown College student, then," Ding had teased when they discussed the issue after the Dow Jones, NASDAQ, and dom.com bubbles had burst and Lucent, AOL, Sun Microsystems, and a dozen other of Julie's favorite high-tech stocks crashed. "As my daughter you'll be entitled to a 75% discount. That's money for two brand new Lexus like your mom's just bought."

"It's not funny, Dad."

"Emily going to Princetown College," Julie had sneered. "Where the heck Princetown College?"

It was a lame joke. Even he himself wasn't too proud of Princetown College.

"No wonder you acting weird recently," Julie muttered, her eyes now glued to the teacup in front of her as if trying to decipher some code in the color patterns glazed near its brim. "Must be little honey. Know that saying in China nowadays? Men be bad the instant they become rich; women to become rich have to be bad. Something like that."

Speaking of bad women! Ding retorted in his mind. "You know I'm not rich."

"But you rich in the eyes of young gold-diggers in China, *Da-jiao-shou!*"

"Mom!" Emily intervened again. "Yeah, Dad, you're Ding *Jiao-shou*, Professor Ding. Princetown or Princeton, what difference would that make to them?"

"Okay," Ding straightened in his chair and folded his arms on his chest. "You really want to know? I'll tell you why if you really want to know."

Ding told them about Tom, his kid brother, and his parents. The gist of a long, convoluted story.

For a while his wife and daughter sat there and listened and didn't even make any sound breathing.

"What a story," Emily looked up when Ding finished. "It'd be noble of you if it were true, and a good cause—"

"It is true, every word and comma and quotation mark of the whole thing!" Ding sipped from the teacup again. It tasted unbearably stale.

"You expect me believe this?" Julie's eyebrows knit together.

Ding nodded affirmatively.

Tom had offered, most sincerely, to reimburse him for all the expenses and lost income. Moreover, Tom and his family would love to contribute to Emily's college education if Ding's efforts would lead to definitive closure about his long lost brother, one way or the other.

Ding decided against letting the other two members of his family in on the offer. He wanted to save Julie the embarrassment of an about face change of attitude.

Emily's eyes continued to look for tell-tale signs in her dad's face. Julie turned hers away as if looking for a window to see how late it was outside. These Chinese restaurants. They all looked like some abandoned warehouses renovated with a shoestring budget.

"I can give you the address and phone number for verification, my dear closet FBI agents," he tried to joke again.

The two dear "FBI agents" gave him a dirty look at the same time.

The waitress came with the bill and three fortune cookies and left with the empty plates, teapot, cups, and anything else that was messy and wrinkled on the table.

"You hoping my dad help you, right?" Julie turned her eyes back to Ding. "If I believe your story for a second."

Ding nodded vaguely. He must have thought of his father-in-law when he said yes to Tom about a week ago: the old professor, at the time a college sophomore, was among the tens of thousands of Chinese People's Volunteers who crossed the small steel bridge on the Yalu River under the cover of darkness on October 25, 1950.

Julie picked up a fortune cookie between her long fingers, opened it, and read slowly: "A lost ounce of gold may be found; a lost moment of time never." She frowned.

Emily reached for one of the remaining two cookies and opened hers: "Your future will be limited only by your own timidity."

"Mmmm," Ding mocked, "The sky will be the only limit for Emily then, right?"

"Dad!"

Ding grinned and put his credit card next to the bill and sat back in his chair.

"Dad? Your turn!"

"Okay," Ding picked up the last cookie in the plate, tore it open, and read his fortune, with affected enthusiasm: "A life without romantic adventures is a life not worth living at all.'"

Julie gave him another dirty look, grabbed her purse, and walked out, ignoring the "Good night!" and "Thank you!" and "Come again!" from the waitress who came to pick up the bill and the credit card, and the owner who was busy organizing things at the register.

"Nice going, Dad," Emily stood up, too, "Really nice, Dad."

5

Julie used to take charge of packing whenever the family was going somewhere. Even if Ding had already packed for a conference or something, she would take everything out and rearrange according to her concept of organization, distribution, and aesthetics. She hadn't done so this time. In fact, she hadn't packed for him for quite some time now. The accumulative effect of little things during the last few years too.

The evening before his departure, when he had just squeezed everything into the hard-cased bag, Julie sailed in and threw something on his desk. A small plastic packet with two silhouetted human figures locked in a frenzied embrace.

"It come in handy when *Da-jiao-shou* and his little honey, you know," Julie tried to project genuine concern in her voice, yet the martyrdom look in her moist eyes betrayed how she really felt. "Have all fun in the world you want. Just not bring anything funny back home."

The trio, Ding, Julie, and Emily, tagged onto a long line at the Air China check-in.   They didn't talk.   Their eyes would meet occasionally. When that happened, Emily would hold the eye contact to see who would blink first; Julie would dart her eyes away and let them wander around as if she were looking for someone.

Finally, it was Ding's turn. He handed his ticket along with the passport and Green Card to the Air China agent. He hadn't applied for citizenship yet. He was in no hurry. He wanted to wait until he was emotionally ready. Both Julie and Emily had received their naturalization certificates and letters of congratulations from their congressmen earlier this year. Their oath ceremony was set for early September.

"Be careful, Dad," Emily had said the day she and her mother received the long-awaited documents. "Anything you say and do at home now on will and can have international repercussions."

"Dad, don't forget us," Emily said while hugging him before he boarded the plane. She stepped aside and nudged her mother forward.

Ding hesitated, then gathered Julie in his arms, clumsily, and bent to print a kiss on her rouged cheek.

Ding hadn't spent the last few days before departure imagining a rendezvous with his phantom little honey. Instead, he had gone through the files in the big envelope Tom had trusted to him and searched through microfilms and microfiches in the college library which few people cared to use much nowadays. By now Ding had garnered enough information to sketch out a contour of the Korean War for his students if the topic would ever come up in one of his classes:

North Korean People's Army crossed the 38th Parallel on June 25, 1950 to "liberate" their brethren in the South and, within months, drove the South Korean army to Pushan, a port city near the southern tip of the peninsula;

Gen. Douglas MacArthur staged a near impossible invasion at Inchon on September 15, 1950, and soon pushed the North Koreans back to their side of the 38th Parallel.

Tens of thousands of "Chinese People's Volunteers"—among them a college sophomore who would become Ding's father-in-law many years later—marched across the Yalu River between China and North Korea under the cover of night October 25, that same year.

The ensuing offensive and counteroffensive campaigns went on for the next two years resulting in more heavy casualties than clear victory for either side.

The tug-of-war during the armistice negotiations in a small village called Panmunjom dragged on, one of the thorny points on the table being whether to repatriate all POWs or to allow them to go anywhere they wanted to.

On this thorny point the American side eventually won because when the armistice was signed thousands of North Korean and Chinese POWs didn't choose to go home.

On this the American side lost, in a way, too, because 21 young American GIs refused to be repatriated and chose to go to Red China.

America was scandalized. Stunned. Despite the apparent inconsequential number of 21 compared to the thousands on the other side.

How could these American boys, brought up in the freest, richest country in the world, educated in schools that taught not only reading and writing and arithmetic, but also George Washington, the Declaration of Independence, and the Pledge of Allegiance to the flag, all trained in the army that had defeated Hitler and put Old Glory on Iwo Jima, Okinawa, and elsewhere in the world—how could they have chosen to turn their backs on family and friends, home and country, to embrace the way of life of the enemy they had fought on battlefields?

The Communists must have concocted some evil tricks to scrub the minds of these vulnerable young American boys clean of what they had been brought up to believe in—some kind of demonic psychological surgery, indeed.

This theory was readily clasped by so many puzzled Americans who were dying for explanations, Ding couldn't help smiling as he recalled scenes from *The Manchurian Candidate* he had checked out from Blockbuster only days ago. The film was quite engrossing and Ding was more than convinced of Frank Sinatra's talent as an actor. Nothing else.

Or, as some pensive psychiatrists figured, there must have been something quirky in the upbringing of these young men that had made them particularly susceptible to Red China's brainwashing games: poverty, alcoholism, crime, syphilis, polio, cancer, low IQ, and so on. These young men must have been sick, "diseased," somehow, because there was nothing in America—its culture and socioeconomic system—that would have caused their defection.

Another interesting theory, Ding thought. Several of the 21 "turncoats"—as they were dubbed contemptuously—did come from slum and poor rural backgrounds and broken families. He wondered, though, that if this theory held, its reverse would have to be true, too: People growing up in privileged socioeconomic environments and "happy" families were somehow immune to anything that would be deemed, even remotely, unorthodox or heretic. How would this theory explain Sgt. Richard Corden of Providence, RI, one of the leaders of the 21 defectors, who had an IQ of 134? Ding had never had an IQ test, but his daughter did: 136, which made Emily eligible for the gifted program offered by Provincetown West High—not much of a gifted program if anyone were to ask Ding what he thought of it. Emily's IQ had failed as a foolproof safety lock and failed spectacularly. She had fallen for the most heretic "contemporary" dance her dad had ever seen, its satanic tunes and lyrics and all, despite the best "classic" education he had tried his best to provide.

Maybe, just maybe, there was something in those tunes and lyrics, something subliminal, that he wasn't able to appreciate because they were intelligible only to people with an IQ of 136 and higher?

"Dad, now you sound more like a prof. from Princeton!" He could picture Emily's eyes sparkling with a knowing smile.

The bone-shattering shake having subsided, the engines quieting down to an easy hum, the Boeing 747 was now cruising thousands of feet above the blue waters of Long Island Sound toward the open sea.

Emily's IQ, Ding wondered, did she get it from her dad or her mom? And her folly. He couldn't in clear conscience take all the credit for the good things in Emily and let Julie take the blame for their daughter's imperfections. After all, Emily was the daughter they had created between themselves and nobody else.

In the days and months after the 21 American young men went to China, their mothers, and indeed the mothers of hundreds of other American POWs, took a beating from pundits, army analysts, and people in powerful positions. A book called Generation of Vipers by a popular writer advanced the theory that American mothers of the modern times, being liberated from the chore of raising a large family and keeping house by the advent of home appliances, now had time to dote on their sons, who grew up being "mamma's boys," weak both emotionally and physically. It was as good as saying that these young soldiers never outgrew some twisted Oedipal complex they suffered during their pampered childhood. Some of these people went so far as to blame American mothers for all social ills plaguing the country at the time: alcoholism, suicide, schizophrenia, neurosis, impotency, homosexuality, and promiscuity. An Army sergeant, as quoted in a Saturday Evening Post article, dismissed those POWs who had collaborated with their captors as spoiled and pampered kids: They had "no guts here"—the sergeant pointed at his belly—"or here"—pointing at his head. "Too much mamma."

Talking about adding insult to injuries. Ding thought. As if these mothers hadn't suffered enough. Most of the mothers of the 21 American boys were struggling through a very tough life and were not in a position to pamper their sons anyway. At least three of the 21 "turncoats" had served during WWII and received a Bronze Star for heroism: a Cpl. Howard Adams from Texas, a Cpl. Andrew Fortune from Michigan, and another one whose name

Ding couldn't recall at the moment.

Eventually, all but one of the 21 "turncoats" became disillusioned and returned to their family and country.

After the midnight snack—a tiny piece of sweetish bread—and the last page of Virginia Pasley's 21 Stayed, Ding turned off his light.

The airplane buzzed quietly in semi-darkness. Most passengers were drowsing uncomfortably in their crammed seats. Dozing off in the seats next to his were an elderly couple, Isaac, a retired rabbi, and his wife Ruth, going to China for an international conference on a recent discovery of an early Jewish settlement in Xinjiang.

Ding tilted the seat all the way back and tried to fall asleep too.

Of the 21 American GIs who refused repatriation, 16 were Protestants of various denominations, four Roman Catholics, one Greek Catholic. How did religion figure in each of these young Americans' decisions? What about Tom's kid brother? Where would he fit in all this?

A brilliance flashed across his closed eyes. Ding opened his eyes lazily and saw lightning through an uncovered window. Another crazed lightning shot up the sky in the far distance. Nobody else seemed to have noticed. Ding fell back in the seat and tried to have some sleep again.

6

So many new high-rises, glassy, shimmering under the misting glow of early morning sun, whole forests of them, having sprung up since he passed through this city not too long ago, some burgeoning from the foundations, some arising halfway into the sky, and many already reaching their staggering summits all but ready for the ribbon-cutting ceremonies to begin; movie-screen sized in-your-face billboards along the expressways vying for attention: GE, GM, Citibank, Microsoft, Marlboro, KFC, McDonald's, vistas of Pu Dong New District, new Euro-American styled residential compounds, and brand new golf courses of lush green; small, modest domestics alongside of much cockier BMWs, Lexuses, Cadillacs, and Lincoln Town Cars with tinted windows, all caught in the same endless streams, moving forward in uneasy, spasm fashions, honking and jostling unpredictably between lanes to overtake their peers . . . Minus the Chinese characters and Ding could fancy himself still in New York rather than Shanghai. All seemed like in a dream.

His taxi driver from the airport, a man in his 30s, helped Ding place the large luggage in the trunk of his Santana, a sedan manufactured by a joint venture called Shanghai Volkswagen. With a neat crew cut, a pair of white gloves, the man was efficient and taciturn, the very picture of practiced professionalism.

The moment Ding stepped out of the Santana at the train station an hour later, a group of men and women—all with rollers, carrying poles, or simply ropes, all looking sunbaked, tired yet eager—swarmed over, grabbed the straps of his carryon and the handle of the hard-cased bag, and pulled in seven, eight directions at the same time.

"Hands off, all of you, now!" Ding hollered like a military police ready to shoot to kill anyone who dared to disobey the order, took a quick glance at the mob, all shocked by his sudden outburst, and pointed at an older man. "You!" The rest of the mob, mumbling protests of the arbitrary, unfair decision, rushed to meet other taxis arriving with fresh hope of work and income for the day.

The man Ding had hired on the spot was in his early 60s, short, wiry, muscles visible in his arms and legs. He had a single-wheeled pushcart which squeaked on the rough pavement outside the train station.

The waiting hall for his train was packed with businesspeople carrying important briefcases, tired travelers who looked as if they hadn't slept for days, and sweaty migrant workers holding onto their personal belongings stuffed in used plastic bags. They were all going somewhere, big cities, small towns, east and west, as announced by the train schedules flashing across a large electronic panel.

Ding found a "seat" in one of those long, crowded rows of hard benches and sat down. Across from him was a young woman, not strikingly pretty or anything, but her features—her clear eyes, pointed nose, and her small mouth—were all neatly placed. Her skin, soft, pale, showed only a hint of makeup. What made her stand out was her clothing. All pink. A pink blouse of some fine material Ding couldn't name, finely tailored with cloth buttons and embroidered laces. Pink skirts, which reached down to her knees, just enough to reveal her shapely long legs with translucent panty hoses. A pair of slipper-like pink shoes with exquisitely needled patterns. And a large, silky pink cape spread around her young shoulders. The look in her eyes was blank, faraway, oblivious to whatever was going on around her in this noisy, sweltering waiting hall. Next to her shapely leg was an expensive looking carryon, also pink, and a flashy, pinkish bag from some expensive shopping plaza; atop the half-filled shopping bag was a hardcover book: Health and Nutrition During Pregnancy.

She looked like a bride—Ding thought. If so, where was her groom? Her husband? Her family? Who sent her on this trip all by herself?

Oh, yes, Ding suddenly realized, she could be one of those little honeys of some obscenely rich upstarts, rich not owing to their creativity, enterprise, honest hard work, but through contacts and loopholes and abuse of power; she had become an inconvenience and was being sent back to her own parents.

Ding was no fiction writer but had enough imagination to fill in all the details—flowers and jewelries and tears and sobs and false promises and threats and all roiling underneath that pair of pretty, bored eyes—enough details to fill the pages of a full-blown novel.

All this while, as he was imagining the story which led the young woman to the seat across from him, Ding was carrying on a small chat with the old porter. Or rather, the old porter was monologuing about his parents who had died when he was still a little boy, about the 30 years of lonely life in a poor, inland province where he was banished, about the relatives who wouldn't want to have anything to do with him when he finally returned to Shanghai, unmarried, childless.

It was quite a walk along the platform. For some time, Ding was conscious of the "little honey" in pink among the crowd, pulling her small carryon behind her. When he boarded the train at the far end of the platform, he turned one last time: she was gone.

The old porter sweated profusely as he dragged the heavy trunk onto the train and lifted it onto the rack. Ding pulled out two 20-yuan notes from his wallet. The old man took the money, checked, and handed one 20-yuan—wet with his sweat—back to him.

Seven hours later, Ding was at the door of his in-laws. When it was opened, Ding thought he had perhaps made a mistake, thanks to jet lag and the fierce streaks of a setting sun slanting in through the hallway window.

"You must be Jie, I mean, Dr. Ding," the young woman said in English, perfect American accent. "C'mon in!"

She opened the door wider and reached to grab the handle of the heavy trunk.

"I'm good," he said bravely and carried the luggage to the middle of the living room as if it were nothing at all.

She looked familiar. He must have seen her somewhere. Like Samantha, a brainy student in his Humanities 101, except that this woman looked a couple of years more mature. The warm gaze, which was saying "I care about you," reminded him of Rachel, Emily's best friend, but not quite. Yes, more like the Helen Hunt in As Good As It Gets, except that she looked more cultured and except that she was a brunette. Her hair, effusive, several inches over the shoulder, rippled gently under the breeze of the ceiling fan.

Professor Zhu, his father-in-law, was pleasantly surprised. His hair, combed all the way back, was as thin and gray as Ding saw him the last time, his voice as loud and hearty.

"What's wrong with you, Jie? Why didn't you let us go to Shanghai to—"

"Oh, look at you!" Ding's mother-in-law hurried out from the kitchen with a big smile on her face. "All sweat and dirt and. . . Go and take a shower and change so we can all sit down and eat. I happen to have prepared a few—"

With that, she hastened back to the kitchen.

Somehow Ding and Julie's mother had never warmed up to each other, much against the old adage of mothers being always fond of their sons-in-law. Mrs. Zhu had retired for years now from a job at the Propaganda Department of the Provincial Government. She took much pride in her cooking skills, which, Ding had always felt, were a bit exaggerated.

"Professor Zhu," "Helen Hunt" said. Her Chinese had only a slight trace of foreign accent. "I'll have to run now. I'll come another time."

She turned and shook Ding's hand, her warm gaze on him.

"I've heard so much about you," she said in English. "By the way, I'm Greta."

"Jie. Nice to meet you, Greta," Ding tried to sound like a Princetown College professor. "Hope it's not all bad things."

"Not at all. Professor Zhu is most proud of you!" she turned to Professor Zhu. "Right?"

"What do you think?!" the old man beamed. His English, though slow, was clear and sure. "I was the one who set him up with my daughter . . . Hahaha."

Greta. Yes, she had a hint of Greta Garbo in her, too. Her voice was a bit low in pitch, like a clarinet, although she didn't speak English with a European—Swedish?—accent.

Greta picked up her things—a few books and a stack of paper—from the glass top coffee table, smiled, and turned to leave.

Ding opened the door for her and watched her and Professor Zhu slowly walk downstairs. Before he closed the door, the phone rang. Loud. Persistent. Almost impatient. He hastened back and picked up the cordless on the coffee table.

"Hello?"

7

The cemetery was on a large hillside covered with pines and evergreens. It was a sea of tombstones, rows and rows of them, each marked with the names and dates and pictures of the dearly departed. As Ding and his mother made their way up the steep hill, he caught glimpses of families laying wreaths here and burning paper money there and bowing to pay respects further down. The air, being broiled by an overzealous sun, was muggy, drowsing. Ding was startled when suddenly there came the shrill wail of a popular festival song blasting from brass instruments leading a small procession on its slow, sad journey uphill.

By the time they found themselves in front of the right tombstone, Ding was soaked in sweat. His mother, a retired teacher, was gasping for air, too.

Father gazed at him kindly, as usual. Ding loved the old man. He remembered sitting in his lap learning his first characters with flash cards, riding on his bicycle to go and fly the paper planes they folded together, watching his Adam's apple moving up and down rhythmically while reading from "little people" cartoon books for his children. And he had despised him, too. How many times had they fought since he was a young adolescent? Over nothing, really. Government policies, sometimes. He despised his father for having to agree with whatever the newest government policies happened to be, new policies that nullified policies issued by the same government only days ago that nullified . . .

"You're too young, Jie, too ignorant to appreciate!" father would declare, his voice trembling with anger, and frustration.

"You're just too spineless!" was on the tip of the son's tongue, but he had to swallow it. He didn't have the guts, and the heart, to say it. He had seen father being forced to kneel on shards of broken glass by the Red Guards, with a heavy blackboard hanging from his neck from a thin wire, and to shout slogans to "down with" himself. He had stood by the curbside watching father being paraded through the street donning a tall cone-shaped hat, his name on the hat being condemned in bloody red ink.

Still, he had despised his father. Pitied him. Loved him. And hated him.

Ding stood in front of father's tomb speechless, tearless. His mind went blank. Mother sobbed quietly as she cleaned the headstone with a towel she had brought along. As he bent to pull the weeds that had grown from cracks in the cement cover, he felt a sudden rush of soreness in his nose, in his eyes; he struggled to hold it back.

"Jie," his mother said when they turned to leave.

"What, Ma?"

"You and your dad, whatever between you—" mother sighed and stopped.

On the way home Ding surprised himself by telling the taxi driver to make a stop at father's—his, too—middle school. Suddenly, from nowhere, came this urgent desire to see the place he hadn't visited since graduation, a few plain brick and shingle structures in a blue-collar section of the city surrounded by crowded alleys, small mills, and unsightly sewage ditches. Ding could still picture the school yard teeming with wild weeds during those hot summer days, of him and his classmates reciting through the Little Red Book in mindless singsong voices as cicadas shrieked in the trees outside and loudspeakers mounted on trucks broadcast the latest quotations from Mao in the distance.

Now the school gate was wide enough for two cars to go in abreast of each other. Inside the gate was a campus alive with lush green grass, young pines, cherries, chrysanthemums, and high-pitched choruses of students practicing English after their teachers in new multi-level buildings of contemporary design.

"Told you it's changed," mother murmured after she said something to the security guard, who nodded and let Ding in.

He strolled around the campus with the air of a casual visitor, looking for something that could even remotely connect him with this place that had morphed beyond recognition. Surrounded by new residential complexes crammed with tall, red-roofed buildings, it looked rather arbitrary, and pretentious, under a cloudless mid-June sky.

He found it. Huddling in the back of the campus, behind the new, seven-story Central Building, was an old, small, one-story structure; the white lime paint on its walls had long chipped off, exposing underneath a fiery revolutionary slogan in dark red ink. What looked like a warehouse now, an eyesore to be toppled down any day to make room for a new tennis court, or a swimming pool, had long been buried in his memory, yet would raise its hideous head when most unexpected, a nightmare that refused to awaken to sunny, blue sky. Something had happened here many years ago, in another reincarnation of his. Something on top of seeing father being brutalized. Humiliated. "Downed with."

8

"Mmmm, that's like finding a needle in the sea." Professor Zhu took a sip of the freshly made tea and placed it back on the coffee table.

"I know," Ding said, nudging the pile of paper and photos sprawled on the coffee table away from his father-in-law's teacup.

Professor Zhu picked up a photo from the pile and gazed at it.

It was the first time Ding had had a chance to talk to his father-in-law more seriously since he came back about a week ago. In addition to supervising a dozen or so graduate students, Professor Zhu sat on several university committees and province-wide program review and accreditation boards. He was every bit as busy as when Ding was still a young graduate student under his wing.

"Forty some years ago," the old man looked up and murmured, as if he were teaching a graduate seminar session, "Forty years…like a cloud that drifts into the sky and then it's gone, before you know it. Jie, you've seen photos of me dressed in uniforms when I crossed the Yalu River. I was about the same age as this fellow, a college student, idealistic, naïve, really, if you look at it from today's vantage point." He chuckled, replaced the photo on the table, and smoothed back a tress of gray hair on his forehead with his fingers.

Zhu was a junior intelligence officer during the Korean War. His job was to assist interrogations of POWs, organize files, translate documents, and perform other such errands as they arose.

"Those American GIs," the old man sat back in his cushioned chair and continued. "Most of them 18, 19-year-olds. They were so scared. You could see it in their eyes. The way they cast furtive glances at you when being led into the interrogation room, as if they would be led out to face the firing squad at any time. When I crossed the Yalu River singing that 'Resisting America, Assisting Korea' song, I was bursting with hatred for the American imperialist aggressors and their running dogs. But when I saw these poor American boys, shaken down with fear, hunger, and cold, I felt sorry for them even though I was quite brash with them at times.

"These American boys. They were like our young Volunteers. Okay, our young Volunteers were brave, and fired up with anger and what not, but they were scared, too. Taking on the Americans in a war like that? Americans who have bombers and fighter jets and, yes, nukes? Have we swallowed leopard's bile? Ah, who wouldn't be scared going into battlefield for the first time, having F-51s, 82s, whatever, diving at you and machine-gunning like mad? And who wouldn't tremble, if not pee in the pants, when B-26s, so many of them, hell-like, swarming in and letting loose those god-damn eggs from the sky? I didn't get to go to the front often, but the first time a bomb landed on top of our bunker, the whole earth shook and rocked like the end of the world. I don't remember how I dropped like a piece of dirt on the ground and crawled under the table with whatever I was holding in my hands. Half of the bunker had collapsed. I could've been killed or buried alive there."

Ding had heard bits of the same story before, but this was the first time Professor Zhu, a decorated veteran, had allowed fear, rather than heroism, to be the dominant theme. War is a strange, monstrous beast, Ding thought. It has been so ever since Eris threw a golden apple for Hera, Aphrodite, and Athena to contend for; since the Three Kingdoms romanced each other in bloody battlefields for dominance on epic scales; since Cain struck down his brother out of jealousy and anger at what he perceived to be God's favoritism; since Christopher Columbus stepped off the Santa Maria and set foot on what he thought to be India for the first time, and since. . . . Once this beast gets hold of any tribe or country, it would not let go until it has sucked dry all of its juice and air and sense and dignity. Things haven't changed much since the Trojan War and since way, way before then. The only difference is that now humans can kill each other more efficiently and on a much larger scale, stones, slingers, spears, and swords having been replaced with weapons that can kill by the hundreds, by the thousands, and by the tens of thousands from the safe distance of a continent or an ocean away.

"Jie?"

Ding woke up from his reverie and grinned.

"You might want to start with some library research: books, records, archives and so on. Who knows what you may find. In the meantime, I'll chat with some of my buddies."

Ding nodded.

"Be cautious though, Jie," the old man added, an afterthought, perhaps. "I don't think everybody will be thrilled by what you're trying to do here. So, do the best you can, but don't try to be a lone hero, I mean the I-alone-can-save-the-world John Wayne type."

Part II
Winter 1953-54 —

9

His eyebrows knit as he tried to understand what Peide was saying, and then, putting the furry hat back on, he took a step forward and unbuckled. A hot beam shot into a patch of snow, which hissed and turned dirty yellow instantly.

"Now the monkey's put his personal seal on the place!" Peide gibed as the hot beam dissipated into a few half-hearted drops.

Fastening the pants, he turned and stared into the eyes behind the large wire-rimmed glasses.

"You'll understand one day, Shanmeng," Peide grinned, undid his pants, and shot a long stream onto the same patch of yellow, shriveled snow.

Shanmeng shrugged, humped to shift the weight on his back, and trudged ahead again.

The sun that had been teasing the skyline gave in finally, the last of its orange rays quivering through the shadows of maples, pines, walnuts, bamboo, and bare branches of nameless trees. The mountain, though not marked by cloud-kissing peaks, nothing, indeed, but tall hills covered with patches of brown, inky green, and residual snow, which seemed to roll endlessly, had given their feet quite a run for the last few days.

"Look, Shanmeng," he heard Peide mumbling from behind, "Seriously, it's not too late yet. We still can turn around and go back—"

Back to where? That small wood-framed house atop a hill that whizzes spasm-like even when there is not a whiff of wind in the air? The house inside whose walls "If you want to fuck up your future with this girl, fine, but do me a favor: Don't call this place your home anymore!" "Fine!" and such insane exchanges were routine like salt and pepper on the dining table? He had made peace with himself, with his past, and with the entire world, and was more than ready to begin anew.

"You want back watch Joe DiMaggio play?" Shanmeng snapped in awkward Mandarin, with feigned anger, "Go ahead, but you go alone!"

The trail through the long reverse slope became viscid and slippery. The warm sunshine during the day must have given the frozen ground a temporary thaw. Once he slipped but regained his balance quick enough to avoid a fall on his butt. This is nothing compared to those days. He told himself. Those days of forced marches through slush and freezing rain that snaked on and coiled into each other with no end in sight.

The last streaks of sunlight had faded away. Dusk thickened. The world around them seemed dizzyingly quiet, except for little creeks dribbling through dead leaves, mussy ferns, soggy, half-melted ice and snow, and the misty drone of a mini waterfall crashing down somewhere.

And the muffled sound of a dog barking.

Did I imagine it? Shanmeng listened but didn't hear anything again.

After a few sharp turns, the trail dipped precipitously. He turned to check on Peide who was following close behind. Behind them the mountain, the endless rolling hills, loomed and blocked half of the sky.

Something twinkled not far ahead in the valley. Shanmeng sniffed and fancied smelling something sweet in the air. A knot tightened in his belly. The twinkle drifted in their direction like a glowworm, a coded message. A small dark shadow dashed toward them, barking furiously.

"Come back, Sportie!" A voice hollered sternly.

The dog had already reached them. It bounced around and snuffled their legs and boots and buttocks, growling all the while. A young farm dog that looked not too different from the German shepherd he used to have.

Its owner limped closer. Yes, the man's right leg had a noticeable limp. A few steps behind him was a child. The dog ran back to its owner, and then to the child behind, whimpering joyously.

Peide broke into vigorous strides to meet the approaching man, little pieces of mud landing all over his rear end.

"Comrade Old Ma?"

"Captain Chen?"

The two men shook hands and patted each other's back like old friends. Shanmeng didn't catch everything they were saying— Comrade Old Ma's local accent was a bit hard for him, but he understood enough to appreciate what was going on.

Peide—Captain Chen—turned and introduced him. Comrade Old Ma, the village chief, grasped Shanmeng's free hand.

"Welcome, Comrade—" he turned to Peide for help. "Oh yes, Comrade Mack . . . what? That's too much of a tongue twister for me. How about Comrade Ma, like my name? That'll make us family five hundred years ago! Hahaha!" His grip was forceful, his palm rough as the bark of an old tree.

"Shanmeng, Mountain Dream, I like better, Comrade Old Ma," he tried, conscious of his labored speech.

The village chief burst into a hearty laugh. "Plain Old Ma is good enough too!"

He emptied the pipe against his muddy heel, stuffed it into a pocket, and reached for the heavy bundle straddled on Shanmeng's back. Shanmeng cast a quick glance at his right leg.

"Strong as a steel rod," Old Ma chortled, punching his leg a few times with a tightened fist. He didn't look old at all despite the stubble around his firm chin and sideburns. His eyes glittered in the darkness as he spoke. "This old horse can still give anyone a good race! Want to try me?"

As if remembering something, Old Ma turned to the child behind him. A girl of seven or eight. Sportie was licking her hand playfully, wagging its tail.

"Stop it," the girl giggled shyly.

"My worthless daughter," Old Ma grunted. "Told her not to come, but she—"

Shanmeng felt the girl's large eyes on him as she tried to control the dog. A tress of hair fell loose from the headscarf tied under the chin.

"Okay, let's go home," Old Ma said. "The buns must have frozen again."

He threw Shanmeng's bundle on his broad back and led the way. Peide exchanged a glance with Shanmeng and hastened to walk alongside Old Ma. They chatted jovially as they strode in the direction of the village. There's absolutely no turning back now. Shanmeng thought as he followed with long, vigorous steps. Old Ma's daughter and the dog trailed not far behind.

The three men sat down at the old Eight Immortals dinner table in the main room of Old Ma's home. The table was made of some rare hardwood. Its smooth top shone warmly under the ardent glow from the two large oil lamps. The carved pattern around the edges and the tiger-claw legs lent the table an aura of dignity that would befit the august presence of a king.

Old Ma's wife and Fuli, the young daughter-in-law, busied themselves with bringing food from the kitchen to the dinner table: a large earthen pot of chicken and radish braised in brown sauce, a sea-sized bowl of well-cooked soybeans with a mount of salted pork slices on top, a plate of two meaty silver carps steamed with ginger and green onion, some green vegetables, and of course, a plateful of steamed buns.

Shanmeng took a deep, savoring breath as a pang of hunger washed over him again.

"Nothing to eat," Old Ma's wife apologized when she and Fuli handed everyone a bowl and a pair of bamboo chopsticks.

"I tried the river this morning," Old Ma said as he poured Shanmeng, Peide, and himself each a cup of homemade rice wine from a white porcelain pot with a long beak, "and caught only these few skinny fish. What a shame. The water was too damn cold."

He raised his cup. "Three days in the mountain under such

lousy weather. . . you must be dog tired! The only way to make you feel like men again is good wine, good food, and good. . ." He checked himself, grinned, and turned to Peide. "Why don't you take the lead, captain?"

"All right! We're all family here and I won't stand on ceremony!" With that Peide raised his cup and emptied it with one gulp. His face turned red instantly, his eyes glinting warmly from behind the glasses. "Good wine! I . . . feel like ice on fire . . . hahaha . . ."

Old Ma looked very pleased and turned to Shanmeng. "Now, your turn, Comrade Mack. . . Shanmeng."

Shanmeng placed the cup to his lips. It felt cool. A puff of sweetish aroma flushed his nostrils. With a toss of head, he could dump the whole thing into his mouth, like he had done too many times with shot after shot of vodka, scotch, or whisky during the last semester of senior high to get stoned. No, he didn't want to do that anymore. He sipped tentatively. He let the wine stay in his mouth for a moment, and then swallowed it slowly. It tasted soft. Supple. Unassuming. He could sense its fragrance rising to his head, and then oozing deep inside him. He shuddered as a current of warmth rushed over his entire being and then emptied whatever was remaining in the cup with one gulp.

"How do you like it, Shanmeng?"

"Good wine!" Shanmeng nodded affirmatively, still registering the taste in his mind.

"What did I tell you!" Old Ma's eyes shone with delight. With a long, appreciative "ahhhh" he emptied his cup and reached over to pour his guests and himself another round of wine.

"Don't make our guests drink on an empty stomach, old man," Old Ma's wife scolded from the door of the kitchen. Her lined face beamed with smile.

Shanmeng picked up a slice of pork and stuffed it into his mouth. He had all but mastered the intricate finger-coordination in the use of chopsticks. The pork tasted fatty and a bit salty but had a rich flavor that mingled well with the lingering fragrance of the wine in his mouth. He chewed rigorously. "I. . . not mind eat this. .

. rest of my life."

Everybody burst out laughing at his funny accent. Sportie, frightened by the outburst, growled from under the table.

"I. . . not mind eat this. . . rest of my life!" Ah Bao toddled to the big dinner table and mimicked with food in his mouth.

Old Ma laughed again.

"Ma, he eats with left hand," Ah Bao announced his new observation proudly.

"Ah Bao!" The boy's mother hollered from the small table in the corner.

Shanmeng smiled and patted Ah Bao on the head. His hair felt so soft. Yingzi hurried over to lead Ah Bao back to the small table. The tress on her forehead danced in the rustle.

"I want to eat at the big table," Ah Bao whined and resisted.

"The little brat!" Old Ma said. "No manners at all! Come over, Ah Bao!" He picked up a meaty drumstick and turned to give it to his grandson. "Now, get lost!"

"Isn't he a little treasure!?" Peide marveled.

"He is," Old Ma smiled. The smile faded instantly.

Where's Ah Bao's dad? Shanmeng wondered. Noticing Old Ma's face, he swallowed the question with a slice of tender fish.

"Be careful with fish bones," Old Ma's wife said, beaming, as she came over to help Shanmeng and Peide with another ladleful of chicken and radish.

"You come and eat with us, big sis?" Peide invited.

"Oh, no, I ate already." Old Ma's wife went to join the others at the small table in the corner.

"General Ye once told me," Peide picked up the wine pot to pour for Old Ma, "if you hadn't left, you'd have made a division commander by now."

Old Ma shook his head with a smile. "That son of a gun! He was as heavy as a water buffalo when I carried him off the battlefield during the Long March."

"General Ye wanted me to tell you," Peide lowered his voice to a whisper, "not to worry. He's doing the best he can to. . ."

Old Ma nodded as he listened, a cloud flitting across his face again.

An hour later, when they had emptied all the dishes on the table, Old Ma arose with the wine cup in his hand, his face glowing, his shadows flung large on the walls and lime-coated ceiling: "Comrade. . . Shanmeng, a friend of Captain Chen's is a friend of mine. You're at home now. You have my word!"

He thrust back his head, tossed the wine in his mouth, and showed everyone the bottom of his cup.

10

The rooster sounded fierce and unyielding, as if it was putting its dear life into singing the first note of the new day. Roosters from far and near joined in. Then dogs. The chorus filled up the world with a sound that could wake up just about anyone, living, dead, or hibernating, even the trees and bamboo and rocks on the hills still shrouded in the predawn haze. Then they all stopped, roosters, dogs, and whatever beings had made up the choir. They must have realized, somehow, that it was still too early to rise and start the day. After all, this was deep winter and there was not much for them to do anyway.

Shanmeng poked his head out of the warm quilt and peeked. There was no Peide—Captain Chen—sleeping soundly at his feet. No Sportie raising its head, its eyes sparkling with alertness. No Ah Bao crying "I want to pee" and Fuli's soft, sleepy-eyed voice telling her son to be quiet, which was followed by the sound of a beam of liquid shooting into some wooden, earthen, or porcelain container, then by Old Ma and his wife mumbling to each other in their room. He, Shanmeng, formerly Simon, was alone in his new home, in the bed of his own home for the first time in his 23 years of existence in this world. Where's Peide now? He wondered. Did he camp in the same caves and underneath the same flying rocks?

Was he afraid while forging along the trail twisting through the forested mountain all by himself? Peide, a veteran soldier, and armed, should be okay.

His eyes having adjusted, Shanmeng could make out just about everything in his single-roomed home: stalwart wood beams that gave the hut a firm framework; A-shaped ceiling where large patches of lime coating had peeled off; and a small leaky window through which slanted pale light of the new day. In the far corner of the room was a waist-high stove of deep-red bricks that looked worn yet clean. The bamboo-framed bed, upon which he had spent his first night in his new home, was a bit small for him. His feet could feel its smooth, round edge at the other end. But it was comfortable enough. In between the stove, the bed, and the doors was the dining table, knee-high, discolored, surrounded by neatly arranged—all except for one—stools.

Old Ma had invited Shanmeng to stay at his place for as long as he wanted to: "My home is your home! Don't ever forget that." But Shanmeng didn't want to be in the way. The village chief's home wasn't big enough for the family of five—Where is his son, Ah Bao's dad?—and adding him and the need to set up the make-do bed in the main-room every evening would make the guest a nuisance soon enough.

Old Ma said he hadn't had time to fix up the hut yet, having received General Ye's letter only a few days ago. Since it was still dead winter, there was little he could do except for having it swept and dusted.

Shanmeng couldn't wait to see it, though. He had been through so much that anything he could call his own and could shelter him from wind and rain and snow would be good enough.

The hut didn't seem much bigger than Thoreau's cabin, he thought. But he wouldn't know. He had never visited. And what did it matter anyway? The dark, eyebrow-shaped shingles on the steep roof, weather-beaten, covered with dead leaves here and there, were aligned into long columns, one facing up, one down, to form passageways for rain--so different from the hilltop house etched with such ambivalence in his memory.

According to the elders of the village, Old Ma had said, the hut was built by a man about three or four hundred years ago. At the time there were no more than a few dozen families scattered around this part of the valley.

"The soil was so fertile, they say, the flowers so sweet, and the peaches big and juicy, it was like. . ."

"Peach Orchard outside the World?" Peide offered.

"Exactly!"

Delighted with what he saw when he first came here, a small bundle on his back, the man decided to stay. He built the hut from the ground up with little help from his neighbors. It had taken him months and months. But he was not in a hurry to go anywhere. Like everyone else in the village, he sowed his own seeds, picked his own fruit, and sat drowsing under the sun whenever he felt like it.

"Sounds like the kind of life someone has been dreaming of living for some time," Peide said. "Right, Shanmeng?"

"Oh, I don't blame him," Old Ma chuckled. "Who wouldn't want to live like that forever? The problem is whether you can."

The good life the man was living lasted for only a few years. One day a band of uprising peasants happened to pass through. The next day came mounted troops of the Imperial Army hot on the heels of the fleeing rebels. Like everyone else in the village the man, a hermit really, ran into deeper mountains and never returned. That was how this hut had become a sort of public property for as far back as folks could remember.

"A few tramps and people of that sort, you know, have spent nights here, once in a while," Old Ma sighed, smiling. "Otherwise, this place is used for temporary storage and locked up the year round."

Does that make me a tramp too, sort of? Shanmeng mused, but his thought was interrupted by Peide, who patted him on the shoulder and said to Old Ma: "Hey, Old Ma, don't you worry now. You've got a custodian of this property for free. This one is here to stay for good."

In front of the hut stood a large ginkgo tree, ancient, knotty, its long, scraggy branches reaching upward into the sky, a nice canopy for the hut during the summer. Did the long-lost hermit choose this spot to build his nest on account of the ginkgo tree? Or he planted the tree after building his nest? Shanmeng wondered.

"Oh, you should see the tree when the leaves come out!" Old Ma marveled. "It's the most eye-catching in late fall, like a huge mushroom of gold, I mean, you can see it from the hilltop outside the village. Yeah, it'll brighten your eyes even from that far away!"

Shanmeng put his arms around the tree. It proved too thick for him no matter how hard he stretched his arms, his face brushing against its gnarled skin.

"Need any assistance?" Old Ma put his arms around the tree from the other side. Their fingertips barely touched.

"By the way," Old Ma said when they gave up the attempt and stepped back to admire the tree again. "This tree is a female. It bears seeds in fall, lots of them."

"There you go, Shanmeng!" Peide said. "Told you this would be an ideal place for you!"

It smelled so fusty when Old Ma unlocked the door and they all stepped in, but clean enough. There were no fossilized bodies of flies, wasps, roaches, or God forbid, snakes. Not much furniture either.

Before they had time to check out the place more thoroughly—there was not much to check anyway—the men were joined by Old Ma's wife, Fuli, Yingzi, and of course, Ah Bao, and Sportie. They brought with them the new cotton-padded quilt Shanmeng had slept in the night before and a whole bunch of other things he would need to start his life here. While the women fussed with setting up his bed, kitchen—cooking utensils, flour, soybean oil, salt, a large chunk of homemade ham, some salted fish—and putting other things in order, the men stood there watching, amazed. There was nothing they could do to help.

Every time Yingzi had arranged the stools neatly around the

small dining table, Ah Bao would stride on one of them and ride it around as if it were a little pony, cheered on by an excited Sportie running alongside.

"Ah Bao!" cried the little auntie, still a child herself. She sounded frustrated.

"It's all right," Shanmeng said to Yingzi. "Let him have some fun."

Yingzi watched Ah Bao riding his "pony" with a pouty face. What else could she do except. . . .

"Shanmeng?" She turned and looked Shanmeng in the eye, shyly.

"Yes?"

"Call him Brother Shanmeng," Old Ma's wife hollered from behind the stove, her face lit by the fire she had started to prepare lunch. A sort of housewarming. Fuli was busy cutting something on a board at the stove's counter.

"Brother Shanmeng," Yingzi flushed, a quick glance at her father. "What's Xinjiang like?"

"Xin. . . Xinjiang?" He turned to Old Ma, and Peide. Both winked to him meaningfully.

"You must have had a drop too much yesterday, my friend," Peide said. "How could you forget your birthplace, where you're from?"

"Oh. . . that Xinjiang," Shanmeng understood. Why the heck hasn't anyone told me about this?! "My Mandarin. . . still not very good. Xinjiang, mmm, a beautiful place, mountains, rivers, trees. . ."

"Everyone in Xinjiang, I mean everyone's nose is as big as yours, and everyone's hair as--?"

"Yingzi!" Old Ma's face glowed with anger.

"Useless girl!" the girl's mother arose from behind the stove and looked unhappy, too. "I should have taught you more manners!"

"Oh, no worry," Shanmeng felt bad for the little girl. He had been like this when he was Yingzi's age, so curious about things, and asking too many questions for his own good. "Yes, you're right, just about. Everyone's nose is big, and everyone's—"

"Yeah," Peide stepped over and reached to pinch Shanmeng's nose between his fingers, "as big as a red pepper!"

Shanmeng dodged. Everyone laughed. Ah Bao ran around the room shouting: "Big as red pepper! Big as red pepper."

His mother stopped whatever she was doing at the counter and came over to pull Ah Bao in her arms: "You have no manners, either!"

Shanmeng stretched lazily and yawned and felt delicious all over the body. The light from the window looked bright enough now. Yes, time to get up even if there was not much to do at this time of the year. He removed the warm quilt and rolled out of bed.

The air was chilly. There was no fireplace or heating stove in the hut. He had seen *kang* in the north, a kind of "bed" built with mudbricks and connected to the cooking stove through some kind of mudbrick airway. Whatever residual heat coming from cooking would go through the *kang* and heat it up before its smoke was released from the chimney. What a clever way to use energy efficiently! There was no such thing, though, in the southern part of the country where people didn't have heat inside their homes at all. It seemed their skin was better adapted to fending off the cold.

He shivered while putting on the blue cotton-padded pants and winter jacket, which had been chilled overnight.

A flimsy layer of ice had formed in the water vat nestled against the stove. When he dipped the gourd ladle in to fill the wooden basin, the ice cracked into tiny glassy pieces.

The water had a biting feel to the fingers at the first touch, to the skin of his hands, and to the cheeks when he dipped his face in the basin to savor the chilling freshness as it flushed to the head. When he couldn't hold the breath any longer, he blew the pent-up air into the water through his nose and mouth at the same time, producing a loud, bubbly stir in the basin. As he dried with a towel, a wave of glowing warmth swept over him from head to toe.

The door's threshold was made of a chiseled rock about half a foot high and four feet long. Its edges had been smoothed to a dull shine by the tread of the long-gone hermit and its many wayward guests through the centuries.

Bordering the threshold was a small patio of dark-green bricks. Across the surface of the patio was marked indentation, three or four inches wide and half an inch deep, apparently engraved by raindrops from the eaves above the neatly aligned bricks.

Beyond the patio the ground was all mud: brown, frozen mud. He could see deep, variously shaped footprints left by his guests yesterday. Some were large, positively "sculpted" by the feet of Old Ma, Peide, and himself. Some were of a medium size: they must be from the lighter feet of Old Ma's wife and Fuli. The smaller ones were imprinted by Yingzi and Ah Bao who had insisted on walking home by himself. And the smallest, but most numerous, flower-patterned prints belonged to Sportie, who was bouncing and running around in unpredictable zigzags and half circles. All these footprints crisscrossed each other's paths rather whimsically yet formed some most intricate, amazing patterns on the mud ground in front of his home. My home! How sweet it sounded to his ears. He had never had a home of his own before, but had seen homes built, had seen homes flattened into smoky ruins, by the hundreds and by the thousands. He had seen whole villages and towns smoldering in flames. He cringed as the pictures tumbled back in his mind. No, he told himself. It would do no good dwelling on that now that he was thousands of miles away from where it all happened. I'm not Simon anymore. I'm Shanmeng, Mountain Dream. I'm more than ready to start anew.

11

He treaded along the mud road marked by frozen footprints and hard-edged tracks left by wheelbarrows, breathing in the frosty air slowly, deeply. Except for an occasional pine and other evergreens, the trees and bushes were all dead brown. It was bleak winter everywhere.

Before long the mud road led him to the presence of an opening, a vast open space—no trees, no bushes, no shrubs, no nothing— which shimmered under the pinkish light of a burgeoning sun.

Twin-Sun River? It must be. What else could it be?

It looked more like a lake that extended far and wide for thousands of acres until it reached the misty contours and inky green silhouettes of rolling hills in the far distance.

A gusty breeze blew across the surface of the river. Shanmeng shivered, regretting not having on the fur hat when he left home. This is nothing—he reassured himself. Nothing at all compared to what you've been through.

Slowly he went down to the river's edge. From there the river felt as vast and endless and imposing as the sky; its surface, iced over, dazzled under the orange intensity of the sun emerging from behind the hills.

He bent to feel the ice. Its biting freshness reminded him of another body of water. A lake of similar size in a faraway place, in another part of the world. In the dead of winter the temperature there could drop 10 to 20 degrees below zero—Fahrenheit!—and the lake would freeze so deep and rock solid that he and his friends could skate on it. Although quite a good swimmer, he was clumsy on the ice and would trip and fall crashing on his butt, more often than he could have bragged of, and someone dear to his heart would glide over, like a dream, and give him her warm, slender hand.

Shanmeng returned to the mud road along the river. Old Ma had said that all of his village, a bit over two hundred households, were living on this side of the river, which shaped like an enormous teardrop if viewed from the sky. From its southernmost tip the river narrowed into a small tributary that flowed for miles and miles until it found its way into the Yangtze River, which rolled eastward night and day surging through towns and cities and farmland before pouring into the Pacific Ocean. Where he was, near the southernmost tip of the enormous teardrop, the river was not all that wide. He could probably swim across it in 10 minutes or so.

A sound, a splashing of water, broke the quietness of the early morning. He looked ahead but couldn't see anything except for the long twigs of a huge willow cascading over the riverbank. Shanmeng hastened his pace and soon passed the willow.

The sound came from someone down at the water's edge. The sleeves of her cotton-padded coat pulled up to the elbow, she was rolling an article of clothing vigorously on a large, smooth rock. Then she dipped the clothing deep in water, shook it hard, picked it up, and rolled it on the rock again, adding to the forcefulness the weight of her upper body. It was a pair of straw-colored shirts that looked familiar. Next to her was a basket filled with clothing that had already been rinsed and wrung dry.

The young woman, feeling the presence of someone watching from behind, perhaps, turned. It was Fuli, her face reddened by the cold breeze rippling over the river. The young woman stopped rolling the clothing between her hands. The opening in the surface of water at her feet, greenish, pure, about five or six feet in radius, calmed down like a mirror again. Behind her was the glassy body of water that stretched endlessly toward the sun-kissed hills in the misty distance.

"Morning," he faltered. He hadn't said a word to the village chief's young daughter-in-law since he came here two days ago.

Fuli smiled shyly. She wanted to stand up, but stopped in the middle of the effort. Her legs must have gone to sleep. She must have been squatting like that at the washing station for some time by now.

A few more things in the big basket and in the pile on the rock looked quite familiar. They were mingled together with washings of the Ma family.

"Thank you very much for washing my clothes," he wanted to say, but somehow didn't say it. It would be frivolous of him to express his gratitude to the young daughter-in-law alone like this? And flippant? He didn't know. As he was thus debating with himself, the right moment for saying anything was gone.

Perhaps both felt the awkwardness of the moment at the same time. Fuli turned and resumed her work with a bent head.

Shanmeng went on his way. For quite a while he could still hear water splashing from behind and its echoes across the river.

He ambled on for he didn't know how much longer. Ten minutes? Half an hour?

The sun had risen above the hills, showering the world with a radiant glow of warmth. Shanmeng turned and retraced his steps at a faster, more urgent pace. When he reached the huge willow at the bend, Fuli was not at the washing station anymore. The rocks still looked wet. A film of ice, tentative, had already formed in the opening where Fuli had rinsed a big basketful of clothing. He turned to glance at the woods on his right. A narrow trail cut through the trees and bushes and soon disappeared.

What shall I have for breakfast? Shanmeng wondered. Porridge? Pancake? A couple of eggs sunny side up? They all sounded good.

12

Shanmeng had upturned the soil in the garden for the fifth time. He wanted to get it ready for spring. His garden consisted of strips and patches of land of various shapes and sizes scattered within a stone's throw of his hut. Within the perimeters of the garden was a little peach orchard half buried in chest-high dead weeds.

These pieces of land had only a vague resemblance to having been cultivated before, by the long-gone hermit, for sure, and by whoever had sojourned here long enough to see seeds germinate and blossom to fruition. By the time Shanmeng arrived, however, weeds had long taken over and formed a food chain of generations feeding on the carcasses of their parent generations. The weeds had succumbed to the onslaught of winter but had not completely fallen yet, a massive entanglement of prickly mess, a wall of resistance to any effort to tame the land they stood on.

"Damn weeds!" Old Ma marveled when they returned from a tour of the village. "They can grow just about anywhere, soil, cracks in the bricks, the face of a dead rock, even your roof. Rain, shine, drought, flood, they don't give a crab. So damn cocky!"

Shanmeng was amazed, too, more by Old Ma's outburst than by the untamed wilderness around him.

"You can always come to our place and help yourself," Old Ma continued. He bent and grabbed the thistly stem of a weed and gave it a good yank. "Whatever we have on our table, you can have them, too." Old Ma flung the weed far into the wilderness and clapped his hands. "Mmmm, this time of the year, you won't see much green in our garden, either. Anyway, if one day you're tired of walking to our place, we can come and give these weeds a hard time. Hahaha."

Shanmeng didn't wait though. The next morning, he got up early, washed, ate a bowl of congee, and headed for the weeds with a spade.

That hermit, now a mythologized figure in his mind, might have used this very same spade to colonize the land around here and to build his hut, Shanmeng thought as he swung the spade left and right striking down half-dead thistle, shamrock, clover, mustard, ivy, wild oats, whatever in his path. Now and then a spiny vine would prick the skin of his hands or leave a hurtful scratch on his face, but he didn't mind. He worked furiously and stopped only to wipe away salty sweat oozing down the forehead, and to doff the cotton-padded jacket and pants. Before an imaginary pipe of tobacco could have been smoked to its last blink, an area of weeds, the size of his hut, had been felled.

He had never worked on a farm when growing up but had seen mules pulling plows in fields that stretched for miles; seasonal workers harvesting corn, beans, potatoes, and fruit, their soulful folk songs drifting over like long-forgotten dreams; tractors, when they arrived on the scene, cluttering, dragging rows of plows behind them, kicking up an expansive cloud of dust.

Shanmeng spat into his palms and waded further into the

weeds, brandishing the old spade that began to shine near its cutting edge. A long, twisty stem caught between his legs, its sharp thorns giving his skin an irritating, itchy kind of feel. He bent to untangle the stem with careful fingers when he heard a familiar voice booming from yards away.

"Hey, you're an impatient early bird, too?"

Shanmeng turned to look.

Old Ma waved and dived into the weeds with a long-handled sickle. Wherever the sickle went, in a beautiful arc, weeds dropped like nothing, clueless of what had just happened to them.

"Yeah, they're such a pain now," Old Ma said when he had caught up with Shanmeng. "But they are such good firewood, burning inside the stove like hell, sputtering, and giving you a noseful good as tobacco."

Toward the end of the day, they had cleared the weeds in the orchard and beyond and raked them into piles to the side and were upturning the soil to let it freeze and thaw through winter. "Best way to wake up the soil, you know," Old Ma said.

Where weed roots were creepy and deep, Shanmeng had to kick the spade really hard. The upturned soil, brownish, dark chocolate like, had a damp, have-never-seen-sunshine kind of odor. Now and then he would see earthworms, chopsticks long, having been cut into halves, convulsing in spasms of pain and wriggling into deeper soil.

And fresh soil turned up with such ease and neat cadence wherever Old Ma's spade went, his sleeves rolled up high, the muscles in the small arms bulging like iron. This old horse, Shanmeng thought as he tried to catch up with the man about 20 years his senior, I wouldn't want to race him any day.

"Don't dig too hard," Shanmeng hollered breathily.

"Why?"

He meant to say "Mind your leg," but was that really what he had meant to say?

"See, this is us, America, where we are," Mrs. Davis had said to her third-grade pupils, and then turned the globe a full half circle, "this is China, the Sleeping Dragon, according to Napoleon. If you dig hard and long enough in your garden, yeah, you'll end up in China."

"Really?" young Simon was amazed.

"Yes, be careful, though," the teacher said, a smile in her voice. "You might emerge from underneath some family's kitchen stove, and they might be cooking something hot and delicious there."

The class burst out laughing. A few minutes later, when the teacher had moved on to Europe and the war that had just broken out there, Simon raised his hand again.

"Mrs. Davis, have you ever tried?"

"Tried what?" the teacher didn't like to be interrupted while in the middle of explaining things, but she seemed fond of the earnest kid with deep-set eyes.

"You know, digging in your garden, your backyard?'"

Mrs. Davis doubled up laughing. "I'm sorry, Simon," she said when finally getting hold of herself. "I shouldn't have laughed. It's just a folksy kind of saying. Seriously, one of my great aunts did go to China as a missionary many, many years ago. She never returned."

Now, about 15 years later, he, Simon, was in China. He hadn't needed to dig in the garden or backyard. He was flown to this part of the world in a big cargo plane. He hadn't come to visit or do missionary work, but to fight a war. Thank God, he thought to himself, that's all over now.

Old Ma's eyes were still on him.

"You dig through the earth, you know, you be on the other side."

"The other side. What would that be? Not Xinjiang, I guess?"

"Xinjiang? Oh, no, but new, sort of, too," Shanmeng hesitated, then said it anyway. "Meiguo, you know."

"Meiguo, hmmm, nice name. Is it really a beautiful country, though?"

"Yes, very beautiful country!"

"More beautiful than here?"

Shanmeng's body stiffened. His breath quickened. His eyes searched in the face of the man not far from him but detected no quicksand, no trap there.

"Well. . . ."

Old Ma laughed. "Just kidding!"

The laugh in his eyes withered right away, as if struck by a deadly frost.

By now Shanmeng had learnt to be self-efficient in his kitchen. He knew how to start the fire, even when it rained, and the weeds gathered from outside were not that dry. He pressed his face close and blew gently, persistently to encourage the flittering sparks. Damp smoke would thicken until the balled weeds burst into flames and washed his face with choking black steam. Once the fire caught on, it would burn briskly, sputtering, giving out a sweetish smell.

One of his favorite dishes he had learnt from Old Ma's wife was a mix of rice, cabbage chops, and salted pork slices cooked together in one simple deal. The juice coming from the fatty pork gave the cooked rice and vegetables a faint shine and a delicious aroma and taste. He would eat it while it was hot, savoring each mouthful that felt like a piece of the noon sun.

Making steamed buns with yeast didn't look that difficult now either. He knew how much water he needed to make good dough— neither too hard nor too soft and sticky. He would roll the dough on the small dining table until it was perfect, put it back in the bowl, cover it with a damp rag, and wait for it to rise. That would take a couple of days this time of the year, but, as Peide had said, he was not in a big hurry to go anywhere.

He still wasn't too good with the right amount of soda. Old Ma's wife? She didn't need any spoon to measure at all. She simply tilted the bowl containing the diluted soda and rolled and bent to sniff a couple of times and added a few more drops and rolled a bit more and the dough was as right as could be. When the buns were ready, they were so bouncy and smelled so good. The first time trying on his own, he overdosed. The buns looked yellow as the bread his Camp buddies baked using an empty gasoline barrel but had a strong sulfur kind of smell to them. He felt so thirsty after the meal that it took bowls of water to extinguish the fire in his stomach. The second time around he was too miserly with soda. The buns refused to rise. They looked listless and tasted so sour. Worse, they gave him heartburn that lasted for a whole day afterwards.

His home had acquired a new roof and a bright, fresh look inside, too.

Right after the Spring Festival the village chief gathered a few men who came with barrows of shingles—yes, those dark, eyebrow-shaped shingles—a ladder, and other tools and material. They swept off the rotten leaves and dead weeds first. Then they removed all the broken shingles and fixed the cracks with lime, mud, and straw mix before installing the new shingles in arrow-straight columns and perfect alignment. It was quite an event that day. Everyone in the Ma family pitched in: Old Ma's wife and Fuli bringing in water and food cooked from their own kitchen, Yingzi running small errands whenever she could, and Ah Bao and Sportie wandering around cheerfully.

As the men worked on the house, they talked and joked and made the work light and fun. Shanmeng sensed that he was the main source of the excitement because he "caught" them glancing at him whenever they thought he wasn't looking.

"Ask Red Hair himself!" he overheard two young men whispering between themselves.

Red Hair? He hadn't been here long and was already given a not so flattering nickname! Would they call him Big Nose soon? Yet, the two young men didn't look mean at all. So he pretended not to have heard.

"Sh. . . Shanmeng, you're from Xinjiang?" Yucai, one of the two, asked, eventually, while passing shingles to Old Ma on the roof.

"So I've told you!" Old Ma said hoarsely.

"Where on earth is Xinjiang?" Fugui, at the bottom of the ladder, asked hesitantly.

"Xinjiang?" said Huifa, a thirtyish man, who had seen a bit of the world beyond the mountains. "Northwestern China, I think, bordering the Soviet Union. But I'm not sure whether they are Chinese or Russian. Their hair, eyes, and nose—"

"No, they're not Russian," said Yingzi, who had just returned with a few more shingles. "They're Uyghur, a Chinese ethnic minority."

"Hey, Chief Ma," Huifa laughed, taking the shingles from Yingzi. "See your precious daughter here? She'll blossom into something and make you mighty proud one day!"

"Told you to go and play elsewhere," Old Ma glowered down at Yingzi. "What do you know, erh? Useless girl."

"The book Sis' Fuli gave me to read says so," Yingzi mumbled in protest, clapping her hands to rid the dust, and led Ah Bao away from the grown-ups.

Yes, Shanmeng thought, as he watched the girl leave, a mix of curiosity and stubbornness in the same person could be a recipe for joy, pain, or both. He knew this firsthand. What would it be for Yingzi?

"Is it true, Chief Ma," an older man asked, "your daughter-in-law will teach at the school?"

"I don't know," Old Ma sighed. "I haven't decided yet."

"Well, that school building has been dead like since the old schoolmaster left. Somebody has to teach the kids; otherwise, they'll all grow up useless illiterates, like us, right?"

Old Ma nodded without saying a word.

13

"Xinjiang! Xinjiang! Where's the goddamn place?"

The question had been playing in his head like the refrain of a hated song days after the roof was fixed and the burning smell of the new lime coating had all but dissipated. He dug out the old pocket Xinhua Dictionary from the bottom of his bag and turned its wrinkled pages back and forth but couldn't find anything about the two characters except for their spellings: 新疆, New Frontier. Too many strokes for each character and too many curves and sudden turns in impossible directions. Mastering them would not be too unlike conquering new frontiers. He tossed the dictionary on the table and stared at the oil lamp. Why had it seemed so fascinating and so goddamn easy when Peide showed him the first time about three years ago?

He, Simon then, had just been handed over to PVA, the Chinese People's Volunteer Army. Like all of his fellow POWs who had survived the long march through the war-scarred mountainous terrain in freezing rain and despair, he was sickly and no more than a shadow of his former self. And he was in a foul mood. He did let the nurse address his head wound and eat whatever food handed him, cracked wheat day after day at first. Beyond that he was a dead log. However, when a young PVA officer droned on and on in clumsy English about the evils of American Reactionaries to waken his conscience or consciousness, and to convert him into a "Progressive," Simon almost lost it.

"Can you just shut the fuck up?" he looked up and muttered weakly.

Stunned, the officer scowled at the young American sitting on the mud floor, speechless, and stomped out.

Soon he heard footsteps coming in. No one said anything for a while. The very air he was breathing quavered with nervous expectancy.

"Never in my wildest dream imagined this place, Korea, could be this damn cold," the newcomer murmured. Perfect American accent. What the heck . . .?!

Simon lifted his head slowly. The person who had just spoken turned away from the barred window. A Chinese face. Large, ridiculously large wire-rimmed glasses on his nose.

"You. . . an American?"

"I was. . . until about four years ago," said the officer, Captain

Peter Chen ("Call me Peter, or Peide, Nurturing Virtue," he told Simon later). "Let me guess, you're from New England, Boston area, probably."

Not exactly, but close. Simon was impressed and nodded vaguely.

"What happened to the morons who sold Babe to the Yankees, do you happen to know?"

Simon barely shrugged. He didn't know and he wasn't in the mood for such conversations with anyone, not to say a PVA officer under such circumstances.

"Mmmm, okay," Captain Chen said suddenly, "are you game? Let's play a game, not baseball or anything, but. . . let's see."

He stepped to the middle of the room. Simon watched, feigning no interest at all.

Captain Chen stood with his legs wide apart, arms resting on the outside of legs. "What is this? What does this symbol stand for?"

Simon shook his head. What the heck am I supposed to know?

"It's *ren*, 人, Human."

So?

"And this?" Captain Chen raised both arms level to the shoulders, bird-like.

Simon shook his head again. Okay?

"It's *da*, 大, Big, meaning a human being is big, a big deal."

Sounds interesting.

"And if you add another horizontal stroke above my head, like this, it becomes *tian*, 天, Sky, or Heaven. A human being is a big deal, the biggest deal, under the sky."

"How...how do you know all this stuff?"

"Well, I worked hard on it when I first returned to China," Captain Chen said, his eyes glinting. "When I was young, watching my parents slave in the laundry day after day, the last I wanted was to talk like them and eat their food and...well, what did I know then!"

Before leaving, he pulled out a dictionary from his pocket and tossed it to Simon.

"If you're interested, I'll be happy to help."

The next morning, Shanmeng got up early to wash his clothes at the riverside. He had repaired whatever looked like a washing station that had fallen to long disuse. From there he could see a wide, V-shaped opening between two hills in the eastern sky, almost level with the surface of the river.

About halfway through the laundry basket, the sky began to blush with the pale rays of a sun freshly astir from below the horizon. He stopped rolling the underpants on the rock and watched.

Soon the sky churned quietly with ever more intensity of light and before he had time to refill an imaginary pipe, the sun burst free from whatever was holding it back and peeked in between the two hills, an arch of fire, its fiery rays melting the sky and the river into fierce scarlet splendor.

As the arch of fire swelled into a ball of gold ablaze, one half of the sun kept rising, following the heavenward trajectory while the other half continued to sink, as if being pulled downward by something from the bottom of the river, the heart of the earth.

All of a sudden, the sun split into two, one in the sky, one on the mirror-like river, both dazzling in their ever-elongating splendors. As the one in the sky rose higher and higher, the one on the river weakened and faded and then disappeared altogether.

Dang... dang... dang—a metallic sound, not too different from the church bell that had been encased deep in a corner of his memories, though of a sharper, higher pitch, came rolling from across the fields of baby wheat that had survived the long winter. It shook the air in a measured, unhurried cadence, yet Shanmeng felt a rush of excitement, and urgency, which he couldn't explain.

Following a foot path winding through the wheat fields, and a chorus of young voices that arose after the bell had stopped, Shanmeng soon came in front of an old one-room structure of bricks and shingles in the midst of tender green—nondescript, the deep-red paint on its wood-framed window long faded. Upon seeing him, the kids inside stopped reading aloud; several couldn't help giggling. Noticing the pupils being distracted, their teacher opened the door and stepped outside to see what was going on.

Fuli looked different from the village chief's daughter-in-law and Ah Bao's mother busy cooking and cleaning and doing laundry at the riverside. It was not just the blue jacket with open collar that she had on, or her short hair, which, together, gave her a livelier, more refined presence that separated her from all the other women in this mountain village, but also a sense of who she was that Shanmeng hadn't noticed before.

"Oh, it's you." She looked surprised.

"Yingzi mentioned a book, Xinjiang," he ventured.

"Oh, that book," Fuli smiled. "It's not really about Xinjiang."

"I. . . I leave. . . Xinjiang long time ago, and. . . ."

Fuli nodded understandingly. "Sure, and I have a few other books."

Shanmeng nodded gratefully.

Fuli returned to the classroom and the chorus of young voices rose in the air again.

As he turned to leave, Shanmeng noticed something hanging from a tree next to the school building: a piece of bombshell, about a foot long, gnarled, with crooked edges.

From that day on, a favorite pastime of his was to sit against the wall of his home warmed by sunshine and turn the pages of the books he had borrowed from Fuli. Some of the words he recognized right away. Many, however, were strangers and he had to look them up in the old Xinhua dictionary.

Peide said when he first returned to China, his Mandarin was very bad, having been wasting away from disuse for too long, but it bounced back fast enough once it breathed the air of his native soil. For Shanmeng, though, he had to work hard to acquire the new language, a word, a phrase, and a sentence at a time. He already had a feel for it. Nearly three years of dogged, fascinated efforts at the Camp had not gone for nothing. He could understand most of what Old Ma and the folks were saying here. He was not quite used to the accent yet, but he liked it. It was open, hearty, and without any guile. That was how he felt about it.

Sometimes, tired and not wanting to exert himself anymore, he would close his eyes and let himself loose in the serenity of it all. As he drowsed, he would fancy hearing something in a language, which, upon waking up, he couldn't remember, perhaps a stream of voiceless sound winding down a creek, now open, crystal-clear, now hazy, littered with pebbles, and half blocked by formidable rocks, a stream that would eventually wind into a much larger stream that would tumble and rumble until it poured into something primal, wild, boundless.

He was yet to experience the thrills of dreaming in Mandarin. That, Peide had told him, would have to wait until he was very fluent in the new tongue.

14

He heard it, tenuous, like a dream drifting over from faraway. Yingzi, Ah Bao, even Sportie, heard it, too. They all stepped out of his home to listen.

The branches of the tall ginkgo and the long, arching limbs of willows skirting the river were already showing a hint of tender yellow; the peach trees in the orchard behind his home were alive with kindling buds on their young, purple-red twigs; and the sea of baby wheat far and beyond were turning a vibrant green, its dewy blades glistening under the early morning sunshine misting over fields and hills in the distance.

They heard them coming a-chirping from far and high as the rising sun melted away the chills in the air and warmed their bodies still clad in padded jackets.

They caught glimpses of them, a whirling blur of shiny blue-black, clean white, and streaks of vivid red—silk strings tied to the birds' little feet the autumn before, Yingzi explained—as they appeared in the sun-bathed sky, one close behind the other, racing, diving precipitously only to soar again, and painting dizzying circles and curves around his home, around the tall ginkgo, a-warbling all the while.

Then, they darted in from the front door, a startling rush of air over the heads of the awe-struck humans, and dogs.

They floated on their sharply angled wings under the vaulted roof of beams; they chased each other up and down and left and right at unpredictable speeds; they perched tentatively on the beams, their long, forked tails quivering nervously, only to dart out from the back door, a resonance of colors.

They wove in and out of his home in this fashion for a few more rounds before settling on a beam, a song gushing from their bronzing throats, now in duet, now in chorus:

"What are they saying, I mean, singing?" Shanmeng asked curiously.

"Pa said they are singing: No borrowing of your charcoal /No borrowing of your rice /Only borrowing your home /To give birth to our babies."

"No borrowing of your charcoal /No borrowing of your—?"

"Rice," Ah Bao finished it for him. "Only borrowing your home /To give birth to our babies! Babies, hahaha!" Ah Bao began to run around riding his imaginary horse again.

"Be quiet," whispered his little auntie in an authoritative voice. "You'll scare the swallows." Then she turned to Shanmeng, in the same hushed, mysterious tone: "Pa said swallows are good birds. They bring good luck to people."

The swallows. How did they know that this long-abandoned hut had become a home again and was ready to receive "guests"? What kind of good luck would they bring him? He was already lucky enough to be where he was now. What more luck would he need? Was there such a thing as too much good luck? Shanmeng mused as he sat on the stone threshold of his front door watching his guests start to build their nest, a straw, a twig, a piece of sticky mud at a time, layer upon layer, with perfect alignment.

Within days a well-knit, rice bowl-shaped nest appeared on the beam.

Now, at the end of the day, when Shanmeng returned from his garden and sat down at the table for supper, the swallows roosted in their nest overhead, crooning now and then.

Shanmeng's garden flourished. The vegetables grew with a vengeance that both delighted and baffled him. The soil, having slumbered for so long, suckled the seeds and seedlings as if it couldn't wait to see them ripening to their full promise.

The radishes were large, the size of his fists, fleshy, and juicy. Whenever he had a fancy for them, he would pull one up by grabbing its luxuriant stem and pungent leaves. He would wash it, cut it into fine, noodle-like slices, marinate it with a bit of salt, and then sprinkle some sesame oil. There on his table would appear a salad dish of snow white and fresh red, which tasted almost as good as that made by Old Ma's wife, or Fuli.

He didn't have olive oil or any other dressing to make real spinach salad. But he knew how to improvise. He heated a spoonful of soybean oil (he couldn't be too extravagant because cooking oil was expensive) in the wok, put in a sprinkle of salt and ginger and green onion slices, and oh, the oil and everything in it would sizzle and smell so good. He would then drain the oil and pour it on a large bowl of fresh, meaty spinach leaves.

Growing up, he hadn't really craved soup although he liked Grandma's chili, especially on cold, snowy evenings, and Ma's cream chowder all right. But he had been hooked ever since that bowl of chicken soup at the Camp. The small, skinny chicken had been boiled and broiled until the meat and bones had all but melted away in the big cauldron. It was the longest wait for Shanmeng (still Simon back then), and his buddies. There were no more than a few hints of meat in the small bowl he had, and he could count the oily rings floating on the surface. He had to force himself to go slow with every little sip to savor the full flavor every drop in the bowl had to offer.

He had learnt to make chicken soup with ginger, green onion, and whatever vegetable he fancied for the day: radish, green cabbage, or spinach. It tasted good and he would always have a second bowl. Somehow it never tasted nearly as delicious as the small bowl of soup he had relished at the Camp.

Was he going through some metamorphosis, like a butterfly? Shanmeng sometimes wondered. One thing for sure: He was not the same person who had dumped his first cracked wheat meal as unfit for human consumption. He almost died for his stupidity if Harold, a tall marine who had fought in the jungles of the Philippines, hadn't intervened. "Eat it, kid," the marine had ordered, "if you don't want to die!" He had since developed a new set of taste buds and stomach and digestive system. And a new pair of eyes, too. Toward the end of his time at the Camp, he had all but shed sensitivity to the facial differences between his captors and himself. Somehow, they all looked alike, cousins of sort, their kinship going way, way back, to the beginning of time perhaps.

In this small mountain village thousands of miles away from where it had all happened, he was still something to be noticed. His eyes. His nose. His mouth. His auburn hair. He could see that in the eyes of anyone in the village who saw him for the first time. But the curiosity was fading. People were getting used to him. One day he'd be one of them. To the Ma's he was already family. Sort of. He was a Ma, too, according to the village chief. His Mandarin wasn't that good yet. He hadn't picked up the local accent. But he was getting there.

The cucumber vines had grown long, luxuriant, hanging onto the supports he had made of bamboo and tree limbs, their heads reaching skyward lustfully as if they didn't know when to stop. New bright yellow flowers budded here and there as old ones morphed into baby cucumbers the size of his pinkie. The longest cucumber, however, was already the full measurement of a chopstick.

The tomatoes hadn't ripened yet. Like the cucumbers, Shanmeng had staked their stems and learnt, against his instinct, to prune each plant to a single or double stem by removing all the "suckers" from the leaf axils. Some of the tomatoes were big as a ping-pong ball, hard and green. Once he picked up one that had fallen, took a bite, and oh, he couldn't spit it out fast enough. It tasted so puckery.

The pink peach flowers, whose sweet fragrance had attracted so many bees, had long fallen. In their places were baby fruit, clusters of them, all over the limbs and twigs, half shielded by dark green leaves: they looked cute, promising, and vulnerable. Every morning his heart would ache at the sight of a few more fallen on the ground. Nightly winds? Sparrows which fooled with things they couldn't really handle? Or squirrels, of which he hadn't seen any?

Yes, even in his sleep he could hear his plants grow. And he could hear other sounds that were musical to his ears, too. The baby swallows and their young parents in their nest. More exactly the baby swallows in the nest and their Pa and Ma perching on a beam close by. One day, one of the baby swallows fell from the nest. Luckily the bird was not badly hurt. When picking it up from the ground, Shanmeng could see thin blue veins under its pinkish skin where soft feathers didn't cover completely. He pulled the dining table under the nest, placed a stool on it, and climbed onto the stool to place the bird back to its home. Its siblings sounded overjoyed, but the look in their eyes betrayed unease at seeing the face of a giant visitor so close.

In his sleep he could hear cooing sounds from a different source: the small coop in the corner not far from the front door, about three feet high and six feet long, its roof a sheet of bamboo loosely strung together for air.

About 20 days into warming a pile of eggs with her warm body, turning them up and down tirelessly, Brownie had a mystified, expectant look in her eyes, as if she had heard something. A baby chick moving inside an egg? Another egg cracking open?

Before long twelve cute little chicks emerged from under the ruffled feathers of their mama.

Shanmeng picked up the baby chicks, one by one, and placed them in a large reed basket, each a ball of fluffy, soft yellow. They started to chirp right away, all twelve of them, their voices tiny, pure, a dream trickling over from afar, little stars twinkling on steel-blue sky.

Brownie, a gift from Old Ma's wife, would lead her children to wander around for fun and for food. They stuck together wherever they went. Whenever one of them found itself falling behind or straying, it would rush to rejoin its mama and siblings lest it would get lost. The mama hen clawed and raked among little mounts of dead leaves and old wheat straws and, finding something—loose grains, little worms, or a fat insect, she would coo and call her children to the feast.

One day, as the chicks and their mama were thus engaged, there was a sudden commotion and they fled back as fast as legs could carry them, as if they had seen a ghost, Brownie squawking in a most mournful, combative way, more than ready to fight to death to defend her children. Shanmeng hurried outside to see what was wrong and thought he saw a large black rat scurrying into the shady bushes of loose bamboo and shrubs.

Shanmeng had acquired two little piglets, too. He wasn't sure if he was expanding too fast but couldn't resist when Old Ma mentioned that Old Chao had a litter ready to sell.

Old Chao, a wiry old man, his skin sunbaked, leathery, had a bouncy growth the size of a steam bun on top of his left arm. "Oh, that?" Old Chao chuckled as they walked to his pigsty. "That's punishment for me being greedy."

A bad flood hit when Chao was still a young fellow, and all the crops were destroyed. Having nothing to eat for days, Chao picked up a dead weasel from the bushes and skinned and cooked it and ate a big bowl of it and more. The taste wasn't bad, and his hunger was satisfied. But soon afterward he noticed a growth on top of his left arm, a bud at first, which kept growing until it was in full bloom.

The mama pig, sprawled inside the pen under the warm sun, looked old, her ribcage quite visible. She was grunting appreciatively as the six or seven baby pigs busied themselves with her large, swollen teats, jostling for better positions all the while.

Every one of them looked cute with its smooth hair and little tails wagging contently.

Noticing the presence of visitors alongside of her owner, the mama pig became vigilant; she lifted her head and grunted with displeasure. Old Chao stepped in and placed cabbage leaves near the mama pig, who sniffed and started to nibble tentatively. Before Shanmeng realized what was happening, Old Chao had grabbed a baby pig in each hand; the piglets, being held upside down by their feet, screamed for their lives; their mama, alarmed, rolled on her feet and charged with heart-wrenching noise of fear and fury, the remaining of her children still hanging on to her teats.

Now the guttural noise of the piglets in the new pen behind Shanmeng's home added to the constant chorus in his world.

He had begun to dream in Chinese, too, although he couldn't recall much of the dreams the next day. One day he woke up in the middle of night, scenes of himself being chased by two huge characters: *fengbao*, 風暴, Fierce Storm, still vivid in his mind. He rubbed his eyes and listened again. Nothing. My mind must have been overworked last night. How to spell the word again? "*Feng. . . fengbao*, fierce storm. . . long downstroke to the left, horizontal followed by vertical with right turn and hook, downstroke to the left, vertical, horizontal. . . horizontal with fold, horizontal, vertical. . . Damn, too many strokes and kicking left and right and up and down. . . and inside outside. Whoever invented this language must be nuts. . . crazy, he thought, and went back to sleep again.

The sky, leaden with low, dark clouds that were torn to pieces by thunderous lightning now and then, seemed ready to collapse. The chickens, young as they were—a few having just budded into little roosters, sensed something bad was afoot, too. They didn't dare to venture outside the home anymore. The Pa and Ma swallows stayed on the beam close to their babies, too, who were all but grown up, restless, loved to hop onto the edge of the nest to test their abilities to balance, their wings and forked tails quivering tremulously. Even the two pigs, now robust youngsters, grunted anxiously as they lay drowsing in the pen.

Then, the sky collapsed, rain tumbled down, cheered on by thunder and lightning that threatened to open the earth for the crazed water to go. Shanmeng's small hut rocked from roof to foundation as if it would cave in at any moment. From a finger hole in the front door, he saw columns of water rumbling over the brick patio to join the muddy rivulets plowing down the slope toward the river and branches of the gingko tree being tossed around in a most wacky dance; beyond the tree was a vast wet blur.

The rain raged on all day and throughout the night.

The next morning, he opened his eyes to a deafening quiet. There was a visible drizzle in the air, but the worst seemed over. He put on the "raincoat" Old Ma had given him a few days ago: a broad-brimmed hat and a two-part cape all made of reed leaves neatly braided together. He must look ridiculous in it, like a straw man, a scarecrow. When he opened the door and stepped into the drizzle, he knew why it was good. He could breathe easily, hear what was going on around him, and walk without any hindrance at all.

The fruit trees had been all but shaved bare. Broken branches and twigs were scattered around. Everywhere on the ground, soaked in puddles of muddy water, were fallen peaches, fallen before they had a chance to ripen. The vegetable garden didn't fare better, either. The cucumber vines and tomato stems and their supports had all collapsed whichever direction the thunderstorm had struck. None looked like it could be revived.

The river itself was no longer a sheen of translucent green. Muddy, shivering under the constant drizzle, it threatened to overtake the bank and spread beyond.

It rained on and off lethargically for a day or two and then poured again nonstop for days with rekindled madness. Despair began to appear in the eyes of the villagers. Everybody said they hadn't seen anything like this in forty or fifty years. What was wrong? Why was Heaven being so angry with them this year?

Ten days later the river had swollen so much that Shanmeng

could see it without stepping outside: a wrinkled sheet of muddy brown billowing from close to the base of his home to the hills in the distance, a water world indeed.

With the flood rising at this speed, Shanmeng's home would be buried under water within days. He had to evacuate fast. That was the village chief's order, too: All residents living in lowland had to abandon their homes and find shelter with those on higher ground.

"That's the true spirit of Mutual Aid," Old Ma hollered hoarsely, as he waded through the muddy water from house to house with a broken branch as cane.

Had the hermit, Shanmeng wondered as he packed, the architect of this hut, its very first inhabitant, foreseen flood of such magnitude when he chose this spot? Probably not. He had failed to foresee many other things, too.

Shanmeng cut more than a dozen tall, thick bamboo in the backyard, tied them together into a small raft, placed all his furniture—his bed, dining table, and what not—on them, and fastened it to the ginkgo tree.

The two pigs in the pen met him anxiously, sniffing his legs like dogs. He put a rope around the neck of each and led them to Old Ma's home, its ground a full house higher than Shanmeng's. By now the pigs were around 100 pounds each, robust and willful. Excited by the sudden excursion, they were sprinting this way and that way; their leashes got braided together now and then. Shanmeng had to rely on his own weight to slow them down. Even the pigs, though, sensed something was wrong, very wrong, when they had to wade through a long stretch of muddy water that reached their raised chins. From then on they were as submissive and well-behaved as pigs could.

Next, Shanmeng had to move the chickens to safe ground. He was glad that he had only Brownie, the mama hen, and six young chicks to worry about. Where had the others gone? He knew the answer only too well. He had seen Old Ma's wife slaughtering chickens: Her left hand holding a squawking chicken from under its wings, vising its head between thumb and forefinger, and sliding the kitchen knife there a few times; blood would gush into a bowl of water spiced with a bit of salt; the poor chicken would squirm and kick until it stiffened.

Shanmeng squirmed with the chicken every time he had to do it, his eyes half-closed. He had been a soldier. He had killed before. But to kill with a knife like this and to pull the trigger from a distance weren't quite the same thing. When the light in the chicken's eyes had dimmed completely, the rest was easy.

It took him a while to catch all six young chickens, tie up their legs with strings, and place them in a basket. The real trouble was Brownie. She was settling down in the nest atop the coop again, for the first time since she had hatched, with the same dreamy look in her beady eyes. Wanted to hatch again? That soon? When Shanmeng lifted her from the nest, she whimpered as if she were being glued to it. There was no way he would leave her there. God knew what would happen. Once placed in the basket, Brownie hunkered down in the make-do nest right away. Halfway through the stretch of knee-deep muddy water on his way to Old Ma's, Shanmeng felt an uneasy movement from the otherwise quiet Brownie and stopped to check.

She was in the middle of something: Her eyes shiny with selfless focus, the small comb atop her forehead reddening, all her feathers, taut, all caught in an tremendous effort. The tip of an egg, an oval ball of fresh, pinkish life, peered from her behind.

"Easy, easy," Shanmeng said softly. "There's a good girl."

He wanted to wait till the birth was over, but the egg seemed stuck in its passage, barely moving. He resumed his journey, groping ahead with his feet underwater carefully. The young chickens all kept quiet, perhaps out of respect to their onetime mama hen.

When he finally reached Old Ma's home, Brownie trembled in the basket, and then made a half-hearted attempt to sing. An egg, still warm, marked with a small streak of fresh blood, was in the basket.

Huifa, Old Chao, and a couple of other families had moved in with Old Ma's, too. His house already in the water, Huifa's face was overcast all the time. Even the cheerful Old Chao would lose his temper with his wife now and then. It was hard to imagine how he had coaxed the mama pig into going along with evacuating for her own good.

"Everything will be fine in a few days," Old Ma said after a hasty supper of pancakes and porridge that had taken his wife and Fuli quite a while to prepare. "I don't believe the sky has really cracked open. Jade Emperor has had a long pee. That's all."

Jade Emperor indeed was taking his time to pee, a long, draining pee, swelling the river to the base of Old Ma's house, too. Between the drops, people ran out and tried to catch fish with harpoons, baskets, and rags of old mosquito nets framed with sticks. Whenever someone caught a silver, a black carp, or a sharksucker, there would be a cry of excitement. The fresh catch added to the food on the Eight Immortals table, which proved too congested for the hosts and their long-staying guests.

News of houses caving in and another kid drowned in the flood kept coming in. Old Ma decided to evacuate everyone to a level area, the size of a thrashing ground, on the hill outside the village.

Once on the hill Shanmeng could see the enormity of it all, the continuous body of brown water accented with treetops, occasional roofs demarcated by hills that seemed a bit lower than he remembered and spreading to the edge of the sky. Like a piece of painting by a crazed artist who had poured ink on the paper, added a few impatient brushstrokes here and there, and walked away.

They needed to set up tents first, 人-shaped tents framed with thick bamboo and covered with reed sheets and wheat straw. 人. Human. The very first character Shanmeng learnt from Peide, who illustrated for him with his arms and legs.

The sound of the village bell—heart-rending, urgent, one on the heel of another--still lingering in the air, Old Ma led a few young men going from house to house in the village looking for folks who had difficulty evacuating.

As the villagers were busy cutting trees and bamboo and carrying the old, the sick, and the very young to the camp being built on the hillside, there was an aura of resignation and quiet determination to survive. What would happen would happen. What was the use of sitting around and sighing and blaming Heaven, Earth, Jade Emperor, or Dragon King of the Sea?

Shanmeng was helping the Ma family build their tent. The only man, adult man, of the family was running around taking care of the whole village.

Shanmeng told himself to be calm, like the villagers, but his body had a mind of its own and kicked into a crisis mode in spite of himself. He waved the ax in the rain like a mad man.

Old Ma's wife and Fuli carried the tree branches and bamboo he had cut to a spot they had chosen. The older woman's hands trembled as she tried to pick up something long and heavy. The simple, kind woman was only in her mid-forties, but looked at least ten years older, her face lined with worries, worries she must have kept mostly to herself.

Fuli, a lot younger and stronger, could lift the things he had cut all right. Her hair and her face were dripping with rain, sweat, a mix of both. Her short-sleeved blouse and satin pants, wet like water, stuck to her body, showing her vivid curves. Shanmeng's heart ached watching her carrying a long, thick bamboo struggling up the rain-drenched slope to the campsite.

The rain stopped suddenly. Streaks of furious sunshine pierced through the clouds and shone on the tents of various sizes that had been hastily set up. Shanmeng hurried back to the village to help move the kids and "valuables" to the camp. No one could tell when the sky would crack open again.

Nearing the entrance of the village, Shanmeng saw Sportie dashing toward him, barking urgently, whimpering. "What is it, Sportie?" The family dog turned around and led Shanmeng to Old Ma's home, where kids were crying, screaming, among them, Yingzi.

"What happened, Yingzi?" Shanmeng asked.

Yingzi, her face twisted by tears, pointed at a small wooden tub in the water, capsized, still drifting further away from land. "It's Ah

Bao!"

Shanmeng ran into the water and swam toward the tub. Upon reaching it he dived and searched, with his eyes open, in an ever-expanding circle.

The river felt so different from before the flood when the water was so translucent he could see things in vivid detail as if he were in an enormous aquarium: the hairs on water chestnut stems, a lotus root peeping out from slimy mud, the eyes of a curious carp wanting to check him out, and fresh-red feet of ducks rowing in the greenish water, which, startled when his head suddenly emerged in their midst, would explode, and fly away, quacking, water splashing in all directions. He did swim to the other side of the river at its narrowest place where he saw wild geese nests full of fist-sized eggs.

Now the water was muddy and gave his eyes such a bitter, gritty feel. But his eyes soon adjusted. He could see tree trunks and shrubs, but where the heck was Ah Bao?

As he surfaced to breathe again, his head hit something like a sandbag. Something bloated, rotten, and revoltingly stench. It was a dead pig. He waved it away with his hand and at his touch, it dissolved into a thousand pieces of mushy flesh revealing pinkish skeletons underneath.

He took a deep breath and went underwater again and searched in an even bigger circle. Still no Ah Bao. His lungs swelled fast. His arms and legs began to stiffen. Be calm! Damn it! He ordered himself. Hold a bit longer!

He saw a shape not far to his right, his heart in his throat.

Ah Bao, so small down there by a tree trunk, his limbs outstretched but not moving, like a fish allowing itself to be carried by the undercurrent. The boy was naked. His open-seat shorts were not on him anymore. He must have lost it during whatever struggle he had put up while drowning.

Shanmeng grabbed the boy from behind and kicked to surface. A loud cry met him when he emerged. Screaming. Commotion.

With Ah Bao in his arms—the boy's eyes closed, face pale, colorless, belly bloated with water, body limp and without warmth-

-Shanmeng sprinted in the muddy water, almost tripping a couple of times.

"Ah Bao! Ah Bao"

Old Ma's wife collapsed. Fuli screamed and reached to touch her son. Yingzi cried and sobbed and kept mumbling unintelligibly. A crowd swarmed around them.

Shanmeng laid Ah Bao on the ground. Fuli fell on her knees, picked up her son, and rocked him in her arms.

"Put him down, Fuli," Shanmeng said, his face and voice contorted with emotions.

Fuli looked at him through tearful eyes and laid her son on the ground again.

Shanmeng tilted Ah Bao's head back with one hand while lifting his chin with the other, pried open his mouth and teeth to see if there was anything blocking the airway, and, finding none, turned the boy's face to the side. Then he sat astride Ah Bao, placed the heel of his right hand on a spot above the navel, and pressed with a quick upward thrust, gently.

"C'mon, Ah Bao!" he pleaded while pressing rhythmically. "Don't quit on me!"

He tried to stay focused, conscious of all the eyes on him.

"C'mon, Ah Bao! Ah Bao is a good boy!" His was the only voice speaking as the entire world watched on.

A few minutes later Ah Bao's lips stirred. A streak of brownish water began to ooze out.

15

The water had receded to its level before the flood three months ago and become clear again, yet dead branches half hidden among the shrubs and broken limbs dangling from a tree here and there still reminded people of the deluge that had all but destroyed their lives.

Weeds were growing luxuriantly on top of new graves in the village cemetery by the hill. These were unmarked mounds of earth underneath which were buried coffins, hastily made of trees cut from the hillside, for a childless old couple, who, feeble yet stubborn, had refused to evacuate; a middle-aged man who had gone out of his family's tent on the campsite to pee at night and tripped and smashed his head against a rock; a father and his young son who defied the orders by Old Ma and sneaked back to the village for the last two sacks of seeds and had their mud house collapsed on them; and several toddlers who, when their older siblings were not watching, wandered into waters too deep for their own good.

Most of the houses, those built with fired bricks, remained standing despite the debris and slimy mud and everything else that lumped inside and outside alike. The village chief's Eight Immortals table, having been exposed to the elements, lost all of their shine. Shanmeng's ancient furniture: the bamboo-framed bed and dining table, looked even more faded. A number of houses of mud walls, however, had to be rebuilt from ground up. Some of those that had not crumpled looked too dangerous for human inhabitation.

On the night of the worst thunderstorm, wind and rain pounded on the thin roofs and walls of the make-do tent so viciously that Shanmeng felt it could be torn away from the trees and rocks it was fastened to at any moment. When the storm did punch a hole into his tent, a peal of water poured in and soaked everything: his clothes, bags of grain, and books he had borrowed from Fuli. They had been air-dried now—the books. He had never seen a book that looked so bloated, its pages all but mushed, that he had to pry them separate one by one gingerly and lay them under the sun. The books dried up eventually and, with the new knowledge they had absorbed, looked puffy, twice their pre-flood size.

Now, while drowsing in bed in the evening, Shanmeng would hear a lone rooster, Brownie, and a young hen nestling in the coop;

the lone pig in the pen behind the hut; its sibling was gone, a few months prematurely, the way pigs were destined to go: Shanmeng had donated it for the big wok during the campaign to rebuild homes and reseed the fields. The swallows were all still here when he returned after the flood had receded. By early autumn, when the trees around the Twin-Sun River showed a hint of rusty red, the baby swallows were ready to test their wings. Cheered on by their Pa and Ma they emerged from the nest, one by one, leapt into the air, and fluttered out from the front door, carving circles and curves around his home, a-chirping all the while. They soared and disappeared into the sky.

Now, ambling in the quiet early morning breeze, Shanmeng would hear leaves drifting across the tree-wreathed river—yellow, rustic red leaves, like butterflies, like dreams—and large patches of vibrant orange and deep red murmuring in subdued tones on the hills in the distance.

One morning, thus ambling, when near the bend where stood the big willow overlooking the river, Shanmeng heard voices, soft, almost indistinct, yet familiar.

"Mama?"

"Mmmm? Ah Bao?"

"Mama?"

"Ah Bao? Are you hungry? We'll go home and have breakfast in a minute."

"Breakfast! Breakfast! Hiii!"

"Yes, breakfast. Congee and an egg for Ah Bao. How about that?"

"Breakfast. Congee. Egg. . . ."

When he gained to the other side of the bend, Shanmeng saw the mother and son team. Fuli was finishing the last article of clothing in a large basket. She tossed a shirt into the water, shook it hard, picked it up, and squeezed, water rippling far and wide. Ah Bao, in a gray padded jacket, was standing behind his mother.

When Fuli was done with the shirt, she straightened up, grasped the basket with one hand, and gave the other hand to her son.

"Let's go home."

"Home! Home!" Ah Bao repeated enthusiastically.

Propped awkwardly between two tall branches, Shanmeng reached to grab the last peach half hidden among the leaves of a twig close to the top of the tree. It was large, light golden, and promised to be as meaty and juicy as any he had harvested this year. Once his fingertips secured the fruit, Shanmeng yanked; it came off, a bit of the twig and leaves still attached. He jumped off the tree and went in the direction of the Ma home.

Old Ma had aged visibly since the Flood. His days old sideburns now became weeks old, and he was more taciturn.

Hearing footsteps, he looked up from the Eight Immortals table to see who it was, and then turned his eyes away, and sucked at the pipe again. Old Ma's wife peeked from inside the kitchen, gave Shanmeng an awkward smile, and resumed cutting at the counter, her lined face marked with old teardrops. Fuli and Ah Bao were not at home.

"Old Ma," Shanmeng asked, "what's the matter? What's happened?"

Old Ma shook his head.

"Is Ah Bao okay?"

The village chief nodded vaguely. Relieved, Shanmeng sat down at the table. "Look, Old Ma, I'm terribly sorry about what happened to Ah Bao—"

Old Ma looked up slowly. In that pair of eyes was something Shanmeng had never seen before: coldness, puzzlement, and something on the brink of hatred. It lasted for only a few seconds, and then he sank on the stool again and sat there, without a word, as if frozen at the table, a poor replica of his former self, but it was enough to make Shanmeng shudder.

As Shanmeng neared home in leaden spirits, he saw a small figure under the golden canopy of the gingko tree.

"Yingzi?"

The girl turned and smiled. Her attempt at brushing away new tears with the back of her hand only smeared her face more.

"Red. . . Brother Shanmeng."

She struggled to stand up, but Shanmeng had already sat down next to her. The chilliness of the ground cut through the padded pants instantly.

"What happened, Yingzi?" he asked softly.

"Pa didn't want us to tell anyone," Yingzi said, her chest heaving. "But I came anyway."

"Then don't tell. . . but, is everyone okay?"

Yingzi shook her head. They sat like that for a long while, neither saying anything. Ever since what happened to Ah Bao, there had existed some kind of bonding between the two for apparent reasons even though they had never talked about it.

"Jian'er is back. . . from Korea," Yingzi mumbled suddenly, as if she couldn't hold the burden of secrecy anymore.

"Jian'er? Who's Jian'er? From Korea?"

"Old Chao's son, remember Old Chao, with that big thing on his arm? But my brother. . . ."

Ah Bao's dad? Shanmeng had been wondering about Ah Bao's dad since day one. He had been dying to know. Now that he was on the verge of knowing, Shanmeng felt, to his own surprise, that he didn't really want to know anymore.

"My brother, Heshen, Ah Bao's dad. . . he won't come home no more."

"What happened?"

"He's been forced to go to Taiwan or South America by the American devils!" The girl's eyes were lit up with anger.

Shanmeng cringed at the expression which he hadn't heard for so long that he had all but forgotten it had ever existed. "You, stinky American devil!" the North Korean officer had screamed and pointed a pistol between his eyes. "This stinky American devil. . .his attitude is really bad," he had overheard the young Chinese PVA officer complaining to Peide . . . But to hear it from Yingzi like this?

Old Ma told everyone to leave when Jian'er came to see him before going home to his parents. Later that evening he made an announcement at the dinner table.

"Heshen won't come home no more," he muttered through clenched teeth, his face ashen. "Think of him as dead. I don't have a son anymore."

Yingzi's small shoulder heaved with emotions as she narrated. Shanmeng didn't know what to say to comfort the girl sitting next to him. Heshen, Yingzi's big brother, Ah Bao's dad, Fuli's husband, the son of Old Ma and his wife—had been forced to go somewhere else other than his home? Could he have refused repatriation. . . too?

Silence fell over the two again; they were too immersed in the new shared knowledge, and pain, for words.

"Where is Ah Bao," he murmured after an eternality, "and your sis?"

"Sis is taking Ah Bao for a long walk."

Shanmeng wandered around after Yingzi left. He couldn't sit at home. He couldn't cook and eat like nothing had happened. He needed space, much larger space, so he could breathe; he needed to stand on higher ground so he could see far without anything blocking the view.

The late afternoon wind blew on his face as he meandered aimlessly, but he didn't feel its bite, or hear the occasional chorus of dogs, roosters chasing hens, and geese in the sky migrating to warmer places before the onslaught of winter. Soon he found himself going toward the hill outside the village where they had set camp not too long ago. Here he could see far and breathe much more easily.

He worked his way up a steep trail flanked by trees and shrubs. He halted.

About twenty or thirty yards away on a big rock tilted near the edge of the old campsite sat two figures. The rock, the shape of a disc and the size of his hut, seemed in a perpetual flying away posture while being held back by a force too strong to break free from.

The two figures were a mother and a son. They were gazing toward the glimmering river and the hills drowsing in the gathering haze of early evening, behind them, a smaller figure, crouching on the rock, its ears alert, and further behind, the rustic red sky above the treetops. The mother pointed at something in the far distance; the son stirred; the animal wagged its tail.

Shanmeng watched from where he was, his feet frozen to the ground. He didn't know how long he stood there and when he turned and retraced the steps home.

As if driven by a whim, Shanmeng came to the old campsite on the hill again and again. Sometimes he found Fuli with her son here, sometimes, Fuli alone. The two or three of them would sit on the rock without saying a word. The presence of each other seemed the only thing that kept them afloat as tidal waves of doubt, pain, and despondence kept hitting and knocking them about.

"Why?" she blurted out one evening when she came alone, talking to no one in particular. "What gold did they promise you? What girls? Leaving behind me, Ah Bao, your parents. . . ."

He listened silently as the young woman went on, then buried her face in her lap, and sobbed. This very moment, this very scene, and the figure not far from him—it was all like a dream, as if he had seen it before, in another life of his. His heart ached. He moved closer and put his hand on her heaving shoulder.

"Why? Brother Shanmeng?" She lifted her head, her eyes glistening with tears.

He turned, gathered her in his arms, and caressed her rich short hair. She sobbed in his arms, her hands trembling, her fingers cold. He rubbed them until they were warm.

Old Ma, a Long March veteran himself, hadn't wanted his only son to have anything to do with war, but Heshen, stubborn and willful as his father, left home and joined Revolution when he was 16. He was the junior officer who recruited Fuli in 1947, a sophomore at the County High in the small town where Shanmeng and Peide had stopped on their way to the Twin-Sun River valley. They liked each other right away and were married two years later. Heshen was among the first batch of "Volunteers" to cross the Yalu River when war broke out in Korea. Fuli, pregnant with Ah Bao then, returned to this mountain village to live with his parents.

What irony! Shanmeng thought as he listened. He thought he had found a place to be quiet, to be thousands of miles and mountains and rivers away from war and from everything he despised, and hated, but they caught up with him anyway. Should he run again? Like that mysterious hermit? Where could he run? Deeper into the mountains and rivers?

No, he decided, I won't run again. I'm here to stay. I've found everything I've ever wanted here and I'm here for good.

They kept meeting like this for the next two years. Through the misty dusk they saw Nature around them put on a show of colors as the seasons changed, from brown and gray to tender green to purple and pink and yellow to dark green to brilliant gold and rusty red; listened to swallows and sparrows and crows and skylarks and cicadas chirping and flitting away in sun-streaked shadows of pines, walnuts, ginkgoes, and wild cherries and peaches, and seeds and needles and all kinds of nuts and overripe fruits falling on carpets of crisp leaves; immersed in the odor of toppled trees—some of them hundreds of years old perhaps—molded with overgrowth of mushroom-like fungi, blackened barks still decaying and rotting into the dark earth, and the fragrance of warm rays of the setting sun and wild flowers in full bloom nearby and along the river in the distance. When raindrops leaked from the sky, they would run and hide underneath the Flying Rock, their temporary shelter.

He suggested meeting at his place, in his hut, and she said no. "I know what you're thinking, but I can't." And there was nothing he could do to change her mind. As he held her tight in his arms, kissing her hair, her eyes, her mouth, with a thirst that couldn't be quenched with all the water in the river nearby, his hands searching along the curves of her body, she moaning quietly, her eyes closed, her face blushing with joy. Then she would disengage herself, suddenly, grip both of his large hands in hers, firmly, and hold his gaze with such a look in her eyes. He had to stop. He respected her too much, loved her too much, to press any further.

Once home and alone in his bed, his whole body would burn with an urge, the urge of a man at his age, fit and not even 30 years old yet. He would fight it until his hand reached downward, ostensibly to calm himself down, only to stir the fire to a more furious, dizzying blaze, his half closed eyes watching himself kissing Fuli whose body was aglow with the same burning desire, their full-length bodies enmeshed in one rolling ball of fire, despite the frothy cries of Pastor Higgins in the back of his head, cries about sinners in the hands of an angry God, who would hold him "over the pit of hell" like a spider.

The same desperate measure he had resorted to at the Camp, calling in his head the name of his love the whole time, a love forbidden by his parents, with urgency, usually the night prior to a once in a long while chance for bathing, when the loneliness, and hopelessness had reached a killing point. A measure he felt compelled to take to reconfirm his virility which would be cast in doubt after a prolonged interval of feeling no excitement. Each time afterwards he felt even more despondent. He would swear never to do it again, and each time, once started, it would not be over until it had run its full course and melted his entire being into ashen nothingness.

Part III

16

Ding started with the university library, a new five-story building with floor-length windows that glittered under a brutal early July sun. Ding liked libraries with tall windows, but the coral stuccoed exterior didn't quite appeal to him. It exhaled a kind of jolly light-headedness that seemed to be saying to the world whoever happened to be bending over books inside its walls at the time were not serious; they were only flirting with the idea or the appearance of seeking knowledge and wisdom.

The old index card cabinets, rows and rows of them, were gone. He had spent so many hours flipping through drawers of worn, greasy index cards for his master's thesis, jotting down call numbers, titles, and whatever information that would help him hunt down the books and journals in the dimly lit recesses of the old building. He had spent countless hours here leafing through those books and journals and jotting down words and phrases and sentences and whole paragraphs that could be summarized, paraphrased, or quoted in the thesis he was writing, the first milestone of a promising academic career.

Now, flanking both sides of the circulation desk were rows of desktop computers. Great Walls? Haiers? Lenovos? Ding couldn't see clearly thanks to the dazzling cosmic wind flashing across their screens.

Ding sat down at a computer and keyed in Professor Zhu's User ID and PIN. He tried different headings. His command of pinyin wasn't perfect, but was functional:

Korean War

Korean War POWs
Korean War POW Camps
Korean War Truce Talks
American Korean War POWs
American Korean War POWs Who Chose China
21 American Korean War POWs Who Refused Repatriation

He even keyed in the name of Tom's brother in several possible Chinese transliterations. Soon the printer buzzed with a long list of books on the history of the Korean War, memoirs written by Korean War veterans, and newspaper and magazine titles that promised to give the most exciting behind-the-scenes stories of the Korean War based on recently declassified top secret documents.

With the help of a library assistant, Ding found some of the books and carried them to a long table near a window overlooking the new sports field outside. Many of the library's neighbors looked new, too. Coral cement and glass and more coral cement and glass. The president of the university must have made a fetish of that color.

Ding started with the top of the pile on the table, scanning its table of contents and subject and name index for anything that had to do with Korean War POWs.

The book had a chapter on the POW issue, the dispute between the Chinese and North Koreans and the America-led UN side over the repatriation of the POWs. It said that according to the Geneva Conventions all POWs should be repatriated to their home countries, but in an attempt to achieve its dubious goals, the American side came up with this idea of giving the POWs the freedom of choice. That was why and how the bloody war dragged on for two more years on the battlefields as well as at the negotiation tables. This line of representation of what happened didn't square well with what little Ding had read from American historians and Korean War veterans. The American authors claimed that its motive was pure and noble: to uphold the principle of freedom of choice and to satisfy many of the Chinese and North

Korean POWs under its custody who had appealed not to be repatriated.

Ding knew that he wasn't the King Solomon type sent down here to adjudicate a long-standing dispute. His mission was simple: finding a needle in a big sea.

"Dr. Ding!" The clarinet-like voice sounded familiar. He looked up. It was the American girl he had seen at his father-in-law's two weeks ago, with a pile of books in her arms.

"Looks like someone's got a big paper due?" Ding stood up and offered to help the girl unload the books on the table.

"Sort of. I've got it. . . thanks!" the girl said, placing the books next to Ding's. "By the way, I am—"

"Greta! We've already met. I am Jie."

"Good to see you again, Jie."

They shook hands. Her fingers, the long, artist type, felt cool, moist in his hand. Ding pulled a chair for Greta.

"Jie, Outstanding, right?" she switched to Chinese, the same almost perfect tonal control.

Ding nodded. "A tall order from my parents when I was born, you know, and I'm afraid I've failed them miserably."

"C'mon, Jie! You must be fishing for compliments!" The idiom came fast. And hit home. "If I believe everything Professor Zhu has told me about you, about how you didn't start to learn English until you were 19, and how you used to tear pages from your OED, one alphabet at a time, carry them in the pocket, and whisk them out to study wherever and whenever you could—"

"Oh, don't believe him, then!" Ding felt embarrassed, and pleased. "The outstanding one is you! Just listen to your Chinese. More fluent than mine."

"Thank you!" Greta beamed. "I hope you didn't say that just because I—"

"No, I mean it." Ding insisted, and then asked, eyeing her books on the table. "So, what is it you're working on?"

"Long story."

"I've got the time for a novel."

"I'll give you a very short story instead," Greta said. "'Cause there's nothing dramatic, really."

During her sophomore year in college Greta took a beginner's Chinese course to fulfill the general education requirement of her degree program. Hooked from then on, she took all the Chinese language and culture and history courses her liberal arts women's college offered. After graduating with a bachelor's degree in Chinese studies with a minor in art history, she took a year off to work and read on her own to prepare for the only next logical step. And through internet research and her senior thesis advisor's recommendations, she found the place where she could pursue her dreams because Ding's alma mater offered one of the best graduate programs in art history in China. It was the first time that Professor Liu, an authority on classic Chinese landscape painting, had taken a foreign student under his wing. So he invited Professor Zhu to be Greta's co-mentor to ensure her success in the program.

"Why don't you take a breather and enjoy the summer? What's the hurry?" Ding asked, reaching to pick up a book from her pile on the table.

"What are you doing here, then?" There was playfulness in Greta's eyes. "Why aren't you sitting in the shade of a willow by a lake, and jumping into the cool waters--"

"There, you've got a piece of classic Chinese landscape painting already," Ding enthused. "If there's anything that needs to be adjusted at all, to make it truly classic, it's to replace the subject in your painting with an old man: long beard, a bamboo fishing rod—"

"I'd love to paint that myself, one day. Would you model for me?"

"Do I look that ancient already?"

They laughed, then checked themselves. There were not many people in the library. The finals were over a few days ago. Most of the students were gone for the summer, too. At the other end of a table next to Ding's a female student was bent over something. In a chair near another window a young man was leafing through magazines with flashy covers.

"So you teach humanities," Greta lowered her voice a full octave. "At what college?"

"Princetown, a small college in a small town where no ghost—"

"Would lay eggs, right? Pooo!" Greta dismissed the half-hearted self-effacement Ding had attempted. "If I could become a professor in China, when I'm done with my degree program here, I'd be so happy! Size doesn't matter. I mean, size and location of the school don't matter. Even if it's in Xinjiang or Tibet, so what! I'll pack up and go."

"I'd love to visit Xinjiang, and Tibet," Ding said. "But that's not in the plan for my summer."

"What's the plan? I don't mean—" Greta eyed the titles of Ding's books on the table. "They don't look artistic to me at all."

"No," Ding shook his head. "They're about war. War and art. Art and war. They don't seem to mix well, do they?"

"No, war destroys art." Greta switched back to her native tongue. "I don't know how much art has been destroyed since humans waged the first war against each other. And how much has been looted, too. I've read somewhere, oh, yes, a UNESCO report that about 1.67 million Chinese works of art, are being held by more than 200 foreign museums! The biggest among these are, of course, the usual suspects: the British Museum, the British Library, Musée du Louvre, Harvard's art museum, and of course the Metropolitan Museum of Art in New York, I could go on and on. The National Library of France alone holds over 10,000 cultural relics from the Dunhuang Grottos. How did those precious Chinese work of art get to those foreign museums? I don't imagine them having legs and trekking over the long, twisty Silk Road by themselves. Do you, Jie?"

Greta's eyes glinted with passion. Her hands, her long, soft fingers, quivered. Ding was touched. He hadn't been touched like this for some time.

"Do you, Jie?" Her eyes were still on him, waiting for an answer.

"Oh, no. I don't think so," Ding recovered. "There's the other side of the coin, too, if I may. War also creates art. I mean, the horrendous suffering wars inflict upon humankind have also inspired them to create works of art to give expressions to pain, to anguish, fear, to despair, and to the resilience of the human spirit. Right? A quick example would be Guernica, Weeping Woman, and Charnel House, and those black and white pictures of gas chambers and skeleton-like refugees looking from behind barred fences at Auschwitz, and other concentration camps. I can't imagine anyone wants to wage war again once they've seen those works of art."

"I agree, but we don't want to exaggerate the power of art, and literature, for that matter."

They fell silent, to let the weight of what they had just said sink in, perhaps.

"By the way," Greta said as she stood up, eyeing Ding's books on the table again. "Have you been to the Korean War Memorial in D.C.?"

"Oh, yes, more than once. Every time when I see those young soldiers frozen in the muddy fields, being burdened by the guns and ammunitions and grenades and countless other things they hump on their backs, everything about them so muddy grey, so metallic, so vulnerable, I want to cross over and give them a hand, or just touch their poncho, and I just want. . . ."

Greta nodded and mumbled something, but he didn't hear.

17

"I've talked to a few of my Veterans Club buddies," Professor Zhu said over dinner, sipping from a small glass of chilled beer.

The upright air conditioning unit hummed in the corner, blowing cool air toward the ceiling rather than the dining table because Mrs. Zhu was concerned about her husband's arthritis and because her own bones would ache dully even on a hot summer evening like this.

Ding looked up from his bowl and waited, but his father-in-law had just fed a meaty chop of Chrysanthemum Duck in his mouth.

"Jie, you look sweaty!" Professor Zhu mumbled through whatever remained of the duck in his mouth. "Why don't you go and adjust the AC's fan?"

"I'm fine, really," Ding smiled.

"Eat, eat," his mother-in-law urged, her chopsticks busy among the pieces still in the plate. She found a drumstick and stuffed it on top of Ding's bowl of rice. "Julie's favorite part of the duck."

Ding knew that only too well. When they were still dating and whenever Ding had saved enough to take Julie out, he would order a small plate and would insist that Julie have her favorite part of the freshly cooked duck.

"Julie called this morning, right after you left," mother-in-law said, having sipped from the tip of her spoon a few drops of winter melon, seaweed, and ham soup. Her eyes were on Ding's face as she spoke, her face lit up with half a smile. "She and Emily—they both miss you very much."

Ding nodded awkwardly, like when he was still a brand-new son-in-law. He knew that Mrs. Zhu knew that his would be a rather extended summer visit this time. She had never had one unkind word, not even a hint of displeasure, directed at him. But Ding sensed—he didn't know why—that she somehow felt that her only daughter, beautiful, educated, and vibrant, could and should have married better. To her credit, her face did blossom into a big, hearty smile when told that Ding was going to the US to pursue doctoral studies. Toward the end of the 90s, when more and more American-educated Chinese professionals returned with MBA and money and technical know-how to start business ventures in their home country, when newspapers and television programs were filled with stories of tons of money being made by these new elite overseas Chinese, and when Mrs. Zhu and her husband went to visit the mansions the son, son-in-law, or daughter of a Veterans Club buddy had bought in an elite, gated compound, the luster of

Ding's success began to dim.

"I was going to say," Professor Zhu coughed to clear his throat; there was nothing in his mouth to hinder smooth speech anymore, "my buddies at the Club weren't much help. Most of them were foot soldiers and field commanders during the war. They can't give one useful fart about the POWs even if you beat them on the buttocks with a stick! Hahaha."

Ding had loved the occasional slip into colorful language from the much-venerated professor when he was a student of his, but this was serious business now. At least it was so to him.

"They're getting old, senile," the old man sighed and shook his head in disbelief. "Some of them are several years younger than me, but the way they talk and sound and carry themselves, really sad. Then it hit me," he continued, hitting the forehead with the bottom of his palm, "I'm going about it the wrong way! I must be getting old, and senile, too. Hahaha! I mean there is this place, this mosque, I mean this National Museum of Modern Wars not far from the Southern Gate. I've been there once years ago. They asked me to donate things to the museum. What did I give them? Not the medals. No, I wouldn't part from them to save my own life! Now it's just come back to me: a Pak fountain pen and a few diary books, my wartime diaries. Jie, I've been thinking about writing a memoir, something along that line. Been too busy to start organizing things."

"You'd have time if you don't run around as if you were still in your 40s or 50s!" Mrs. Zhu reprimanded, half seriously.

"A memoir? Excellent idea! Why don't you get started somehow?" Ding enthused. "I'll keep an eye on those diaries of yours when I visit the museum."

"I have to warn you," Professor Zhu said, suddenly switching to English, "some of the entries could be personal, mmmm, private—"

"I give you my word that I'll close my eyes if I see anything, you know," Ding replied in English, too.

"Not a chance!" Professor Zhu laughed heartily. "They must have rotted through several times over, being kept in that kind of crabby museum. National Museum of Modern Wars, my butt."

Mrs. Zhu stood up to clear the table, a confused, annoyed look on her face.

18

Ding hesitated when he stepped out of the taxi and saw an armed guard posted at the entrance. The mosque, rather, the National Museum of Modern Wars, had always been here, in an alley not far from the Southern Gate of this ancient city. Surrounded by low, run-down residential houses that could be bulldozed any day to yield ground to new fancy office buildings and shopping plazas, the mosque seemed so out of place. How long could it hold out?

And it didn't look like the mosques one would see in Ankara, Teheran, Baghdad, Mecca, or Casablanca which Ding had long wanted to visit. With its deep red walls, raised eaves, and curved, swallowtail like roofs, it could well pass as a Buddhist or Confucian temple.

The young guard, armed with a rifle and smartly dressed in uniform, stood at attention when Ding approached and waved him in before he had a chance to inquire. Ding continued to march in when someone from the window of what looked like an information room saw him.

"Where do you think you're going?" the man said, hurrying out to stop him. "What're you looking for?"

Ding unzipped his briefcase slowly and showed him a letter from the President of the National Association of Veterans/The Province Conference, Chairman of the Board of Academic Review of the University of. . . .

The man read the letter front and back a couple of times and brought it closer to his nose to see more clearly the still fresh red zeal near the bottom.

"Your ID?"

Ding had anticipated this, but both his old residential ID and work ID had been reclaimed by the authorities ten years ago when he left for America. He had to bluff now. He searched in his wallet. He turned all of his pockets inside out. He fumbled hard in his briefcase with increased puzzlement and annoyance.

"I'm sorry," he said, zipping up the briefcase with regained calmness, "I thought I had it with me. I wonder if I have left it somewhere. . . ."

The man looked him up and down again.

"You wait here," he said and sauntered back to the information room, which, Ding noticed, led to a corridor deep inside.

A very long minute later the man came back with another man in his late 40s, who had the air of a bookish bureaucrat, or a bureaucratic bookman.

"You're a doctoral student of Professor Zhu?"

"Yes," Ding shook the newcomer's hand warmly.

"I'm the Associate Director here, Feng," the man said. "The Director is in Beijing attending an important meeting. I understand you're working on your doctoral dissertation on a Korean War POW topic?"

"Yes. Both Professor Zhu and I feel that this part of history has been overlooked for too long and a careful comprehensive study of what exactly did happen is long overdue. By the way, I like your T-shirt, Director Feng. Where did you get it?"

"Oh, this?" Director Feng pointed at the mountain-and-cloud motif on his T-shirt--and beamed. "I visited the Yellow Mountain last summer. Oh, I thought I would never want to come down again. It was something, so free from any earthly concerns, when so high up there. Yes, I agree with you absolutely. History can serve as mirror for us today and for posterities in the future. Let me show you around."

Ding followed Feng into the hall. The Prayer Hall.

Supported by more than a dozen tall posts forming a constellation of arches, the hall looked spacious and grand and could allow at least two hundred pilgrims to prostrate and pray at the same time. In the middle of the hall was a tablet of scriptures etched in gold. One of the proudest possessions of the entire mosque was an upright tablet of a Qing emperor's decree proclaimed in 1784. Ding took a cursory look and moved on.

Noticing the visitor's lukewarm interest in old relics, Director Feng led him on through a gate in the back of the hall into a deep courtyard, which featured a row of rooms on both sides and another main building, similar to the one Ding had just visited, but about half its size, to complete the long rectangle.

"When the Cultural Revolution was at its worst," Feng explained as they followed a flight of stone steps into the corridor on the left. "You remember those days? Anything that had the faintest odor of a bourgeois, feudalistic relic would be smashed to pieces, burnt down, trampled on. Those reckless, clueless Red Guards!"

This associate director, Ding thought to himself, given his age, could have been one of those young, clueless youths fired up by Mao and their own untamed desire to inflict pain.

They stopped at the first room with a sign that said:

The 1911 Revolution

That was the uprising led by Dr. Sun Yat-sen to overthrow the last emperor of the Qing dynasty. Anything apocalyptic coded in the imperial decree in the Prayer Hall? Ding wondered. That would be truly ironic. He pressed his face against a windowpane and peeked. It was too dim inside to see anything.

"Let me go and get the keys," Feng offered, shaking the large, semi-rustic lock on the door. When Feng hastened back, the Mountain-and Cloud themed T-shirt already looked sticky on his skin.

"Professor Zhu probably wouldn't remember me," Feng said as he opened the door, "but I was a student of his in 1972. Yes, I was one of those Worker-Peasant-Soldier college students, both a blessing and a curse, you know. By the late 80s, I finally had had it. I went back to school, got my master's in library science, and rid myself of the stigma. Young people like you are really fortunate."

"Young people like me?" Ding laughed. "You look quite young yourself, a couple of years older, tops."

The man grinned happily. "I was a diligent student, but at 25, my tongue was so stiff and couldn't tell the difference between [n] and [l], [k] and [g], what have you. My lips would tremble so badly when I tried too hard, especially when I watched my mouth move in the mirror while trying. But Professor Zhu, oh, he was ever so kind and patient."

Ding nodded. He had wondered, every once in a while, in one of his dark moments of self-doubt, if he would have stuck to the marriage to Julie if she hadn't been his beloved professor's daughter.

"Professor Zhu told me he has donated a few things here, too," Ding said.

"Really!?" Director Feng sounded genuinely surprised. "Well, you know, I came here only five years ago, and we're just starting to do an inventory and to develop a computerized index. All in due time."

They continued down the corridor and passed rooms for the wars that had been waged since the beginning of the 20th century.

The Northern Expeditions (1925-1927). The war to annihilate the warlords who had become lawless rulers of different parts of China: Yuan Shikai, Duan Qirui, Zhang Zuolin, Wu Peifu, Sun Chuanfang.

The Long March (1934-1935). Growing up Ding had read, or had been told, so much about the Long March, how the Red Army, led by Mao, scaled snow-capped mountains, and crossed endless swamps to spread the seeds of revolution. Later, he found out that the Long March was actually a strategic retreat, or, to put it more bluntly, the Red Army, having lost its major bases after five major campaigns from the Chiang Kai-shek government troops, had to move to poorer, less accessible mountainous regions of the country in order to survive. But that didn't matter now, because the Communists eventually won. Who could argue with victory?

"When the Cultural Revolution was at its worst," Feng said,

looking for the right key from the long string, but stopped when he saw Ding shaking his head, "a group of Long Marchers, who had impeccable revolutionary credentials, sent a petition to the central government. Somehow, through their contacts, their petition reached the very top, perhaps Premier Zhou Enlai, or even Chairman Mao himself. At any rate, a decree was issued fast enough. That's how this mosque became a temporary, make-do museum of all the precious documents from the 1911 Revolution to the Korean War. After all, there was nothing bourgeois or feudalistic about these documents. Why this city and this mosque of all places? I honestly don't know."

Near the end of the corridor on the left were the rooms for the War of Resistance against Japan (1937-1945). Those eight years were among the toughest in modern Chinese history. Ding wondered whether the rooms had space enough to contain all that happened from the Marco Polo Bridge Incident to the Rape of Nanking all the way to the Japanese surrender in 1945.

The corridor on the right began with the Civil War (1946-1949) between the Communists and the government troops armed by the Americans. From 1921, when a small group of youths formed the Communist Party in Shanghai, to 1949 when they succeeded in taking over the largest country in the world—It had taken 28 years. Not bad. Would anyone of that group of "forefathers" of the "New China" be happy to see what was going on today? Was this what they had envisioned? Would that matter? Ding couldn't help having these wayward thoughts even though he knew exactly why he was here.

Finally, he saw the sign:

Korean War (1950-1953)

It would have been the first sign, the first group of rooms, if Director Feng had started the tour from the right corridor when entering from the Prayer Hall.

Ding had made some progress sorting through the

mountainous piles of documents and files and whatnot for the Korean War. Put together, the two rooms were not nearly as boundless as a sea or even a decent-sized pond, but it took only one person to hide the needle and a thousand to look for it and the odds were not in their favor. And if, as in this case, the trail had been buried underneath half a century of time, any effort to find the needle could indeed be an exercise in futility.

Unless one was extraordinarily lucky.

That was the thought on Ding's mind as he approached the mosque again on this hot, mid-July morning. This time the young armed man thrust out his left arm like a baton and stopped him.

He hadn't come alone. He was with a young woman. A young beautiful foreign woman. She had on a tight sleeveless blouse that accented the vivid curves of her body. Her hair curled naturally where it touched her smooth shoulders. Her nose was not extraordinarily large, but assertive enough, straight, and pointed. Her lips, perfectly aligned, looked full and fresh. And her eyes. A glance from that pair of eyes would put anyone at ease, and leave him restless long afterwards.

Ding had sort of expected an inconvenience like this would happen. He had already caught attention on the way to the mosque museum. He had noticed the middle-aged taxi driver stealing glances at them, or at him on account of her, with envy.

"She's also a graduate student at the university," Ding started to explain, "doing an extremely important project on the art history—"

"No foreigners," the guard cut him short.

"Why don't you wait here, Greta," Ding said to the young woman in English, "I'll go in and clear it up. Won't take long."

"Sorry, Jie," Greta smiled.

No need to say "Sorry," Ding thought to himself as he walked toward the information room inside the gate. Who—what man— wouldn't want to run errands for a beautiful young woman like Greta? Yet, what if Director Feng would not oblige because he felt, legitimately, that Ding was abusing the privilege granted him on account of some real or imagined favor Feng had received from

Professor Zhu many years ago? In that case, should he tell Greta to go home—back to the university—so he could continue his research in those two rooms, or should he leave with Greta? Which would be the more gallant thing to do?

The Associate Director had just made his tea, eased up in his chair, and was ready to peruse the Modern Express and other such papers from a stack on his desk. His office was jammed with stuffed cabinets and stacks and stacks of dusty, yellowed things on the floor.

The annoyance at being interrupted in his morning ritual lasted only as long as it took the man to see who the uninvited visitor was. His face blossomed into a congenial smile instantly.

"Sorry, my office is a bit messy here. Take a seat" Feng pointed him to a chair next to his desk.

"You should see mine," Ding said, but didn't take the seat.

"Mmmm," Director Feng mulled visibly after hearing Ding explain the situation. "I'd love to help, but my hands are tied. We have clear policies: No access to foreigners. Who knows. We may have sensitive documents mixed up in the piles here and there that need to be properly processed. We're still working on it. See what I mean?"

"Absolutely. But you see, this foreign visitor, this American, is working on a master's thesis about Chinese art history. An American working on a thesis about Chinese art history! That means something. That means she's a friend, and she has friends and will make more and new friends. All of her friends could be our friends, too, or at least be more friendly toward us, thanks to the kind of work she does. Don't we need to win more and new friends all over the world?"

Director Feng looked unconvinced, hesitant. "Let me go and see what's going on."

From a distance, Ding saw Greta being engaged in a casual but lively conversation with the young guard. Or rather, she was doing all the talking while the guard listened and nodded or shook his head ever so vaguely.

Upon seeing them coming, Greta flashed them—Director

Feng, to be more exact—a smile, that warm and caring smile. Ding felt a pang of something akin to jealousy. You've got no goddamn right to that feeling, jerk, he told himself. Besides, there was nothing in that smile, that "spot of joy" in her cheeks, that would suggest light-headedness. Or frailty.

Greta reached out to shake Director Feng's hands. Feng grinned, his face lit up with a big, perspiring smile, and shook her hand a bit too zealously.

"Your Chinese is perfect! Where did you learn it?"

Greta explained briefly, the same warm gaze on him.

"The subject of my thesis is Art in China's Revolutionary Wars. I have been fascinated with China ever since I read Edgar Snow, his Red Star Over China. You never know, this young American girl right here may well turn out to be the Edgar Snow, or Agnes Smedley, of the 21st century. . . ."

This American girl does know quite a bit about Chinese revolutions, Ding thought as he watched Greta chattering on. There was nothing in her face and in the easy flow of words that would suggest that she was other than being sincere.

"I'll make sure you, and your museum, be acknowledged when the thesis is completed, and expanded into a book. . . ."

What could poor Director Feng do other than grant her access to the museum? "Sorry, no cameras allowed," Feng said, eyeing Greta's leather camera bag, the smile on his face never fading.

Ding could feel Director Feng's eyes on them as he and Greta walked into the museum, a potential goldmine for Greta, and an endless sea where Ding had tried hard to find the missing needle.

Two days ago he had gone to the university library to check email from school and Emily. Princetown College was still standing, intact. Mike, his officemate, was teaching a summer session of Humanities 101 so he'd have money to fund his summer travel. Except for the few students, mostly local kids who wanted to grab a few fast (and easier?) credits, the campus would look deserted in midsummer when life was supposed to be at its most sappy and dreamy.

Ding received a brief note from Tom and Dora, just to say hello and see how things were going. Ding replied that he hadn't found any solid clues, but he might be onto something and would keep them posted.

The three emails from Emily almost exploded his mailbox because each contained several attachments, pictures of her and her mom at a party with Julie's obnoxious workplace friends, and her and Rachel and other school friends picnicking on lush green grass at Lake Prince. She was in her comfortable summer wear, nothing nearly as wild as that talent show. Each picture took a few long minutes to download.

About half way through the third email—"Oh, before I forget, Mom says hi and wants to know if you're having fun!"—from Emily, he heard a familiar voice from behind.

"So, I thought you've dug your way back to the US."

"Oh, Greta," Ding turned around.

"Sorry to have interrupted," Greta smiled.

"Oh, no, just some emails from school, nothing particular."

They sat and chatted and played catch up like old friends.

There was no way he could have said no to Greta when she said she'd like to tag along. There was no assumption in that warm gaze when she waited for him to answer, but how would he say no? Like how could he have said no during the days when he was dating Julie, Professor Zhu's darling daughter?

Ding spent half of the day showing Greta around in the museum. She didn't exactly let her jaws drop to the floor when she entered each of the rooms, but her enthusiasm was more than infectious. Navigating her way through the stacks and piles on the floor and on half organized shelves, she had an almost religious look on her face. No, she didn't mind the dimness and the mildewy smell at all. She was completely transported to a different time and place.

Director Feng had told Ding that they had considered installing AC units but decided against it because plans were in the works for a permanent site for the museum to better preserve history. The site and architectural plan had not been chosen because the Review Committee, which consisted of eminent historians, veterans' representatives, well-known architects, and the director of the museum, was deadlocked after three days of sequestered meetings thanks to intense lobbying from various interest groups. Now the last two plans had been sent to the central government in Beijing for final decision.

While still in the room for the 1911 Revolution, Greta, with an apologetic smile, fished out a tiny camera from the bottom of her backpack. She used up the five rolls she had with her in about an hour and regretted that she hadn't brought more. Sometimes she would ask Ding to move a poster or artifact closer to the window to have better light.

"Be careful," she would warn as if any carelessness in handling would amount to sacrilege. "I've been to the Smithsonian Museum and Library of Congress," she said while taking pictures of the costumes, homespun cloth, their color long faded, used in The White-Haired Girl, a popular opera about a poor peasant daughter victimized by a vicious landlord. It was staged during the heyday of the Communist revolution to rally the troops and masses. "Everything there had this well-cared for, perfect condition kind of look. Light. Temperature. Humidity. Yes, you feel touched and enlightened. But here, it's history in its most raw, unpolished state. That's why it touches you beyond words."

When they finally advanced to the rooms for the Korean War, Greta couldn't tear herself away from a poster. It featured a mother sending off his son by the Yalu River, the mother looking so aged, simple, and country, so worried despite the smile, her son so young, boyish.

There had to be similar scenes, Ding thought, when Tom's brother, and the tens of thousands of American boys bid farewell to their folks before being shipped to Korea around the same time half a century ago.

Were such posters and pictures pure propaganda or true reflections, at least true among many Chinese, of the spirit of the Chinese people when facing what they believed was aggression from the most powerful country in the world?

"I've always wondered," Greta said, as if thinking aloud, her eyes still on the poster, "why the much superiorly equipped American army couldn't win in both Korea and Vietnam. Now I know."

"Now, Greta, you really sound like the Edgar Snow, Agnes Smedley of the 21st century, at least one in the making."

Greta bowed to an imaginary audience and smiled.

"Let's get started, Jie," Greta said when they returned the following morning. "I don't want to be your excuse for failing this noble mission of yours."

"It'd be a legitimate excuse, being distracted by—"

"C'mon, Jie!" Greta laughed, "Get to work, excuse or no excuse!"

Seriously, though, Ding thought, what if all this search in this hot summer ended empty-handed, a three-month exercise in futility? How would he face Tom and Dora, and tell them, "I've tried, but it didn't work out"? He didn't want to be the messenger of bad news, and to be forever associated with the loss of the last thread of hope.

He had gone through most of the things in the two rooms now. Books. Magazines. Pamphlets. Newspapers. Whatever. Stacks and piles of them. Gingerly. Because they had all become so fragile and brittle.

"Too much acid in the paper," Director Feng had told him during his first visit. "So, handle with care. Who knows, some of the stuff we have here may be the only copy still existent. If we ruin them, they'll be gone permanently. That's why for some of the things we hold here, those from the 1911 Revolution especially, we don't even know if we should xerox them for backup copies. Dilemma, real dilemma. Xeroxing will give you something close to a brand-new copy with much better paper, but you'll destroy the original in the process."

For a while both were so absorbed in what they were doing

that the only sound in the room was their own breathing, and the occasional turning of pages.

"Have you checked this?" Greta hollered from somewhere in a corner at the other end of the room. She was trying to pull out a box from underneath an old bookcase loaded with dusty stacks.

Ding had noticed the box before. It was not big and didn't look like any treasure could be hidden in it.

He grabbed a side of the bookcase and tried to lift it, but it was too heavy. He had no choice but to remove the stacks from the bookcase. As he was busy doing so, his elbow hit something.

"Ouch!" cried Greta, rubbing her head.

"Oh, I'm so sorry!" He meant every syllable of the apology. And felt it.

"It hurts, Jie. Now you owe me ice cream for that!"

"Cherry, chocolate, vanilla, any flavor you want," Ding said gallantly, "as long as you don't sue me for physical and emotional damages."

"All three flavors, and more."

"Deal."

The box was jammed with pocket-sized diary books. Dozens of them. All cloth bound. Velvety. Red, blue, burgundy. They were musky, quaint, damp to the touch.

Greta picked up a book with her delicate long fingers and opened it. "I wouldn't believe this if I'm not looking at it with my own eyes," she marveled.

"You'd better believe it," Ding said, picked up a book, and turned to its opening page:

> *Resist America, Assist Korea!*
> *Liao. Commissar. 3rd Regiment*

Forceful, expressive handwriting, the kind only someone drilled in the old school could have perfected. Ding's Chinese handwriting was okay. He had practiced after several models for fountain pen, but could never write as gracefully as his father, or grandfather. Thanks to the advent of the computer and the Internet, nobody needed to write the long hand all that much anymore.

Ding carried the box to a window, and they sat on the floor to go over the diaries more carefully.

Among the themes of Liao's entries before October 25, 1950 were: Determination to fight the US invaders. Ways to raise the morale of troops. Language challenges—need to find soldiers and officers of Korean origins. A troupe to come and perform for the troops. A feast for troops before crossing the Yalu River.

Apparently, this Liao was a field commander whose dairy entries would not yield clues to the fate of American POWs. Where is this Liao now? Ding wondered as he placed the book to the side. If he hadn't managed to get into any political trouble and was still in decent health, Liao must be a top-ranking general, the commander of a military garrison, or something like that.

One of the diary books Ding examined was by a junior staff officer. He was only 19 years old, but had joined the Revolution in 1946, when he was still a "little red devil." His youth was evident in his handwriting, which was fluent, but not as confident and expressive as that of Liao. Ding wondered how he could sense a person's personality through handwriting. But there was certainly some truth in the old saying that "Handwriting is the man." Some of the entries mentioned American POWs. Sometimes the tone was dismissive, and contemptuous, because many of them had their girlfriends' photos with them. The young officer wondered if carrying those photos would weaken their fighting spirit and how he would feel if he had a girlfriend. Ding hoped, as he placed the book next to the small non-promising pile, that the young officer had survived the war and had a chance to find out what it was like to be in love.

"Hey, Greta," Ding said when he noticed that she was still less than halfway through her first book. "This is no time for close reading. Remember the SQ3R strategy? Here, S alone is good enough, unless you want to camp out here."

"Yes, professor," Greta smiled and began to leaf through the rest of the pages.

Three more books later, Ding picked up another one with a burgundy cover. His heart skipped a beat when he saw the name on the first page. It was in English, cursive, with a distinctive, self-conscious flourish.

As the pages turned, young Lieutenant Zhu switched between English and Chinese. Some entries in English only, some in Chinese, some a mix of both, particularly when he needed to cite a classic Chinese poem to express himself. There was a rendition of Wordsworth's "Daffodils" in classic Chinese verse form. Ding had a lot of respect for old-time scholars like Zhu who had solid grounding in classic Chinese. Ding's generation wasn't that lucky. Whatever he knew of the Tang Poems and classics he picked up on his own as a young teen when they were still banned.

By early 1951, the tone of Zhu's entries began to change. There surfaced a sentiment warmer in tone, the handwriting was bolder, less bridled at times, and hesitant and faltering at others.

One of the earliest of these entries began thus:

> O, my Luve's like a red, red rose,
> That's newly sprung in June.
> O, my Luve's like a melodie
> That's sweetly play'd in tune.

It was followed by an outpouring of joy, of seeing "Rose" everyday, right across from his desk: A mere glance from her was enough sunshine to warm his heart and melt away the brutal cold outside their bunker.

Ding felt embarrassed by such outpouring, which he attributed to youthful inexperience, but blushed when he remembered a certain graduate student giving the very same poem, hastily copied, to a beautiful girl whose English was not nearly good enough to appreciate the sentiment being expressed.

There were days when the young lieutenant felt uplifted by a smile from Rose, who must have sensed how he felt about her. How couldn't she? On other days he would be melancholy, despondent, in the grips of Young Werther kind of sorrow. Ding knew that he was in no position to dismiss it all as the romantic nonsense of youth untempered by setbacks and everything else in life. The pain was real, was cutting to the quick, was heartbreaking. Besides, the young lieutenant was in the midst of war; there were entries about air raids, about deaths, about being scared yet ready to die for the motherland.

Then there entered a threat to this passionate love—one-sided, unrequited, no matter—in the form of a more worldly, charismatic, and yes, much more "stylish," officer several ranks above him, dubbed Four-Eyed. Oh, Rose seemed pleased by the attention paid by Four-Eyed! She smiled, she giggled, and she laughed heartily at the things Four-Eyed said, and each time she thus smiled, giggled, and laughed, the young lieutenant would cringe with pain.

Poor fellow, Ding sighed, appreciating the fact that the poor fellow was to be his father-in-law decades later.

The last few such entries were written apparently by a trembling hand. One of them had the following in the middle of the page:

Till a' the seas gang dry.

How had Professor Zhu felt about this chapter in his emotional history, Ding wondered, when turning the pages of the wartime diaries before donating them to the museum? Rose, apparently, was not the current Mrs. Zhu. Had Professor Zhu ever gotten over it? And who was this Four-Eyed character?

Since many of Zhu's entries mentioned the interrogations of UN, particularly, American POWs, this Four-Eyed character, a superior officer, must have much more intimate knowledge of what had really occurred behind the scenes.

As they stepped out from the Prayer Hall toward evening, Ding saw Director Feng waiting anxiously by the gate. Something has just happened? He wondered. They would have to undergo a pat search from head to toe?

"Well, how did it go today?" asked Director Feng when they were still steps away, an affable smile on his face. "I assume you can write at least ten doctoral dissertations with so much material here," he turned to Greta, "and master's theses."

"Absolutely," Ding enthused, relieved. Where would he be in the world by the time the ten doctoral dissertations—and master's theses—were completed? Would another war, or several more wars, have been fought and won and lost already?

'By the way," Director Feng pulled Ding aside and lowered his voice, "did you mention me to Professor Zhu?"

"Oh, that, sure, yes!" Ding tried to project zeal in his voice. "He remembers you well, and said you were quite a diligent scholar."

"O, good," Feng mumbled somewhat shyly. "As I've told you, this would be my last shot at full professorship in library science. A word or two from Professor Zhu to the other committee members, you know, could make a difference."

"I'll certainly bring this up to him again."

Yes, he couldn't wait—he was dying—to talk to his father-in-law again.

19

The receptionist at the Rain & Dew teahouse led him to a private room at the end of a long, winding hallway. Inside the sliding door were a small leather couch, a table with four chairs, some in-house plants, and a 19-inch TV set in the corner.

A young waitress came in to serve tea and two small plates of melon seeds. Ding told her he would order when his guest arrived. The girl smiled and left.

How should I begin? Ding wondered as he picked up a fat melon seed. It tasted milky and fragrant, but he was never skilful at cracking such seeds and didn't have patience with the process anyway. As always he ended up crushing the seed between his teeth, shell and meat together.

Several times he heard steps in the hallway, but none stopped at his door. He became fidgety and felt the whole thing was a bit presumptuous on his part. But it was too late to call it off now.

Finally, there was a knock; his door slid half open.

"Yes, it is the right one," Professor Zhu peeked and said to the receptionist breathily. "Professor Zhu… Dad," Ding was at a loss how to greet his father-in-law. "C'mon in."

Their waitress came in behind Professor Zhu and asked if they'd like to order. Ding took a look at the menu. "Anything you fancy today, Dad?"

"You know me, Jie, I'm easy."

Ding ordered two glasses of coconut juice and two fruit plates. "That's good for now."

They chitchatted, wandering from family, health, school, society, international politics and back again in no particular order when the old man said, suddenly: "Jie, let's cut to the chase. You know me so well, and I know you. So, what exactly do you want to talk about today? All this secrecy. If Julie's mother ever found out, she might suspect that I—" Professor Zhu chuckled awkwardly.

Ding turned and grabbed his briefcase from the couch and opened it. "This is what I want to talk about."

The old man took over the cloth-bound diary books, felt the velvety cover of the top one with quivering fingers, and opened it. Ding watched the old man's grizzled head bent over the yellowed pages without daring to make any noise breathing or sipping tea. An eternity later Professor Zhu looked up and then leafed through the pages once more, as if looking for something.

Is it all true? Ding wanted to ask but didn't know how to phrase the question without sounding like he was intruding. He knew that he was only fooling himself. He was intruding; he had already intruded by having read the old man's diaries in the first place, and then taken them out of the museum, without permission, and brought them to this teahouse. And he was the old man's son-in-law. What right did he have! What audacity.

And yet.

"It is all true," the old man murmured, as if he had guessed the question in Ding's mind. "Every single word of it."

The tea in Professor Zhu's cup must be cold by now. Ding felt the pot on the table. It was not hot, either. "Shall I holler for a fresh pot?"

"No. It's summer any way."

The old man picked up a melon seed, tried to crack it between his teeth, and then spat it out, a messy mix of half chewed meat and shell.

Ding sensed that whatever the old man had burdened alone all these years, having someone he could trust to talk, and to confide in, would be a welcome relief.

"Did you ever see her, Rose, again?"

"No. Not until many years later. In 1979."

"And she married that Four-Eyed guy?"

The old man nodded. "That was the beginning of her trouble."

The rivalry between the two young men pursuing Rose was lopsided. Four-Eyed won hands down. He might not have been aware of the rivalry anyway. A Stanford graduate who had returned to his motherland in 1946, Four-Eyed was confident, urbane, and funny. After the Korean War was over, he was promoted to the rank of colonel and reassigned to the Department of International Exchanges of the Defense Ministry. By the time of the Cultural Revolution in 1966 he was already a brigadier general even though by then Mao had decided to get rid of ranking and other such relics of the Russian influence. There was some whispering about his trustworthiness thanks to his background, but by early 1967, it wasn't a problem anymore. He had found a patron saint, or a patron saint had offered herself in the form of Madam Mao. A second-rate actress in the old Shanghai before she met Mao, Jiangqing was taken by Four-Eyed's savvy and ready knowledge of America, Hollywood in particular, and relied on his advice whenever she would meet foreign dignitaries.

"Oh, no—" Ding sensed what was about to come.

"You are right. When the Gang of Four was arrested after Mao died in 1976, he was in trouble, too."

Four-Eyed spent the next four years in jail. Although he was not put on trial, he was being investigated as an American agent sent back as a sleeper. That was when Professor Zhu received a letter from Rose. He never found out how Rose had tracked him down during a quiet but desperate campaign to rally all of her husband's former friends and associates to "testify" on his behalf. When Zhu went to Beijing and finally found the address in a back alley—Rose and her two children had to move out of their spacious five-bedroom suite in an elite, gated compound—he all but didn't recognize the woman who had opened the door.

Zhu went to the t investigation team and wrote a 20-page document vouching for Four-Eyed's revolutionary credentials and loyalty on the peril of his own Party membership. During those life-and-death days and nights in Korea, Zhu attested, Four-Eyed had never done anything that was inappropriate or suspicious; he was actually instrumental, the surefire secret weapon, when it came to dealing with nut cases among American POWs.

"That could be because he had some secret understanding, I mean, secret code of communicating with the Americans, see what I mean?" Director Song questioned, his eyes on Zhu's face.

"Possibly," Zhu argued, feeling cold sweat trickling down his back, "but I feel, with all due respect, that it was not the kind of secret understanding you were alluding to. He was very passionate about what he believed in--there is no doubt about that. But there's something else that is hard to describe, something that transcends politics, war, and everything else. It is, shall I say, a kind of human touch, even though I know it won't be politically correct to say so. . . ."

Four-Eyed was set free in the spring of 1981 with a cloud hanging over his head because there was no definitive verdict on his case. He was reduced to the rank of captain and demobilized to the life of a civilian.

"That's what Rose told me in a letter afterwards. In a more recent letter she told me that her husband didn't make it to the new millennium. He belongs to the 20th century completely."

Neither spoke for a while. They sat there sipping cold tea.

"Should I order anything else, a snack or something?" Ding offered.

"No, I'm fine." The old man took a quick glance at his watch. "I think we'd better hurry home. Your mother-in-law must be busy in the kitchen now." As he stood up to leave, the old man added, with an exaggerated tone of secrecy: "And we shouldn't be coming home at the same time."

Ding nodded with a smile. Lieutenant Zhu hasn't returned from Korea yet. Not fully.

"One thing I don't understand, though, Dad," Ding hesitated. "Your diaries. They are so private, an important chapter in your emotional history. I mean, why did you donate them to that museum?"

"I've wondered about it, too. I could never include it in whatever memoir or autobiography I'd write one day. That'd cause trouble, you know. I was hoping that one day someone else might take a look . . . when I'm gone, when both Julie's mother and I are gone."

"And you were allowed to keep diaries, given the nature of your work?" Ding meant to ask but dismissed the question as irrelevant. They were handling all sorts of sensitive, classified information anyway and personal diaries of this nature wouldn't be of value to the enemy while the war was still being fought in battlefields.

"One last thing," Ding said, with the diary books in his hand, unsure whether he should put them back in his briefcase or give— return?—them to his father-in-law.

"I thought the interview, should I say interrogation, was over." The old man's hand was already on the door knob. "Shoot."

"Four-Eyed. . . should know a lot about the Korean War POWs, I mean, American Korean War POWs?"

"You bet, Jie," said Professor Zhu, his forefinger tapping the knob a few times. "I should have been more forthcoming."

20

"I sensed there's more to Professor Zhu than meets the eye," Greta's voice aroused him from the story he had been telling. He wondered why he had told her almost everything he had learnt from his father-in-law about the diaries.

"Aren't we all?" Ding said and gazed outside the window.

A lone student was ambling along a shaded sidewalk. As she turned and emerged into the cement street, she opened a small pinkish umbrella over her head. Halfway across the street she stopped to chatter with another student hurrying from the opposite direction, a book above his head to deflect the early afternoon sun near the end of July.

The place where people meet, Ding wondered. Somehow, this long table by this floor-length window had become a sort of rendezvous for him and Greta. He knew where to find her when he happened to be in the library. And she happened to run into him here bent over things quite often, too. No exchange of phone numbers. No need to call. In this brutal heat of midsummer, what place would be more ideal for them to meet than this reference room on the 4th floor of an air-conditioned university library?

He now came to the library every day to check emails, to do research, and, as an afterthought, to leaf through magazines and newspapers in the reference room. He said to himself that he would sit here for just a few minutes, which would often stretch to a few hours until the library staff came on the intercom to remind the patrons that it would close according to its summer schedule.

On days that Greta didn't show up on the 4th floor Ding would get up and leave and step into the orangey heat of late afternoon feeling listless, as if he had climbed to the top of a mountain but the vista he had wanted to see was not there.

What's going on with me? He asked himself. And he knew the answer. He was letting himself drift into an emotional turmoil he hadn't felt for so long. Ridiculous? Absurd? He would admit so freely, but it made him feel alive, and youthful again.

"So, what's the next step?" Greta asked. She had on a light blue top and white denim today.

Ding shrugged with a "Do I have a choice" expression on his face.

"Can I come with you?"

It was a request all right, but Ding knew that Greta knew that he could not bring himself to say no to her.

She must be a born adventurer, Ding thought. And he, of all people, was headlong, full steam into an adventure, too. What did that fortune cookie say? But this was not a romantic adventure. He was on a mission. He was doing something noble. "For a good cause," as his daughter would say. He wasn't looking for any personal gain—despite Tom's offer to help with Emily's college education—or anything that would advance his career in any way, form, or shade. Yet, ever since Greta appeared on the scene, from nowhere, the whole thing seemed to have acquired a different color. It was not just to carry out a promise he had felt obliged to give, but something he wanted to pursue, something he would love to do every day.

When their plane landed in Beijing, a week later, Ding offered to carry Greta's bag; it looked heavy, its straps cut into her bare shoulders.

"I don't mean to be chauvinistic—"

"Don't be ridiculous, Jie," she said in a playful tone, "women love chivalry from nice men, take that from a woman. But I'm fine. I can race you to the top of the Great Wall!"

She was probably right. The way she walked, buoyant, spry, she could give him a hard run, if not exactly beat him. During the two-hour flight, Greta was busy talking, reading, and checking out the clouds outside the window the whole time, like Emily when she and her parents had flown to Beijing five years back.

"I've dreamed of visiting the Forbidden City and the Great Wall for so long!" Greta said by way of explaining—apologetically?—her apparent girlish excitement.

"Why didn't you apply for studies in Beijing, then?" Ding was going to say, and then remembered what she had said about the best art history program offered by his alma mater.

So much of Beijing had changed since he visited it in 1996. New webs of overpasses and expressways. Forests of glassy high-rises and skyscrapers glittering under the noon sun on both sides of the expressway and toward endless horizons. And yet so much of this ancient city remained the same. The same pride, the same rage, the same frenzied quest to assert and reassert its place in history and in the world, as manifest in the fireworks showering over the 200,000 revelers on the Tiananmen Square celebrating the city winning its Olympics bid only days ago, as manifest in the banners and slogans of hundreds of thousands of youths who had marched here in the recent past, during the Cultural Revolution, the Civil War, the War of Resistance against Japan, and the 1919 May Fourth Movement, protesting, demanding, rioting, and falling down in puddles of young, restless blood.

Would Greta understand these sentiments if he were to share them with her? Would she appreciate?

Greta seemed mesmerized by everything outside the window. She remained quiet the whole ride from the airport to their hotel. Her face had a solemn look.

As their cab passed the biggest square in the heart of the city, Ding seemed to hear a whirlwind of voices, phantom like, which sounded so far away yet so close by that he could reach out to touch. Greta turned to glance at Ding; their eyes met. She understands, Ding thought, even though she might not know all that he knew about this place, and about his motherland.

"Room 2012," the receptionist said and handed him a pair of E-passes from behind the long marble counter.

"Excuse me, Miss," Ding whispered, stealing a glance at Greta a few feet to his right; she seemed attracted by the mural paintings and calligraphy carved on the walls in the tall, arching hall.

"What's wrong?' The receptionist kept her smile on her face.

"Can we have a double bed, instead?" He hesitated.

"Oh, I'm sorry, I thought –"

The hallway's ceiling was low. Its light was subdued. Except for the little wheels of their carryons rolling on the thick floral patterned carpet, and the occasional muffled sound of TV and human voice filtered through closed doors, it was cool and quiet.

Their room at the end of the long, meandering hallway was spacious, the size of his master bedroom at home. The writing desk, the pair of cushioned chairs, and the double beds looked more polished than he had expected. The decors on the wall was tasteful, a more than half-hearted attempt at being classy. The air conditioning unit was already on.

"Excuse me," Greta said and went into the bathroom to freshen up.

Ding drew apart the thick curtain and through the linen he could see the cityscape churning out there under the early afternoon sun. The exhaust fan buzzed in the bathroom, and then, the toilet flushed. Greta reappeared and flashed him a smile. There was not the faintest hint of travel on her face.

He went into the bathroom to wash. After cleaning the glasses, he checked himself in the mirror above the sink. He hadn't been considered the prize to catch among the more daring girls in his college days, but he hadn't suffered any inferiority complex on account of his looks, either: His forehead was full and proportionate to the rest of his face; his eyebrows, arched in the shape of a willow leaf, seemed the work of an assured calligrapher; his nose was. . . He frowned at himself and smiled self-consciously: Don't' be ridiculous.

"So, Jie," Greta turned away from the window when he reemerged. "Business first, then pleasure, right?"

"Sure." Then pleasure?

"Okay, we can always go and see the Great Wall, the Forbidden City, the Summer Place later."

Oh. He should have known.

Ding took out his thumb-sized address book, found the newest phone number in it, and dialed.

Rose, the girl Lieutenant Zhu had had a big crush on half a century ago, sounded warm and more than ready for his visit. She had been expecting him since Zhu's call the day before yesterday.

What would Professor Zhu think if he knew that his son-in-law was not traveling alone? What about Mrs. Zhu? And Julie?

"Wait a sec," Greta said suddenly when they were waiting outside the elevator. "I forgot something."

She hurried back to their room. Ding stood there watching the numbers and arrows on the stainless panel change.

Before long Greta reappeared. She had changed into a light yellow short-sleeved blouse. Her beautiful shoulders were now covered.

The compound was jammed with low buildings, rows and rows of them. Their faded stucco walls and balconies framed in with ill-sorted fiberglass roofs, underneath which hung colorful blouses, T-shirts, shorts, and brassieres, spoke of a bygone era when residence in one of the apartments here was a sure mark of prestige. Now, surrounded by much newer, flashier residential compounds, it looked out of tune with the rest of the world despite its best effort to maintain some residue of dignity. The cracked-up cement footpaths were clean, though, the bushes were trimmed, and the bicycles were lined neatly under fiberglass sheds.

"Why didn't you tell me you have a fried with you, Jie?" Manli, aka Rose, beamed as she let them in. She was taken with Greta right away and couldn't stop being amazed by her Chinese.

"The little English I had," Manli marveled, "I've given it all back to my teachers. Mmmm, I should ask them for a refund!"

Manli, her hair all frosty, was still lithe in movement. When she laughed, there was a youthful ring to her soft voice, her eyes lit up with hearty pleasure. How could Lieutenant Zhu not have fallen for her? Ding thought.

"I know you drink ice water even in winter," she said, handing them each a bottle of chilled water from the fridge. "Lots of ice. Wouldn't it freeze your teeth off?"

Greta smiled. She was quiet and respectful like a girlfriend being introduced to Ding's mother for the first time.

"Greta," Manli said when she sat down in a cushioned chair next to their sofa. "A beautiful name. Like Greta Garbo, right?"

"No more, and no less," Ding offered.

"C'mon Jie," Greta pretended to be annoyed. "I stand on my own, both in name and in person."

They laughed. Their laugh filled the apartment whose design betrayed the mentality of another era which had no use for anything other than straight lines. Even the recent attempts at renovation, hardwood floor, wallpaper, and upright air-conditioning unit in the corner, could not erase the era etched deep in its structures.

"My late husband, Peide, he loved Garbo's films. The way he described her, her haunting beauty, the mystique and just about everything else about her, I couldn't help but feel jealous. That's how I fell in love. Isn't that odd?" Manli paused to smooth back a tress on her forehead. "We were so young, then. And we were at war. Strange thing is, I didn't get to see Garbo in person, I mean her films, until I visited my son in San Francisco a few years ago."

She stood up and walked to a room at the end of the hallway. She was not tall, her waist not slim anymore, but she carried herself with a natural gracefulness. In a minute she came back with three large photo albums. Greta hastened to help her unload the albums on the coffee table.

As Manli turned the pages of yellowed pictures, her husband' life and their life together unfolded for her guests:

Peide, Peter when a little boy, bent over homework at a small table, his parents ironing in the background; Peter, a pair of wire-rimmed glasses on his nose, posing in front of a castle like building on a university campus; Peter, suit and tie and well-groomed, posing in a studio portrait with his father, the son a full head taller than the father, who grinned with pride; Peter and a friend of his, both in Charlie Chaplin's signature attire and posture, posing against a Ford Model T coupe parked outside the Empire State Building; Peter in unfit army uniform, a revolver strapped on the belt, against the backdrop of rough, mud-gray terrain; Peter, next to a Russian-made howitzer, scanning the enemy positions with binoculars, in the manner of a field marshal.

One of the photos was a group snapshot: in the middle was a young female officer in bulky cotton-padded uniform and a furry winter hat, a tress of hair on her forehead; next to her was a young officer who looked familiar to Ding despite the difference in age; way to the left, almost all by himself, stood an officer, donning a pair of by now famous wire-rimmed glasses, his arms akimbo, his gaze confident, apparently the leader of the gang; behind them was a bunker supported by poles and sacks of dirt, behind which loomed snow-covered hills.

Ding wondered at what stage was the triangulated romance when this photo was taken. Lieutenant Zhu's positioning in the photo seemed to imply that he was clinging to hope. Peter, the eventual winner, would have to pay dearly. Not for this particular prize, but on account of things he couldn't have foreseen when he posed for this photo.

"You must have been loved by them all," Greta said as they turned to other pages in the album.

"I was so naïve then and had no idea what was going on in the minds of these young men."

"C'mon, give yourself some credit," Ding joked. "I thought girls were generally more precocious about such things. They could intuit, and, yes, know by a quick glance, how a young man feels about her."

"Speaking like Dr. Romance," Greta teased.

All three laughed.

"These photos," Manli's voice lowered to a murmur. "It is a miracle that they survived to the see the light of day again."

When Peide—Commissar Chen—knew he would be in trouble in the late 70s, he wrapped the photos and diary books in layers of plastic bags and put them in a metal box and buried them in a hole next to the garage for his Volga in a guarded compound they used to live in. When the government decided to build something fancier at the same place in 1995, Peter, a sickly old man by then, went back on a night and dug up the box before it was buried permanently by bulldozers.

"Reclaiming his hidden treasure, like an Indiana Jones film," Greta marveled, "except that this is for real."

"And Peide barely survived it all," Manli said and stood up. "Come with me."

Ding and Greta followed her into the study, the last room in the hallway. It was filled with bookshelves almost touching the ceiling, bookshelves loaded with titles in both English and Chinese. Mounted on the wall above the window was a framed black and white photo of young Peide and Manli, grinning happily, both smartly dressed in uniforms with emblems indicating their ranks.

"Our wedding picture," Manli said, smiling.

Underneath the picture was a desk on which were an old reading lamp and two refined mahogany containers, one for the brushes, and one for pens and pencils. Toward the left corner of the desk stood a color photo in a wood frame: Peide and Manli flanked by their kids and grandkids. Next to the photo was a pair of old wire-rimmed glasses; one of the lenses had visible cracks in it.

Peide had declined an opportunity to move back to his old compound ten years after the case against him was closed. Their son and daughter had chosen to emigrate to the birthplace of their father, to be reunited with Peide's side of the family. For some reason, he never visited America again. Perhaps the psychic wounds he had suffered never really healed. Could any such wound heal at all? Ding wondered.

Manli unlocked a cabinet and took out an old metal box. In it were diary books. Four or five of them. They looked familiar, almost identical to those of Professor Zhu's. Bought from the same store? Gifts from admiring girls the night before the young officers were to cross the Yalu River?

"I've read them through many times since Peide was gone," Manli sighed, her face glowing with fond memories. "He was a born romantic, in his beliefs, and in his feelings. Oh, Professor Zhu said something about what you're looking for. These," she put the diaries back into the box and turned to Ding. "These diaries may give you a clue or two, I hope."

Facing the generous offer, Ding was at a loss what to say.

"Are you sure?"

Manli nodded. "I feel I can trust you, like I trust your father-in-law. He's a good man."

21

"I crave a sandwich, a slice of pizza, or just a plain hot dog," Greta said when they sat down in one of the hotel restaurants.

"What, sick of Chinese food already?" Ding teased and picked up the menu. It was already 9 pm in the evening and the restaurant was still packed with diners of mixed nationalities.

"Not sick of Chinese food, but can't wait to bite into something cheesy, with lots of mayonnaise and mustard, or have a cup of chili, cream chowder, you know."

"Perhaps we should go to a MacDonald's or –"

Ding remembered being sick of having burgers and hot dogs and sandwiches day after day after day when he first came to the US. One day one of the cafeteria cooks, a nice matronly woman, took him to a local Chinese restaurant. When he sipped the first spoonful of hot & sour soup, Ding felt he was ready to die.

Tom's kid brother. Would he miss hot dogs and hamburgers and sandwiches—if he were still alive?

"This is perfectly fine," Greta smiled, returning to the menu. "A momentary fancy only."

"I'll make sure you have ice cream today. Lots."

Ding had difficulty focusing as water gushed from shower head only a thin wall away. He was several pages into the first diary book and except for being taken by the dashing penmanship of Peide, aka Peter, Captain Chen, not much registered. He turned back to the first page, stuffed the index fingers into his ears, and started all over again:

CPC
October 25, 1950

In bold, cursive strokes.

CPC: Captain Peter Chen for sure, Ding thought. Peter must have been proud of how far he had advanced given the short time since he returned to the motherland.

The early entries were more routine: observations of terrain and people; expressions of anger at sights of villages being leveled, women and children fleeing from war zones.

The tone became softer, tenderer, with the arrival of a new junior intelligence officer, who was soon dubbed H. H standing for? Ding wondered. Hanna. Harriet. Heidi. Helen. Helena. Hera. Hilary. Hilda. Holly. The answer was given a few entries later:

> *Helen, thy beauty is to me*
> *Like those Nicean barks of yore,*
> *That gently, o'er a perfumed sea,*
> *The weary way-worn wanderer bore*
> *To his own native shore.*

Ding smiled. What sweet nonsense people say when they fall in love! And the kind of sweet nonsense they say says so much about them! Lieutenant Zhu, younger and simpler, compared his love, the same Manli, to a fresh rose. Fair enough. Peide, or Captain Peter Chen, more cosmopolitan, and flamboyant, would not settle for anything less fanciful than Helen whose face "launched a thousand ships." Manli in her day was, beyond a shade of doubt, a beauty, but was there anything about her features, her eyes, her nose, and her mouth, that could be called "classic"? Or compared to "the glory that was Greece," and "the grandeur that was Rome"? Perhaps, Ding thought, Manli had also become a sort of metaphor for Peter, a "weary way-worn wanderer" who finally returned to "his own native shore"?

The same Manli bent over piles of documents in the dim, cramped bunker in the belly of a charred hill: a glance from her, a smile, a cough, a few murmured words, and her soft movement from makeshift desk to file cabinets, would send dizzying ripples in the hearts of two young officers (and probably more), one seeing a blossoming red flower, the other, the apparition of something much more splendid. Which would Manli have preferred? She chose Peide, of course, but did she protest for being called Helen? Would she have preferred Rose?

She married Peide, the Four-Eyed guy, and that, Professor Zhu had said, "was the beginning of her trouble."

Greta came out of the bathroom finally. She had on a tank top and vintage red shorts with side slits at the outer leg, her hair, still damp, cascading down her back. She grabbed a bottle on the TV stand, drank from it, and came over to the writing desk. Whatever shampoo and perfume she had used, it smelled good.

"Have you found anything?"

"No. Not yet." He stood up and nudged the chair back to make room for Greta.

The air inside the bathroom was still warm, the mirror above the sink streaking with dewy moisture. A plastic bag stuffed with Greta's lingerie, neatly rolled, lay next to the tub, segments of the bra straps coiling outside on the tile floor.

Ding had never been this conscious of his bathing: stepping into the same ceramic tub, naked, where a beautiful girl, an achingly beautiful girl, had stood without a thing on only moments ago; using the same soaps and cute little bottles of shampoo and whatever her long fingers had touched; letting the same hot water gush down his hair, face, neck, and the rest of himself; his wet feet on the damp towels she had used to dry herself. How could he not be self-conscious? How could he not feel a tidal wave of nervous excitement rising inside him?

You asshole! A voice from faraway scoffed as he dried, looked at himself in the foggy mirror, and put on a T-shirt Julie had bought him for his birthday.

Greta, her whole length sprawled on the bed close to the window, her silky hair fanning out on her back, was absorbed in a Peide diary book in her hands, her low-neck tank top, ajar, revealing the curves of her bosom. Ding sat down at the writing desk and continued with the diary book he had been halfway through.

The feelings for H intensified with each new entry. The writer seemed oblivious to the fact that he might have a rival for H's heart. He was confident and never thought his suit could be rejected. Peide, a Byronic type? Ding wondered. He must have had girlfriends before, back in the US, during high school, college, the kind of peppy lover he was. If so, did he share his romantic past with H? Would H care to know? Oh, there was so much she had wanted to know about Hollywood, about Vivian Leigh, Humphrey Bogart, Ingrid Bergman—she had had a chance to see both Gone with the Wind and Casablanca while in college—and Greta Garbo, of course. Peide knew it all. He could deliver the line "Frankly, my dear verbivore, I don't give a damn" as roguishly as any actor by the name of Clark Gable.

Here was apparently another case of wooing a beautiful girl with well-told stories. When would the two find time, find any privacy in a bunker in the belly of a mountain, to tell those stories and to woo and to be wooed when aerial bombing and shelling were more routine than daily meals? Did Peide imagine it all in his own head? It didn't make an iota of difference, of course. He won H, her heart, and her hand. That was all that mattered.

If he loved it so much in America, Hollywood and all, why did Peide give it all up and return to the native land of his parents? Why did Tom's kid brother choose not to return to his? And why did so many Chinese POWs turn their backs on their country and migrate to places thousands of miles away from home? Ding knew that there were no simple answers.

Some of the entries alluded to his work, all written in a sort of coded language. Something interesting came up close to the last few pages of another diary book:

The arrival of AB at C January 1951.

American Boys. Ding concluded right away. What else could AB stand for, given the nature of his work? And C. Camp?

Peide seemed to know AB's well. He knew how to talk to them. He would smile and shake his head at his comrades-in-arms who droned day after day after day about the evils of Capitalism and virtues of Communism until their "captivated" audience had developed calluses in their ears listening to the same words being repeated for the thousandth time.

"Personal touch," he would advise them, "that's the way to go." He could tell where the AB's were from by their accent. Pretty much.

Most of the AB's were easy, already down in spirits. They opened up quickly and were receptive to what was being taught. Many, having repented their war crimes, became "progressive." Some were troublesome, mute blockheads who wouldn't fart no matter what. A few were troublemakers who refused to cooperate. They made things difficult for themselves and for others. One troublemaker, an LS, screamed obscenities during a study session. Another, a RW, stole out of C at night to help himself to some opium-like weeds. An OB tried to organize some underground religious group and poison the minds of fellow C residents. The troublemakers had to be dealt with duly. Locking them up in dungeon like cells? Ding recalled such stories in the memoirs by POWs who had returned to the U. S. Denying food until they have corrected their attitude? Having other POWs criticizing them relentlessly? Peide didn't specify.

An entry about a SM caught Ding's eye.

When the Chinese PVA took over SM and other captives from the North Koreans, they looked more like ghosts than humans, skeletal, unkempt long hair and beard, and sick, many suffering from diarrhea, constipation, dysentery, and other illnesses.

SM had a temper and seemed angry with everyone, the entire world. He would flare up during a study session and then wouldn't fart for days. A nut case. And nobody at C wanted to deal with him.

Since Peide had a reputation for cracking nut cases, SM came under his care exclusively. He chatted with SM, talking about his birth, his childhood, his dreams, his fears, his favorite movies, sports teams. SM never really opened up, but Peide could see the gradual change in SM's earnest eyes that he began to trust. SM told Peide about his childhood in a small town, his troubles with his family (no more than hinted, but Peide didn't pressure for details), his favorite cartoon characters, and his questions which, it seemed, had no answers, and more.

SM became interested in Peide's story about reclaiming the language of his parents. He was intrigued by its sound, the expressiveness of its shape. He wanted to learn. And soon he devoted all his restless energies to learning it, one character at a time.

SM didn't turn "progressive" as Peide and others had hoped, but it was a success story, nonetheless. Instead, he wanted to "disappear" inside China and live in a "Peach Orchard Outside the World" for the rest of life.

SM. What does it stand for? Ding wondered. The needle he had been looking for in the sea? What odds?!

Greta had been reading with her chin cupped in one hand, in both hands, lying on her side, on her back, and on her belly. Now she sat up and turned the pages back and forth a few times.

"Odd," she wondered aloud.

"What is it? Sherlock Holmes?" Ding looked up from his third diary book.

"I'd prefer Miss Marple, or Jessica Fletcher."

"Okay, Ms. Marple . . . Fletcher?"

"Better. Seriously, here's something really interesting."

Ding came over and sat by Greta's bedside.

"See?" she pointed at the diary opened on the bedspread.

It was a drawing. Sketchy. Amateurish. Like a pirate map for hunting down lost treasures. The drawing, it seemed, featured two fat men snuggling in a rather odd position.

"I'd never imagined Peide to be a pervert," Ding chuckled.

"C'mon," Greta protested, "even if he were the kind of man you were insinuating, that wouldn't make him a pervert."

"I apologize, Ms. PC?"

"Jie!"

He turned the picture sideways. One "fat" man looked like a cloud in the sky, his "face," drawn in red ink, like a radiant sun; the "fat" man below resembled a pond, a lake, or a river, and his "face," also in red ink, another sun, an elongated sun? The "sun" in the sky was marked with the letter S; the "sun" below in the river, the letter M.

SM.

The date of the entry: November 17, 1953. Close to the time of the armistice, Ding thought. Any special meaning to this drawing? SM. The same SM he had seen in the other diary books? What odds?

"Some code, you think?" Greta asked, her eyes gazing into his.

"I don't know," he heard himself thinking aloud. "It might be the key to something, but—"

"But the key to the key was known to one person in the entire world alone, and that person is not available for questioning anymore?"

"Exactly."

"Jie, you've been in the States too long!" Professor Zhu laughed so loud that Ding had to jerk his head away from the earpiece. "Two fat men sleeping in the same bed? That's not too bad an idea in the dead winter, but on a summer day like this? Hahaha! What a picture. At any rate, don't tell me you've never heard of the city the drawing stands for, Dr. Ding?"

Ding felt his face reddening. He was glad that Greta was in the bathroom freshening up.

"What about the two suns?" he lowered his voice, "one up in

the sky, and one on the ground, almost intertwined, like the yin-yang totem, except that this is a yang-yang thing? Mean anything?"

"That's still two men cuddling, whichever way you slice it," Professor Zhu laughed again, and then, in a more thoughtful tone. "Two suns intertwined. That I don't know. If Four-Eyed, I mean, Peide, meant anything by it, if this is what you are looking for, then, my hunch is, only a hunch, okay, that it could be a code for where . . . Mmmm, it could be the name of a county, a village, a mountain, a river, a lake; infinite possibilities."

Ding could hear the old man breathing—and thinking—at the other end.

"This is what I'd do," the old man spoke again, much like when he was directing Ding's master's thesis. He went on for several minutes.

"Oh, I almost forgot," Professor Zhu said before hanging up, "Julie called yesterday. She wanted to know how you're doing. She misses you. And guess what, Emily's got her driver's license! She was ecstatic on the phone. Young people nowadays. I don't know what to think of a 16-year-old driving a car on the highway. . . ."

Ding didn't know what to say. If only he could call to congratulate, and to "lecture" about safety. And to talk to Julie, too?

"And, by the way," his father-in-law sounded hesitant, "I don't know how to put this more delicately. Okay, I know you're not traveling alone. No, don't even start to explain. Just want to let you know that I made a right choice many years ago, and still have no evidence to prove me wrong. I am not sure whether everybody else feels exactly the same way, you know what I mean. There you go. So, take good care."

The phone clicked at the other end, and droned. Ding hung up, too.

"Why are you still sitting here? Let's go," Greta said when she came out of the bathroom and was told about the phone call. "Let's pack up and go."

Ding shook his head. "The adventurer wants to leave without some sightseeing? What about having dreamed about climbing to the top of--"

"Mmmm," she lifted her chin and stroked her imaginary beard, an exaggerated look of being torn on her face.

"Besides," he said, "what time is it now? 11:30pm?"

"Okay, Professor Ding," she relented. "Let's go downstairs to have a drink somewhere. To celebrate."

"Celebrate what?"

"The breakthrough! What else?"

22

"You haven't heard of the river?" the thirtyish man in the Office of Military Archives sounded surprised. "Well, it has been in the news quite a bit recently. It's actually a lake and is being developed into an elite resort place. But I don't know if it has anything to do with what you're looking for."

He paused, picked up the sheets again, and glanced at Ding, and then Greta. "Mmmm, PhD dissertation, master's thesis."

He got up from his chair. "Why don't you take a seat, oh, yes, help yourself to some water, and I'll go in to double check on something. Summer here feels like a hot stove, doesn't it?"

Ding pulled out a cone-shaped paper cup at the water station in the corner, filled it, and gave it to Greta. The sweat on her forehead had dried. Her eyes still glistened with the excitement of the flight and taxi ride and everything else. She smiled, sipped from the cup, and smoothed her hair with her long fingers.

They had over two months' worth of acquaintance between them by now. He knew so little about her. Her childhood. Her school years. Her hobbies. Her favorite colors and movies. Yet he felt he knew her so well and knew so much about her. Strange. How should he characterize his feelings for her? Romantic? He wasn't sure. The kind of feeling a man of his age, astride the threshold of midlife, was prone to experience in the company of a young, beautiful, and intelligent woman like Greta? Possible. Whatever it was, it felt sweet, delicious, and somewhat giddy. He knew it was completely uncalled for, and ridiculous, yet savored it gratefully all the same, and with abandon. He felt alive with an adventurous spirit, too; he was ready to take on the world on account of it. His life didn't feel like last night's leftovers being reheated in the microwave. It was a new venture every day. How long would it last?

Five minutes later, the thirtyish man came back with an older man who had a more authoritative air about him.

"Professor Zhu, I know him. Not directly. Read a few newspaper stories about him," Director Jiang beamed. "Where're you staying? You can go back and take a rest, do some sightseeing, and come back tomorrow. We may have more accurate info for you by then. Many places to see. Judge Bao Park. Remember Righteous Judge Bao? His tomb is in that beautiful park. Care-free Creek. Li Hongzhang's Old Residence. He's been exonerated, so to speak, not regarded as a traitor who kowtowed and sold out to Imperialist Powers anymore," the director paused, flashing a quick glance at Ding and Greta again. "As to good restaurants, well, you wouldn't be disappointed. We're the City of Two Fat Men, after all, hahaha!"

Greta wanted to go and see all the places recommended by Director Jiang. "Unless you want to go back to the hotel and rest."

The nights he had spent in the same hotel room with this beautiful, this achingly beautiful girl, the curvy outline of her slender body, half covered, vaguely visible through the subdued light from the bathroom, listening to her even breathing until he drowsed.

He turned to glance at the girl walking by his side. The same warmth in the beautiful eyes. And a coy smile, as if she could see the thought racing through his mind: Don't get any ideas, Jie.

Ding, being the sole tour guide, explained Judge Bao the best he could to a very attentive audience. The judge, who lived about

1,000 years ago, was so revered by the common people that his funeral procession extended for miles long.

"Such a fair and righteous judge, independent, and courageous, is a rarity in Chinese history, and a rarity in China today," Ding said as he helped Greta decipher the words engraved on the tombstone.

"Be a bit more optimistic, Jie."

Li Hongzhang's story was a bit more tangled. Ding tried his best, based on the little he knew, to sort out the messy role Li had played in Chinese history: his attempt to modernize the military through adopting Western technology; his disgrace of being the signatory on some infamous unequal treaties on behalf of the dowager empress Ci Xi, the Qing Government. . . .

"Same thing has happened elsewhere, too," remarked Greta thoughtfully. "A hero vilified as villain, villains celebrated as heroes, hero villains, and villain heroes, and their fortunes rise and fall erratically."

"That doesn't sound like Ms. Optimism to me," Ding teased.

"Even an optimist has to face realities."

Close to evening, they arrived at Carefree Creek Park. The sun was still several feet above the western edge of the sky. The breeze felt warm, but not nearly as brutal as during the day. Couples, families, friends, older people with canaries in hand, were strolling around leisurely.

As Ding rowed their small boat away from the dock, little wavelets from his oars rippled away urgently. Greta stood on the stern and opened her arms toward the sun, strands of her lustrous hair billowing softly in the moist breeze, her silhouette a tall stature under the sky. Then she folded her hands and placed them in front of her face as if she were praying.

"What is it all that about?" Ding asked when she treaded her way to the bow. "I didn't know you were that religious."

"Oh, I just made a wish," she smiled, sat down next to Jie, and took over one of the oars.

"What is it about, if I may ask?"

Classified information!"

Part IV

23

When Shanmeng stepped into the canteen, a long queue had already formed in front of the kitchen counter, everyone holding in hand a small wok, a big bowl, or a wooden basin, chitchatting in excited tones. The two cauldrons bubbled steamily as Big Wang, the cook, gave their content one last, good stirring with a long-handled utensil. Sis Zhang, his assistant, stood by with a gourd ladle, a tired smile showing through her cracked teeth.

The recently built canteen could hold over one hundred people and doubled as a townhall for the village. Overlooking the kitchen in the corner were a large slogan painted high on the wall, its original fresh red ink having been eroded by the steam coiling up from the pit-like cauldrons:

> *Eat to the Full Capacity of Your Belly*
> *Work to the Last Fiber of Your Muscles*

Other slogans were featured on the walls left and right:

> *Overtake Britain in Ten Years, the US, in Fifteen*
> *Twenty Years Work in One Day:*
> *Let Us Dash into Communism*

All these were the brushwork of Fuli, the lone village schoolteacher. Shanmeng couldn't appreciate Chinese calligraphy yet, but he felt the force in each stroke, the excitement, and the hope. This—1958, four years after the Flood—was indeed an exciting, extraordinary time to live in.

Shanmeng didn't understand everything, either, yet he didn't need anyone to explain to him what it meant by "Eat to the Full Capacity of Your Belly / Work to the Last Fiber of Your Muscles." He had enjoyed its full benefit for months by now and he didn't mind exerting his muscles to their full potential in the fields under the scorching sun. As to overtaking Britain in ten years and the US in fifteen, well, if they could really do twenty years' worth of work in one day, then they might have a real shot. They could indeed be dashing, flying, at the terrific speed of an F-20, into Communism.

"You know something, Simon?" Peide had said, one day at the Camp, with a glow in his face, "I'm willing to give up anything, including my life, to make the dream come true, to see that flag flapping in every corner of the world: 'From Each According to His Abilities / To Each According to His Needs!' Being selfish, being greedy, that's only human, that's the most basic human instinct, even at the level of cells. Survival and self-preservation. But the greatest, the most beautiful thing about Communism is to overcome that basic, primitive human instinct. You live not to make money, but to make your fellow human beings happier. In that kind of society, you don't work for the DuPonts, the Morgans, the Rockefellers, and the like anymore. You don't even work for yourself. You live and work for the common good of society, for humanity as a whole. That, in a nutshell, is the difference between the ideal of the country I've returned to and the one I've left behind. . . ."

Shanmeng remembered being shaken by this fiery speech. He was young. All he knew about Communism, its theories and rationales and ideals, he had obtained haphazardly from those crudely printed pamphlets handed to him at the Camp, and all of his knowledge put together would not weigh more than an ounce on a scale, but the eloquence of people like Peide—more eloquent than Pastor Higgins!—was infectious. He hadn't come to China for a Communist utopia, but a "Peach Orchard Outside the World," but they seemed close enough.

People's Commune seemed only one step away from the ideal society of everyone living for the well-being of everyone else Peide had passionately depicted.

Shanmeng still had a bit of private properties. His home, the hut he had "inherited" from that hermit, was still his. And the little orchard in the backyard. He sometimes wondered how he would feel if everyone in the village wandered into his orchard and help themselves to the juicy fruit from the trees anytime, they so desired. Would he mind at all? He knew he shouldn't, but he wasn't too sure. He did give up most of his vegetable strips. He had insisted because all the villagers, including Old Ma, now head of Twin-Sun Production Brigade, had thrown their farmland, their water buffalos and ploughs, and their almost everything else except for their homes into the common lot of the People's Commune. Some had been more willing than others and a few, like the well-to-do Chaos, needed a bit more than persuasion. That was what Shanmeng had heard.

He heard a familiar voice from behind and turned. It was Fuli, and Ah Bao, about seven or eight people behind him. The boy had sprouted since the Flood three years ago. The top of his head almost reached his mother's shoulders, and his face was that of a young lad now.

His eyes met Fuli's and he turned his eyes away casually.

He noticed another pair of eyes that had been watching him intently from two or three people behind Fuli and Ah Bao. It was Jian'er, Old Chao's son, who had returned from Korea over three years ago. Something in that pair of eyes had bothered Shanmeng since day one. Confusion? Fear? Suspicion? Anger? He didn't know.

It was Shanmeng's turn at the kitchen counter now. Sis Zhang grinned and gave him half a gourd ladle of congee. That would be twice the portion for one person, but nobody seemed to notice. Sis Zhang, a matronly widow whose husband and son had been killed in the Flood, had always been warm to him. He didn't want to protest. That would only embarrass him, and her. He was still the tallest in the village, but few seemed to pay undue attention on account of his nose or hair or anything else anymore. His Mandarin was now almost as fluent as anybody else even though he hadn't completely mastered the local dialect yet.

The moon, big, round, golden, was only inches above the hilltops in the distance. It cast a dream-like veil on the river and the world around. Crickets and nameless insects were chirping away in the shrubs and the dark-green leaves of trees skirting the slope where he was waiting. Anxiously.

Seeing the familiar figure from the trail winding up to where he was, Shanmeng jumped to his feet and hastened over. He gathered the figure in his arms and bent to kiss her.

"Fuli," he mumbled between kisses.

"Mmmm. . . ."

"How can I tell Pa?" Fuli said as they sat down on the rock, her soft fingers rubbing his. "He's been like father to me. . . and has suffered so much. I can't look him in the eye and ask."

He didn't know what to say. Old Ma was the last person in the world he wanted to hurt.

"Perhaps we should go to Xinjiang," Fuli said, as if she had just been hit by the idea. "You, me, and Ah Bao. As far away as the edge of the sky."

Xinjiang. Again. He didn't want to hear one more mention of Xinjiang. How he wished Peide hadn't come up with this story. Then again, how else would Fuli and everyone else have reacted if they had known who he truly was in the first place? He had lived with the story for too long not to continue with it.

"I'll do it," he said.

"Taking us to Xinjiang?"

He shook his head. "I've left that place since I don't remember when. I've no family there anymore."

When Shanmeng arrived at the Ma's the next day, the family of five was still at the Eight-Immortals table, a wooden basin in the middle, bowls scattered around.

Sportie came to greet him, wagging its tail. Ah Bao's eyes brightened with a dull smile.

"Have you eaten?" Old Ma's wife asked. She had aged more

visibly recently.

"Oh, yes, thanks!"

He knew that even if he hadn't, there wouldn't be any food left in the basin. Like everyone else in the Twin-Sun Production Brigade, Old Ma's family was entitled to their fair share of whatever was being cooked in the commune's cauldrons, and nothing more.

Old Ma's wife gathered the basin and bowls to take them to the kitchen.

"Brother Shanmeng," Yingzi mumbled, avoiding direct eye contact as she stood up to leave. One more year and she would start middle-school on the other side of the river.

"Why don't you go out and play," Old Ma said when he saw Yingzi going to the room behind the kitchen.

Yingzi turned her head low on the chest and stepped out.

Fuli stood up and gave her hand to Ah Bao. "Let's go out and play, too," she said in a tremulous voice.

"Go out and play," Ah Bao repeated.

Just the two of them in the main room now. Old Ma and Shanmeng. The village chief refilled his pipe and succeeded in lighting it before the matchstick burnt to his fingertips. He puffed away silently. Smoke clouded his face, which looked more sun-browned and leathery than ever before.

"Treat her well," Old Ma looked up and muttered suddenly. "If I hear one word of abuse and any such shenanigans your people are known for, I'll come and kill you myself."

Shanmeng had rehearsed in his mind a hundred arguments if the village chief would object, and a thousand ways, even if he had to beg on his knees, to plead his case, the case for him and Fuli, and Ah Bao. Old Ma must have suspected things, what with his daughter-in-law's frequent nocturnal walks, and whispered rumors. He must have known all along what was coming.

"But leave Ah Bao to me," Old Ma continued before Shanmeng could think of anything to say. He looked the younger man in the eye, as if he didn't know who he was, and turned his eyes away. "Damn that Captain Chen. Damn that son of a gun General Ye."

Something crashed in the kitchen. Shanmeng hastened there and saw Old Ma Wife's small figure bent over a broken rice bowl on the ground, picking up one small piece at a time. He reached to help, but was stopped by the firm hand of the aged woman.

"Don't. You'll cut yourself."

When he came back to the main room, the village chief was gone.

24

Shanmeng wanted to add a wing to the old hut, half of it for the new kitchen, and half as storage space for tools and grain and other things. With the old stove being dismantled, there would be more space in the main room to reconfigure it into a small bedroom and a living-dining room.

A few enthusiastic young men came to help. There were jokes and laughter and things said that Shanmeng couldn't really appreciate yet as they were digging the foundation next to the east side of the hut. The earth was firm and filled with messy tree roots, but it wasn't particularly hard.

At about two feet deep, Shanmeng's spade hit something hard with a grating, metallic sound.

"Must be a goldbrick, Brother Shanmeng!" Fugui, one of the young men, jested.

"Some hidden treasure," echoed Yucai, another young man. "Hidden treasure left behind by that crazy hermit?"

"Get out!" beamed Shanmeng. Everybody laughed.

He dug more carefully nonetheless, watched by several pairs of curious eyes. Soon a large dark green stonebrick revealed itself.

"A brick for sure," Fugui sounded disappointed.

A young man jumped in and lent a hand lifting the stonebrick.

"There's more!" Yucai hollered.

Lo and behold, where the stone brick had been now something else: A square hole, the size of a chess board, walled with small bricks. Inside the hole was a vat, tightly wrapped in layers of oil paper.

"Told you there's gold, and hidden treasure here!" Fugui shrilled.

"You'll share your fortune with us, right, Brother Shanmeng?" asked Yucai, half joking. "At least a gold coin or two for each of us?"

"Sure, if the thing is indeed filled with gold!" Shanmeng promised, laughing.

What if? He wondered as they lifted the vat out of the hole carefully and placed it on level ground.

"Let me open it for you," Fugui offered and, before Shanmeng could say yes or no, he already started peeling off the oil paper.

The first three layers had all but mashed; the next two, however, could still hold.

There stood in front of them an earthenware: still intact, clean with a dull shine.

Fugui put his head close to its mouth and peeked, his nose twitching as if displeased.

"Goldbricks? Gold coins?" someone asked.

"I don't know." Fugui reached in and took out a bundle, longer than a noodle roller, also wrapped in oil paper.

Shanmeng took it over from a confused Fugui and unwrapped the bundle. It was a roll of parchment. A scroll. Yellowed with age, somewhat damp, but quite sturdy. The ink in which whatever on the parchment was written had not faded:

אלוהים מבול נוֹח תיבה יונה קרקע התחייבות

What the heck is this? Shanmeng was puzzled, too. He had never seen anything like it before. A coded message from extraterrestrials?

"Some hidden treasure." Fugui looked as if a goldbrick in his hand had just turned into rock.

"Throw it away, Brother Shanmeng," Yucai urged. "Or burn it. It can't be anything good."

"C'mon," Shanmeng teased. "You don't want to share my fortune anymore?"

The village chief didn't come to the wedding. No one from the Ma family came. There was no real wedding anyway. Shanmeng hadn't been on his knees to propose with a ring. There were no roses. No rehearsals. No floral girl and procession and priest announcing: "Dear beloved . . . we're gathered here to witness . . ."

They did have to apply for a marriage certificate from the People's Commune, which did take a long time to be issued. No other delays and complications, however.

Fuli didn't want to fuss about a wedding. Even for someone with Fuli's status, the village chief's former daughter-in-law, the village school's sole teacher, a widow (Old Ma had let it be known that his son was dead) was a widow after all. For a widow to get married a second time, no matter how young and pretty she was, there was no need to make a big fuss over it.

The young fellows who had helped with the wing and a bunch of others did come and ask for wine and see the bridal room. Jian'er was among them. He was particularly loud and talkative. In the midst of food and jokes and laughter, Jian'er filled himself another cup and staggered toward Fuli and Shanmeng.

"Fuli," he said, his face glowing, "Heshen was like a brother to me, and you, my good sister-in-law. That won't change, right?"

"No, Jian'er. Nothing will change that unless...you want to."

"See?" Jian'er turned and looked Shanmeng in the eye and laughed. "I'll drink to that, Red Hair!"

Several girls and young women, Fuli's friends, came and cracked sunflower seeds and giggled at the jokes told by the braver ones among the young men. Sis Zhang, the cook, and a few other matronly women came out of curiosity but were not impressed.

The DOUBLE HAPPINESS paper cut on the new window looking into the orchard was Fuli's own work. That was the only red color in the décor of the bridal chamber, if there was any décor at all.

Fuli had on a new jacket she made herself with a piece of light blue cloth she had saved in a trunk for years. Widow brides were not supposed to wear anything red.

Finally, all the guests were gone. They were alone in their new home. Just the two of them. Fuli started to clear things on the table. Shanmeng stopped her, held her in his arms from behind, and whispered: "We can take care of that tomorrow!"

They were in bed now. Fuli turned her face to the wall. He reached over and touched her shoulder. She turned back and smiled through teary eyes. He bent to kiss. Her lips were warm, her cheeks tasted salty where tears had washed. She didn't kiss back. She just laid there and gazed at him with such wonder, and expectancy in her large, moist eyes.

He started to unbutton her jacket. Her hands flew up to stop his fumbling fingers. They were cold and shaking.

"Are you all right?" He sounded hoarse even to his own ears.

Her eyes welled up again. The grip of her hands loosened. She closed her eyes.

His fingers worked urgently and soon he was down to the last layer of clothing: a silky blouse embroidered with a small flower above her heart, a fresh red rose-like flower.

Fuli opened her eyes again and smiled shyly.

When he finally wrapped her supple, responsive body in his arms, a dream, long deferred, from another lifetime, was finally blossoming into a dizzying reality. He knew that everything he had been through was worth it. And he wouldn't mind going through everything all over again, and more.

25

In the week following their wedding a rally was held at Red Valley Middle School on the other side of the river. Shanmeng didn't go. He didn't want his "Uyghur" appearance to attract undue attention from folks who hadn't seen anyone like him before.

Fuli had to lead her pupils to join other schools in the area in carrying the red flags and beating the drums for the event attended by hundreds of simple folks and graced by the presence of county Magistrate Wu and other dignitaries. Shanmeng was more than impressed by what Fuli had to tell him when she returned, completely exhausted.

The highlight of the rally was when leaders of production brigades marched up to the podium to vouch for a bigger harvest next year.

"1,000 *jin* a *mu*,"[1] the leader of a neighboring production brigade beat his chest and hollered and was rewarded with thunderous applause.

"2,000 *jin*," another leader shrieked frothily. Thunderous applause.

"3,000 *jin*!"

"950 *jin*," Old Ma announced, hesitantly, when it was his turn, was met with sporadic, lukewarm applause.

"C'mon, Comrade Ma," Magistrate Wu sounded disappointed though he managed to keep a smile on his face. "You're a Long March veteran and don't want to totter ahead like an old granny with bound feet in this Great Leap Forward of ours, do you?"

---

[1] One *jin* is equal to 1.11 pound whereas one *mu* is equal to 797.3 sq yd, or 0.165 acre.

Uneasy laugh from the audience.

"How about 4,000 *jin* a *mu* from the Twin-Sun River Production Brigade?" someone offered from the audience loudly. It was Huifa, the man who had "grilled" Shanmeng about Xinjiang a few years back.

"Huifa, what do you know? Even if I throw you on the scale come harvest time, we'll still be 3,000 *jin* short!"

The audience roared with laughter.

But the fiery excitement had already assumed a life of its own, fiery not so much in eloquence as when Peide had spoken about the ideal society, but fierily eloquent all the same because these people were being fired up by the same simple, raw, primal emotions. Not being an agriculturalist by any stretch, Shanmeng couldn't really appreciate what it meant by those figures, but he was touched, and felt giddy, too.

Once they passed the 5,000-jin mark, Fuli said, Old Ma seemed lost. He looked worried, but the frenzied "bidding" continued with fervor:

"6,000!"
"7,000!"
"8,000!"
"9,000!"
"10,000!"

At the figure of "10,000," everyone at the rally fell silent suddenly, as if a spell had been cast over them, as if they needed a pause to register the significance of that figure, as if they were awed by their own daring of the impossible.

"What do you know," Fuli sighed at the end of her report, "10,000 *jin* a *mu*! Who's ever heard of that kind of harvest? 1,000% increase in production. That's crazy!"

"I'm crazy, too!" Shanmeng picked up his wife and started to fumble with her clothing. She didn't stop him, but his exuberance didn't affect her mood, not right away.

26

Against the pale light of early morning, the window paper looked untainted by rain and wind, the DOUBLE HAPPINESS paper cut in its center almost as fresh red as before. The quilt felt warm and fluffy, but the pillow next to his, creased, was empty. If the roosters had crowed and the dogs had barked, he hadn't heard them. He had been so gone in his sleep, in whatever dreams he was having, and in the peace and quiet and happiness he had found at long last.

He arose from bed and followed a sweetish aroma to the kitchen.

Fuli was adding firewood to the stove. Her face, lit up by the new flames, looked rosy. She smiled when he squatted next to her and put his arm around her waist. Fuli had on a padded jacket, her sleeves rolled up to the elbows. They gazed into the cheery flames sputtering inside the stove; the only other sound audible was their own breathing, even, robust, enkindled by warmth glowing from their young, lusty bodies.

Suddenly Fuli sniffed and hurried to the front of the stove. She had responded to the burnt smell fast enough. Only one bun near the bottom of the wok showed a blackened crust. All the other buns were undamaged; they looked puffy and delicious.

"You almost ruined the breakfast!" Fuli said with feigned anger when he came to her side.

"I know," Shanmeng tried to project remorse in his face, but failed. He hugged her from behind and kissed her hair.

"Don't you see I'm busy?" She giggled and freed herself.

Fuli placed the buns in a wooden basin and covered them with a towel to keep warm. Then she washed the wok clean, put in another batch of prepared dough near the edge of water in the bottom, and covered the wok again.

Once again Shanmeng was awed by the simple gracefulness of his wife's movement, the ease with which she took care of their home, and the soothing domesticity of it all.

He came back to the main room and opened the front door. It had snowed all night, the world outside, the ground, the trees and shrubs, the river, and the hills in the distance now being buried under chastened white.

Snow must be at least one foot deep. There was no way that the canteen would serve meals today. The village school would be closed, too. Through whatever arrangement Peide had made long winters ago, a small sack was delivered to the middle school on the other side of the river once in a while. Shanmeng had since lost contact with Peide, but the sack would arrive all right and brought him toothpaste, sausages, and things he couldn't have deep in the mountains.

It would be Christmas season back in the world he had left behind. He could hear bells jingle, carols echo, and see candles twinkle from windows. He wouldn't be honest if he told himself that he didn't miss those things. But there were many other things that he didn't miss at all. He liked it here. He liked its earthiness, its simplicity, and loved the people here. Old Ma, despite his now less sunny temperament. Old Ma's wife. Yingzi. Ah Bao. And of course, sweet Fuli. He had a family now. A true family. His roots were growing deeper and stronger every day. He was at peace with himself and with the rest of the world. He was happy.

As they slogged through knee-deep snow, Shanmeng suddenly grasped some snow and tossed it into Fuli's face; she shook it off, laughing, snatched a handful of snow, and stuffed it into his collars. The snow felt icy to the skin and began to melt instantly.

"You're bad!" he laughed.

"But you started!"

Fuli had on an old army winter hat, furry, and puffy. She looked handsome with it on. A girl like Fuli, Shanmeng thought, must have caught many eyes when she was still in the army. She would look even prettier when she had on her old uniform neatly folded in the bottom of one of the trunks. The irony of it all! What would she say when she knew who he really was?

Everyone at the Ma's was already up. Old Ma's wife was cooking congee in the kitchen.

"Ma?" Fuli greeted warmly.

Old Ma's wife turned with a smile.

"Pa?"

Without a word Old Ma turned his face away.

"How's my Ah Bao," Fuli grasped her son's hands in her own and rubbed them. Ah Bao's sleeves glossed from being used to wipe clean his running nose. "Ah Bao warm?" She put her winter hat on her son's head.

"Ah Bao warm." Ah Bao lifted his feet to show a small bronze heater on the floor.

"He's fine," his grandfather mumbled.

Yingzi came out from her room with a book in hand. Now that Ah Bao slept in his grandparents' room, she had the room behind the kitchen all to herself.

"What're you reading, Yingzi," Fuli asked.

"Oh, nothing, just a book from a school friend."

"Mmmm, Dream of Red Mansions?" Fuli enthused, turning the pages of the thick book Yingzi had handed to her. "Let me see, my sis must want to be a Lin Daiyu?"

"Oh, no, who wants to be a sickly beauty? Who knows, I may end up cutting my hair and going into the mountains to become a nun."

Her father grunted through his nose.

"This girl is getting more and more senseless," Old Ma's wife shook her head as she carried a basin of steamy congee on to the table.

Shanmeng couldn't make much sense of what they were talking about either. Going into the mountains to be a nun?

"See what I've got here, too," he said and uncovered the basket he had placed on the table.

Yingzi tore off a slice from a bun. "Mmmm. . . it's good."

They all sat down for breakfast. The room fell into self-conscious silence. Except for the sucking at the thin congee, chewing of the buns and pickled vegetables, and occasional whimpering of Sportie underneath the table.

"Pa," Fuli said, to break the silence, perhaps, "you think our village will have that kind of harvest?"

Old Ma looked up from his bowl but didn't say anything.

A familiar theme song began to play from a small wooden box installed high in a corner of the main room. It was broadcast from the People's Commune's radio station. All the households were now connected with wires for the radio service. When the theme song was finally over, a young girl's voice came on.

"I can be a radio broadcaster like that, too," Yingzi announced suddenly.

Old Ma gave Yingzi a "Why can't you just eat?!" look.

"What's wrong with being a radio broadcaster?" Yingzi mumbled in protest.

"Sis," Fuli said, lowering her voice, "that'll be better than being a nun, for sure."

Old Ma picked up a bun and went to chew by the front door. He was champing with gusto, the muscles in his cheeks wriggling visibly, but there was such a lost look in his eyes as he gazed into the far distance.

A sudden sound of motion.

Wings flapping.

And quietness.

Everyone stopped chewing or sucking from the bowl. They all left the table noiselessly and went to the front door to look.

"Shush!" Old Ma whispered.

A big bird had just landed about fifteen yards from the house. It looked tall and elegant with its pure feathers, long neck, all but inseparable from the glimmering white world if not for the black and red colors on its long beak.

And it was alone.

"It must be very hungry," Yingzi murmured.

"And lonely," said Fuli.

The wild goose perched near a willow tree of long, arching leafless limbs steps away from the base of the Ma home, motionless, a snow sculpture, a white dream. Sensing movement from the direction of the humans, it cocked its head to look.

Sportie snarled, ready to charge.

"Shut—" Old Ma tried to rein in the dog, but it was too late.

Alarmed, the bird flapped its large wings and took off, its cries piercing the sun-kissed blue sky.

27

For quite sometime during spring 1959, everyone, even Old Ma, felt that they might—just might—pull off with 1,000 *jin* a *mu* this year, if not exactly 2,000, 5,000, or 10,000 *jin*. After all, they had done everything that could be done, following the instructions handed down from the Commune, which had received them from the County, which had, in turn, received them from the Province, and so on, on how to boost production. And wheat was growing miraculously well. Old Ma hadn't been sucked into the "launch a satellite" or "set a world record" madness, but he was palpably buoyant by the prospect of setting a new record in the history of the entire river valley. Shanmeng could see it in the village chief's gait and hear it in the unknown tunes he whistled while inspecting the crops even though the two hadn't exchanged more than a cursory nod for a long while.

During the autumn months last year, a major campaign had been waged in the fields of the Twin-Sun Production Brigade. Everyone, old and young, men and woman, was mobilized to help prepare the soil for the biggest harvest ever in history. They upturned the soil at least three feet deep and applied a generous layer of foundation fertilizer every few inches deep: a mix of fermented human, animal waste, dead leaves, weeds, whatever. That seemed the logical thing to do. The more fertile, or fertilized, the soil was, the higher the grain production. As simple as that. Theirs was not a brigade that forced its residents to smash their pots and pans and whatever metal they possessed to toss into the slapdash furnaces built on the thrashing ground or someone's backyard. To make steel. Old Ma wasn't that crazy.

Those were dizzying days of sky-high spirits indeed. Red flags flapped everywhere. Loudspeakers, wired on top of makeshift poles, blasted cheery revolutionary songs and exciting news updates. Young men and women raced each other carrying dark, pungent manure to the fields in large bamboo baskets. Everyone's face was lit with a smile, a smile of hope, of dreams, of tomorrow that would certainly be better than today.

The mood was infectious. If Shanmeng had had a moment of doubt why he was here and what he was doing during the Flood four years ago, it was more than washed over by this euphoria. It looked as if they were not too far away from the society Peide had depicted for him. A utopia. A paradise on earth. Almost.

Even during those days, however, not everything was what it seemed to be. Shanmeng had noticed some folks dragging their feet to work at least half an hour late. More than once did he, during his bee break, stumble upon men stretching out in the bushes and puffing away on their pipes, apparently in no big hurry to get back to work.

It had been a mild winter. Nursed by gentle spring breeze, frequent rain, and zealously fertilized soil, wheat soon grew to knee high, chubby, with tender, fleshy leaves. Even Old Chao and folks much older would walk around and marvel that they had never in their lifetime seen anything like this.

Those were among the best days in his life as long as Shanmeng could remember. Fuli continued to teach at the village school, which had added two more teachers to keep up with the pace of population growth. In addition to the pupils under her care at school, she tutored a special, unregistered student at home.

"The book Yingzi is reading. What's its title again?" he asked one evening over supper.

"Dream of Red Mansions," Fuli looked up from her bowl.

"Oh, yes, that's it. Have you read it?"

"What do you think?" Fuli smiled proudly and murmured:

> *Pages full of fantastic talk*
> *Penned with heart-rending tears;*
> *The world calls the author mad,*
> *None his soul hears....*

"You want to try it? It often reads like riddles. I've read it twice and don't even pretend to understand half of it."

Like the riddles in the scroll? He had once, out of curiosity, taken it out from the earthenware and unrolled it. All he found were:

גן-עדן אדמה כמות עצומה נהר מדבר משי דרך

ουρανός έδαφος βουνό ποταμός έρημοςμετάξι δρόμος

السماء الأرض جبل, نهر, الصحراء ثوب حريري طريق

No English, no French—his two years of French in high school should have been of some help here—and no Chinese. That hermit. What kind of being was he?

He'd make some sense of these riddles, one day, Shanmeng thought. And he'd like to understand the mystery of his wife, too. He had caught her sitting at the front door watching the snow outside, her cheeks streaked with dried tears; he had been awakened in the middle of night by subdued sniffling.

"What is it, honey? Not feeling well? Ah Bao?"

She'd shake her head: "Nothing, really, nothing."

Women, Chinese or otherwise, were mystery, Shanmeng decided. Not knowing what to say, he would gather her in his arms and hold her like that until she quieted down.

Most of the time, even during the early days of her pregnancy when morning sickness was really bad, she was sunny and would hum while cooking, washing, correcting her pupils' work.

Her belly was growing rounder day by day. He'd be a father soon. That'd add to the mystery of it all. And its beauty. And joy.

The day Fuli gave birth to their first child was so muggy that everything—dining table, stools, dirt floor, bamboo sheet, even the trees outside—was breathing sweat. Old Ma's wife and the midwife, an elderly woman from a neighboring village, busied themselves with Fuli inside the bedroom as she moaned. Shanmeng begged to go in but was stopped at the door. It wouldn't be good luck for a husband to see his wife giving birth, the midwife explained. So, he had to sit outside the door and wait.

"It'll be all right, Brother Shanmeng," Yingzi said as she brought the water in the wok to boil again.

She would begin middle school this fall. Somehow Shanmeng couldn't connect her with the small girl he had seen the night he came with Peide six years ago. But then, if anyone of his old buddies saw him today, would they recognize him at all?

Ah Bao had grown into a fine young lad, too. Despite the dullness in the bright eyes, Shanmeng felt that the lad knew and understood more than he let on. Ah Bao sat in his lap despite the heat, his hair, damp with sweat, tickling his chin and giving him an indescribable feeling.

He, Shanmeng, would be a father soon! But what did he have to contribute to bringing a new life into this world other than being a passionate, greedy lover on a beautiful autumn evening ten months ago? And Fuli was the one who had been carrying the seed and nurturing its burgeoning and growth during the last three hundred days and nights. Now she was the one who had to labor and go through tearing pain alone without him being by the bedside holding her hand. What an asshole. Did Heshen have to wait like this when Fuli was giving birth to Ah Bao eight years ago? No, asshole, the man was in Korea at the time. Poor Fuli, and Ah Bao. This new life being born at this very moment, boy or girl no matter, would be Ah Bao's sibling. And he, Shanmeng, their father, would do anything, would give his life, to take care of them, protect them, and make them happy.

"I don't want no Sitting Bull, Dancing Wolf's daughter to be my daughter-in-law one day!" The strange yet familiar voice from nowhere, from another world, another lifetime, startled him from the reverie. "And some crossbreeds to be my. . . ."

"The old bastard," Shanmeng muttered.

Ah Bao shifted in his lap and reached to feel his chin. Yingzi looked up from her book: "Are you okay?"

He nodded.

Had he been stupefied by all this anxiety and expectancy and happiness of becoming a father that he had forgotten about those hurtful exchanges? He fretted and cussed and fretted more as the moan inside the bedroom persisted.

Close to midnight, a feeble whimpering sound came from inside the bedroom, followed by a loud, piercing cry. The newborn continued to cry loudly to make sure its entrance into the world would receive all the attention it well deserved. Shanmeng's heart ached. Something warm, mushy, rushed up to his eyes. He couldn't wait to see his baby. He was dying with joy and pain and anxiety. He knocked on the door.

A few long moments later, Old Ma's wife opened the door: "C'mon in!"

The room had a strong, nauseating odor, the odor of new life, and the odor of the sweat and blood that had to be shed for the new life to be born.

"Congratulations!" exclaimed the midwife, washing her hands in a basin of clean water. "The baby has a little rice wine pot between the legs!"

What? A rice wine pot between the legs? That's worse than what the old bastard said!

"Let me see," Ah Bao squeezed to the bedside and pointed at something hanging between the legs. "Rice wine pot."

Oh, that! A quite normal, healthy rice wine pot all right!

"You've got one between your legs, too, Ah Bao!" teased the

midwife.

"That's right," the lined face of the boy's grandma blossomed with smile.

The baby, nestling next to mama, already had on a small, fluffy diamond-shaped belly cover. His eyes—only one pair of eyes, thank God!—were closed, his skin pinkish, and wrinkled. He had mama's hair, rich, lustrous, and dark.

"Baby nose!" Ah Bao marveled again.

What about the nose? Anything out of the ordinary? No, it was a well-shaped, pointed nose without any defects, either!

"Big," Ah Bao said, "like Uncle Red Hair!"

Fuli, her hair messy, her blouse soaked in sweat, flashed him a weak smile.

"Come and feel your brother's hand," she said to Ah Bao.

Ah Bao touched the baby's cute little fingers, gently, worshipfully. Five fingers on each hand. And five toes each foot, too.

By the wee hours of the next morning, a wind began to blow. It gained ferocity by the minute and before long raindrops, belly button sized raindrops, carried by furious, typhoon-like wind, tumbled on the roof and drummed against the windowpanes.

The storm raged on for a full day and then it stopped altogether. Nobody was prepared for the havoc it had wrecked. The sea of exuberant golden green and ripening promise was now a ghastly picture of dashed dreams: chest-high wheat, smashed, whole patches and strips and stretches of it, some still tottering on broken stems, most sprawled on slushy mud.

Had they—folks of the Twin-Sun River valley and beyond—killed the wheat with their kindness, Simon wondered as he stood by the wheat fields, awestruck, by having over-fed the soil with manure and everything else? Less luxuriant and sturdier wheat might have had a better chance surviving the storm.

In the midst of pitiable mash, he saw a familiar figure, who looked small, lost, a statue of shattered hope, of defeat in a gamble he had partaken only reluctantly.

Shanmeng navigated his way toward the man. Upon hearing his steps, the man waded deeper into the sea of dirty green.

The days and nights that followed were relentless, heartbreaking days and nights to bury the crushed dreams with ploughs and spades and anything folks could lay their hands on and to seed soybeans and whatever crops still seasonable to resuscitate a harvest that might somehow arise, however small.

Whatever little wheat they were able to harvest about a month later was sun-dried on the thrashing ground, winnowed clean, one shovel at a time, and bagged and loaded onto two-wheeled carts to be presented to collection agencies as partial fulfillment of the quota levied by the government.

Old Ma hadn't beaten his chest and promised to "launch a satellite," yet 1,000 *jin* a *mu* was still an astronomical figure given the harvest this year, if it could be called a harvest at all. The Twin-Sun Production Brigade wouldn't be able to fulfill a fraction of their quota even if they could track down every single loose grain that had fallen between little cracks on the thrashing ground.

Those must have been Old Ma's hardest days and nights for a long time in his life. The Commune officials were already unhappy with his less than exemplary showing at the rally last autumn although none of them dared to cough their displeasure in his presence thanks to his envious revolutionary credentials. They themselves were under pressure from County officials who wanted to be able to brag when reporting to Province officials who, in turn, wanted to look the best among their peers when they gathered in the People's Hall on Tiananmen Square. They were living in a time that demanded supersonic speed. Tottering on like an old granny with bound feet and China would never catch up with anyone.

Jade Emperor had awakened from one of his long naps again, taken a pee, and had a fitful sneeze. That was enough to shatter whatever pipe dreams people down on earth had cooked up for themselves. He yawned and went back to drowse in his ivory bed again, leaving in his wake misery and despair and millions, tens of millions, perhaps, of hungry ghosts. A new world record, indeed, had been set. A different, most infamous kind.

Most of these Shanmeng didn't know until many years later.

Old Ma visited neighboring production brigades when Commune and County officials came down to see with their own eyes how sky-high grain production was that year. They were not disappointed. They saw mountains of golden grain on thrashing grounds glittering under the mid-summer sun. They grinned. Their joyous laugh echoed in the sky above the fields where stubbles of fallen wheat had not completely rotted. They fished out notebooks from briefcases, scribbled down numbers, thrust them into the hands of proud production brigade leaders, stepped into dust-covered jeeps, and puttered away.

Watching all this happening right in front of his eyes, Old Ma was ashamed. He was ashamed of himself for not having the guts to brush aside the glittery veneer of grain only inches deep to expose the barren, pallid straw underneath, and cry out loud at the officials before they left:

"Look, you block-headed idiots! Open your ball-less eyes and look!"

And he would live with this regret for the rest of his life.

Shanmeng knew, many years later, that whatever Old Ma imagined he should have done would not have been enough to avert disaster. Someone here and there with more guts must have cried foul but no one listened. In some places young militias were posted at the entrances of villages and along crossroads to stop anyone from attempting to get the word out. For many local officials admitting that they now had a famine in their hands and needed help from outside seemed more shameful than letting their own people die of hunger, and die by the dozens, and by the hundreds, and by the thousands.

28

In the beginning it wasn't that bad. Shanmeng could still sit by the bedside and enjoy the sight of Fuli nursing their baby son. Yangyang suckled greedily and suckled until his hunger was completely appeased, until he fell asleep with Mama's teat in his cute little mouth.

"Don't wake him up," Fuli would whisper when she handed Yangyang to him.

Yangyang felt tiny and light in his arms, but filled his heart with so much joy, pride, and an aching sense of the enormity of this new fatherly responsibility. And he smelled so good, the dizzying fragrance of his mama's milk.

Fuli had lots of milk. Her breasts replenished quickly and started to leak before it was time to nurse Yangyang again. The young father volunteered to help, and when he held Fuli's teat in his mouth and suckled, Fuli giggled and tried in vain to hold back the moans that escaped her throat. He felt like a baby once again when a beam of milk shot against the back of his mouth, sweet, ticklish, and intoxicating.

And for a short while they couldn't eat fast enough the chickens and eggs and live fish the Ma's and some neighbors had brought over.

Things began to look bad when all those delicacies were gone and when the grain in the vat neared the bottom with no prospect of new sacks coming from the brigade warehouse.

The collective canteen had stopped operating for months by now. There had been complaints of the two cooks taking things home from the kitchen at night, and of them giving more generous portions to the families of village officials. And now there wasn't anything left even for the roaches and rats to snuff at.

"Whatever difficulty we're experiencing now," Old Ma said during a mass meeting in the townhall, "is temporary. We live in New China, a Socialist society, and we'll help each other out through the difficulty. If I have one single grain left, I'll share that with everybody else. Besides, the government won't sit by and watch us die. It'll come to our help, fast."

As he sat in the corner watching the village chief speaking in such a tremulous voice, Shanmeng sensed that even the man himself was not convinced by everything he was saying.

That same evening, when the meeting was over, Old Ma was locking up the place when he was startled by a shadow jumping off from a window.

"Who is it?" He hurried over and caught the shadow before it could get on its feet and run away. "Huifa? What're you doing?!"

Huifa fell on his knees right away. "Chief Ma, Uncle Ma, the kids are starving to death..."

Old Ma glowered at Huifa and saw the bag in his hands. "That's seeds for spring next year. Our only hope. The whole village counts on it!"

"What am I supposed to do, Uncle Ma? I did all I could to have food for my kids, I can't just watch them. . . ."

Old Ma, torn between pity and contempt, yanked the bag from Huifa. "Go home. Don't ever let me catch you again."

"Thank you, Uncle Ma, I'll never forget your kindness . . . I'll pay you back in my next life. . . ten times over. I'll—"

"Just go!" Old Ma never told anyone about this until many years later.

Soon all the grains were gone. People began to eat chow for pigs and other livestock. When there wasn't anything left to feed the animals, they had to be slaughtered.

That was what Old Chao did with the old mama pig. Huifa came and offered Old Chao good money—three times more than what it would have been worth—for the pig's dry, wrinkled hide and meatless bones, but the old man wouldn't sell.

"I can cook up a cauldron of soup that'll last us for a week, to say the least," the old man mumbled through toothless mouth. "Money isn't worth anything. It isn't even worth the paper it is printed on now."

One day they slaughtered the water buffaloes, the dumb, loyal, hardest-working beasts they had counted on for plowing, planting, and harvesting since time immemorial. They slaughtered these beasts for meat, bones, hides, and everything else because they were hungry and because there was nothing else to quiet the blinding noise in their stomachs.

The day they slaughtered the water buffaloes on the thrashing ground, folks who could still manage to walk came to see and to receive their share.

The water buffaloes, weakened by hunger, their bony ribcages more visible than ever, didn't put up much of a resistance at all. The oldest one had tears in his big eyes as he fell on the knees slowly to receive the sharpened knife at the neck.

It was one of the saddest days in the history of the village.

At first Old Ma insisted on touring the village once a day to check on his people. But before long he became too weak to do so. Years later Shanmeng knew that Old Ma and his wife refused to touch whatever little food they had so that Yingzi and Ah Bao would not starve.

Sportie had become old and gaunt by this time. Its eyes were dull, its ears hanging listlessly, and it wouldn't bother to bark at the sight of anyone tramping along the dirt road outside. When Old Ma put a rope around its neck, Sportie whimpered, kicked, but it wasn't much of a struggle for its life. It was Old Ma who had to pull hard, gasping for air, as the dog, all of its length, head to tail, dangled from the top of the front door.

Yingzi cried, but what could she do to save Sportie? Ah Bao thought it was some play at first, but stopped laughing when the dog stiffened, the light of life in its eyes dimmed, and when it didn't respond to his touch.

Yingzi refused to touch the meat at supper that evening.

"Eat, useless girl!" her father ordered.

Yingzi dipped her chopsticks into the earthenware and picked up a morsel. No sooner had she started to chew than she jerked away and doubled up in a fitful vomit. Old Ma picked up another piece of dog meat and stuffed it in his daughter's bowl.

"Eat," he said weakly, "when it's gone, it's gone."

Ah Bao looked around the table while chewing with relish. "You eat," he urged his grandma. "You eat!"

"No, Ah Bao eat," Old Ma's wife shook her head. "Grandma not hungry."

Rumor came that people in neighboring villages—villages which had bragged sky-high grain productions—had spotted kids' little shoes and jackets in the bushes and shrubs.

Folks here shook their heads in disgust and disbelief. But in the heart of their hearts, they sensed that the rumor might not be too far-fetched.

One day, when Yingzi went with her mother to pick weeds—young, green weeds had become scarce—the old woman swooned and fell, like a dried leaf, and never got up on her own again.

Hunger wasn't new to Shanmeng, though. He knew what it could do to the body, and the spirit.

29

He hadn't had a chow for a whole day. He hadn't had a decent chow for days by now. His body, awash with sweat, trembled spastically as he staggered along the narrow trail, each step causing fireworks to splutter in his forehead.

A young captor, not older than 15 or 16, barely taller than the M-1 rifle he was shouldering, urged him to keep up with the long file of old and newly captured GIs snaking up an ugly hill of barren brown. The young boy, toothy, his face filmed with dusty sweat, sounded strange, even charming, but the high-pitched tone was masculinized by a passion less than friendly.

Pfc Simon Mackenzie bit his lips and dragged his body along. He felt light as a dream, a bad dream; a whisper of wind could sweep him away and toss him to he didn't know where.

Forms and bundles sprawled every whichever posture by the road side: fellow former army soldiers and marines, mostly 18 or 19-year-old boys, who couldn't go on anymore, some already stiffened, the limbs of others still moving in a vague attempt to crawl, to wave away proffered aid, or to give feeble expression to whatever was on their mind as numbing coldness zeroed in on them on the frozen foreign soil far away from home.

Simon had no desire to join those forms by the roadside; he wanted to keep going as long as he could still breathe. For what? He didn't have the faintest idea. His mind was foggy, unable to deliberate anything this deep and heavy. But that didn't matter. He tried to keep his eyes locked on "Battle of Leyte" on the knapsack of the tall marine ahead of him, who shuffled ahead, left boot, right boot, with a smooth cadence as if he wanted to measure the hardened earth accurately. And he knew that he could trust the marine, and that he owed it to him that he was still breathing.

The day after they had been taken prisoners, so many of them, infantry soldiers and marines and whatever, they were forced to march northward for 16 hours without stopping once for water or food; they marched through tough terrain at gunpoint of North Korean captors who didn't hesitate to kick ass, hit with the butts of M-1 rifles, carbines, or shoot if anyone dared to show defiance.

When finally, they couldn't drag themselves one more step ahead, order came from the front for them to stop. Their captors began to hand out food. Cracked wheat. A handful for each captor and captive alike.

Simon was disgusted upon receiving his "meal" from a North Korean officer. It felt so coarse in his hands, so dry, and unfit for human consumption.

Prior to today he had been bored with canned C-rations and developed an aversion to them. Now he salivated for them, if his cracked lips, parched mouth could still salivate.

But this cracked wheat in his hands? He didn't want it to have anything to do with his lips and mouth at all. So he let his palms open. The cracked wheat fluttered to the dirt ground, all of it, where it belonged.

The young North Korean officer was stunned. He grabbed Simon's collars and hit him in the face left and right. "You, stinky American devil!" he screamed in broken English.

Simon saw red-hot lava erupting in his forehead, his cheeks singeing.

Still fuming with rage, the officer drew his pistol and pointed it between Simon's eyes, only a mocking inch away.

It'll be all over for me now, Simon thought as he stared at the dark hole of the tube. With a pull of the trigger, he would be a goner in a fiery splash of colors. Strangely he was not afraid. He was calm and ready to end it all. Right there.

Someone intervened.

"Easy, easy, officer," he heard the guttural voice of the tall marine; a strong arm pulled him aside.

"Kid," that voice was speaking to him now, like a commanding officer, "get on your ass! Scrape up the food, every bit of it. Now!"

The man's arm was on Simon's shoulder, steely, forcing him down, until his knees hit the ground.

As he scraped and picked up a tiny bit between his fingers, Simon looked up, confused, and saw the North Korean officer still glowering at him with the pistol in hand.

"See?" the tall marine licked the cracked wheat still in his free hand. "It's good. It's good food!"

The officer grunted through his nose and turned to check on the other GIs in the long line.

"Are you nuts?" the marine said as Simon stuffed a mix of cracked wheat and mud into his mouth. "You'd have got yourself killed! If you want to die here, in this God-forsaken place, that's not

too hard. Every coward could do that, the stupid antic you put on."
Then, in a softer voice, "But you've got no right to do that. You
want to eat, and to live, and to make it home, even if the food tastes
like shit. And this, this cracked wheat, is not that bad, not that bad
at all."

No, it wasn't that bad, Simon nodded vaguely as he tried to
swallow it down his parched throat.

"And the native people," the marine continued, shaking his
head, when Simon got on his feet again, "only the Good Lord
knows, may have lived on this thing for thousands of years."

That was how he got to know Harold.

Cpl. Harold White had fought in the Battle of Leyte during the
Philippines campaign of 1944-45 under the command of General
MacArthur and was awarded a Bronze Star for his courage in
combat. He returned to his family's tenant farm in Tennessee to
recover from a wound in his shoulder, but soon grew sick of the
bleak prospect of it all. His parents, now older, were still struggling
to make ends meet. His two brothers didn't want to till the soil like
their parents, yet, thanks to their skin color and lack of skills, they
couldn't find anything in the nearby town. They were restless and
quarrelsome. Harold didn't like the plow a bit better than his
brothers and felt unfulfilled by the odd jobs he was able to find in
town. The day he heard on the radio that the North Korean
People's Army had swarmed across the 38th parallel, the news was
a godsend to him. He enlisted again.

Harold told him all this later as they lay in the woods—so that
American fighter jets and bombers wouldn't spot them from the
sky—trying to loosen up the limbs and drift off to a nap.

"The Good Lord knows," Harold chortled, his eyes gazing into
the cloudy sky. "I may be destined to be a soldier, but I don't see
why I can't, one day, marry a beautiful girl, and have a bunch of
kids!"

It was dusk. The world all around dimmed and blurred. They
started to march again. They had been marching northward for
about a week now. Soon they would reach the Yalu River between

Manchuria and North Korea. He didn't need anyone to tell him that. He still had the map of Korea, of East Asia printed in his mind. Not just from that geography class he had taken with Mrs. Davis, his third-grade teacher. At the boot camp Colonel Eagleton, a decorated WWII veteran, had pointed it out for them:

"See that country there, right across the Yalu River from Manchuria of China? Yes, that's where you're going, son, to do a little police action. See, it's shaped like Florida, long and slender, probably a bit smaller, with the 38th parallel cutting right across at a mid-point like Orlando, separating the Communist North Korea and the Democratic South Korea. Right now, the two Koreas are caught up in a little quarrel. As President Truman said, you boys will be back for Christmas. Personally, I don't see how it would even take that long."

The good colonel had conveniently forgotten to mention that the weather in Korea couldn't be more different from that in Florida. Christmas was still about a month away, but the prospect of them going home for Christmas was bleak like the early evening sky.

Harold had said he would give anything to be able to go home and celebrate Christmas with his folks. If that would happen at all, through a miracle of sort, he might leave home again, after only a short stay, to serve another tour of duty somewhere to appease whatever was restless inside him.

What was Simon's story? How did he get into this big mess? Well, he didn't even know where to start if he were to tell the long, messy story. He was not running away from plows and furrows and the cheerless prospect of a life on a small tenant farm. He had never worked on a farm, but he wondered what it would be like growing things with his own hands and living a life of basics, stripped of anything that would even remotely suggest luxury. He didn't know. The way he had reacted to the cracked wheat was not a good sign. It was no more than a reflex, an instinctive aversion to something that looked offensive to his palate. Cracked wheat was bare basics, unsoftened by sugar and butter and anything else that would make it more palatable. But it could sustain life all the same.

It had sustained life in this part of the world, and perhaps elsewhere, for thousands of years. And what else, what luxuries, had he, Pfc Simon, a prisoner of war, thought he was entitled to from his captors if his captors had been sucking life from the same thing, coarse, nutty as it was, all their life—many of them could have been peasants growing the wheat before war started?

And he thought of what he had said to a beautiful girl about Walden in another lifetime of his. He blushed.

The knapsack he humped cut into his shoulders and sank him down, earthward. Could he still handle it if he were to carry also his M-1, grenades, ammos, and many other things? He felt relieved that as a captive he had been released of those tools of death on his shoulders during the forced march.

There was a hole in the top corner of his knapsack, round, the size of a coin. The bullet could have hit him, penetrated his shoulder blade, his spine, and bled him to death, or paralyzed him for the rest of his life. But he was lucky. It came from a trajectory that was not perpendicular to his person. In the heat of battle, when rifles, machine-guns, mortars were roaring all around, no one could choose what angle a bullet or shrapnel would hit him.

The drizzly air soused his face—forehead, eyebrows, nose, cheeks, chin, and blurred his vision. He dabbed with his damp sleeves, but it didn't help much. The trail became slippery. Soon it began to sleet. Light. Unhurried. Yet it made it more difficult to maintain the pace they had been going. Even Harold, the tall marine, had slowed down, every step a near slip accompanied with slushy sound.

This goddamn North Korean weather. It was still late fall by the calendar, but the cold could already shrink you a few sizes down. And the sleet, a mix of rain and snow, seemed worse than either alone.

A flush of sweat swept over him now and then. He was feeling weaker each new step. He must look like that ridiculous grasshopper in the fable, gaunt, a sorry shadow of its former self, that could be blown away by a mere breath. The first time he read the fable as a young boy, he laughed as if a funny bone had been tickled, picturing the grasshopper—who had been fooling away its time during summer, crawling to the ant's well-heated home to beg for food in the dead of winter. Did he fool away his time during warmer, sunnier days, so to speak? Would he lose count of days if he had to drag on like this forever? Would he lose the sense of who he was? Would he even know whether he was still breathing? Breathing. It used to be easy, natural, instinctual, now each breath, a conscious effort.

He staggered on, keeping his eyes on the tall figure in front of him.

Suddenly he bumped into something hard, his half-awake forward trajectory had been interrupted. His body broke into another cold sweat.

"You okay?" The familiar guttural voice in the predawn dusk.

They had stopped. Their captors were giving orders in broken English. They would eat and set camp for the day.

Simon looked around. He could make out shadowy mudhuts here and there. Collapsed roofs, and tottering walls.

The sleet had stopped, too.

The captors were handing out "meals."

Cracked wheat, again.

It still tasted rough and nutty and dry to the mouth. It was still difficult to chew and swallow down the parched throat. But he now chewed with relish, like a dog that hadn't seen food for days, knowing that it would fuel the fire in his body so he could keep breathing, so he would not freeze into an icicle when he woke up again.

When they finished chewing, they were told to find a spot nearby for shelter. The captors needed not worry about the captives attempting to run away. They had been marching for days and nights and had covered so many steep hills, precipitous ridges, and deep valleys of tough terrain and bare brown earth that nobody would have a chance of surviving even if he could get away.

Simon, Harold, and a few dozen other captives found themselves herded into a small hut not far from the trail. It had large holes in the roof and its walls tittered on collapse, but it would provide some shelter, nonetheless.

As the former infantry soldiers and marines dropped on the frozen ground, everyone sighed and moaned out of pain, fatigue, and tense anticipation of the respite to their stiffened joints and sore muscles. They huddled together for lack of space and for warmth.

"Fuck Truman, some kind of police action he sent us to do!" a marine cussed.

"Yeah, fuck MacArthur, too. If he can't get me home for Christmas, I'm going to kick someone's ass real hard!" an infantry man echoed.

"Try fucking in your dream!" Someone snickered.

"I wouldn't mind, if you'd get me a pretty girl, Korean, American, Japanese, no matter!"

"You think I'd be that charitable if I could find one?"

Titter, jeer, heehaw came from all corners. Then, a hushed silence fell over everybody and left him to nurse whatever thought was on his mind.

Simon found himself lying face to face with Harold, so close he could feel the marine's breath on his face. Harold's chocolate face was clearly chiseled with prominent cheekbones. His garlic-shaped nose, reddened by cold, had a few wet hairs sticking out. His eyes, large, open, glinted with quiet cheerfulness. Simon recoiled at the first flush of Harold's warm breath in his face.

"You stink, too!" the marine grinned, as if saying.

Simon shifted his position slightly and turned his face toward the sky. The sky he saw through the hole in the roof was clear and bare. He tried to put a lone star there and focused on it. The longer he gazed the bigger and brighter the star became. He didn't know what constellation it belonged to, whether it was close to or far from the solar system, or even if it were a member of the Milky Way. That didn't matter. The imagined star lifted him away from this half collapsed mudhut on this ridgeline of a cold country to a place thousands of miles away.

When he woke up toward the evening, a dust of snow had fallen on his blanket. He—all of them—must have slept like the dead.

They got on their feet and marveled about the snow.

Their captors hollered outside and along the trail.

They started to march again.

The wind whistled and cut to the bone.

The western part of the sky was streaked with bloody red from the setting sun. The hills nearby and in the far distance were covered in snow. The world was entombed in white.

He struggled on the steep trail, gasping for air. The cracked wheat had long burnt itself out in his body. How long could he hold on to life?

Sprawled by the wayside were bodies of young soldiers and marines who had died of cold, of hunger, of sickness, of having surrendered to a wish not to fight for life anymore.

What would happen to them now that they were dead? Simon thought. Who would bury them? Would the bodies rot fast? What would happen to his body if he fell and didn't pick himself up again? Would it stay for long? Would that matter?

They clambered through the night silhouetted by pale snow. By midnight Simon reached the top of the hill from where he saw behind him a long, tortuous line of shadows still struggling up the slope while ahead of him another line was already creeping down into the dark valley. It would be high noon on the other side of the globe. Would people know what was going on here? Would they care? Would he care if they cared or not?

Someone slipped and fell on the snow. Simon stopped to lend a hand to pull the fallen one up again. Another one tripped and rolled down the wayside and vanished. No one stopped.

Something buzzed in the early morning sky.

It droned in the misty air and boomed and within seconds fighter jets and bombers roared overhead. They flew so low that Simon could all but make out their serial numbers.

Fuck them flyboys! He cursed. Couldn't they see that they were not North Korean, Kim Il-song army, but good old American GIs?

Fighter jets hovered around and dived, their machine-guns

clattering, bombs exploding left and right.

The captives scurried in all directions, screaming for their lives.

In a minute, the planes were gone, en route to their destination northward, the Yalu River, perhaps, leaving behind a deafening echo, several large, grotesque pits in the snow-covered ground, and more than a dozen bodies—maimed, charred, still smoldering—scattered here and there, and the rest, who had escaped death, moaning in pain, fear, and anger.

Where the heck is Harold? That was Simon's first thought when he got on his feet again.

"Harold?" he called, but no sound came out of his parched throat.

There was a commotion on the other side of the trail. He hastened over. Not far from him to the left was a dirt mount in the snow fouled with shrapnel, patches of dark red, and body parts seared beyond recognition.

"Harold?" he hollered as he ran toward the mount. No Harold.

He stumbled over a bundle on the ground. A knapsack with broken straps and burnt holes. Near its bottom were words, half singed, but still recognizable: Battle of Leyte.

"A sort of lucky charm," Harold had told him with a big smile on his face.

"Harold!" he screamed.

Someone scuffed over. It was the same North Korean officer who had almost executed him not too long ago. The officer shouted angrily, flourishing the same pistol.

On the trail the line of captives was already teetering ahead again.

30

Everything eatable was all but gone. Twin-Sun River had been combed several times over by the five or six villages in the valley with fishing nets, bamboo baskets, and anything that could trap a carp, an eel, or a shrimp. Vegetables in the garden became the primary source of nutrients and when that became scarce, weeds by waysides and tree skins had to step in to fill the otherwise empty woks.

Pure vegetable meal—boiled cabbage chops, carrots leaves, and what not—had a sickening smell to it when you had to have it day after day. You could have gulped down two or three bowls of such a meal, but your belly would still feel empty. And it didn't take it long to travel through the entire digestive passageways.

Once in a long, long while a wagon would wiggle and creak down the dirt road with a few sacks of dried yam slices and corn or wheat flour, the wagon being guarded by armed militiamen from the Commune, which had received the emergency supply from the County, which had finally reported to the Province, half-truthfully, the famine that had been raging on and taking massive tolls. These sacks of food would be divided, as equitably as possible, among the households, considering age, health, gender, and other such vital factors.

Sprinkling a bit of corn and wheat flour onto the grassy mash bubbling in the wok and the meal would smell more palatable and last a bit longer.

The dried yam slice was another story. It had a sweetish odor and taste and didn't have to be cooked. But you had to chew long and hard, till your mouth was sore with exhaustion. So Shanmeng learnt to soak it first, bring it to a boil, and let it simmer until it mashed like congee.

"One *jin* of yam meal, two *jin* poops," Old Chao was once heard saying, "and when you turn to look behind, it's actually more."

The old man isn't too far off, Shanmeng thought whenever he visited the outhouse.

And the sweetish yam meal didn't quite agree with his stomach. It gave him a dull heartburn that would leave him no peace between the meals.

Fuli's breasts had fallen flat, too. Yangyang cried so much because he sucked and suckled with all his might and little milk came out of mama's teats. What else could she use to appease the baby but spoonfuls of yam mash?

Fuli had thinned so much. Her skin had lost the soft luster of the days right after she gave birth. He didn't need a mirror to remind himself how he looked. What's going on? When will it all be over? Will I lose my wife, and my son? Sometimes he suspected that all this trouble was caused by him, by his coming into the lives of people he hadn't even known to exist. Otherwise, how could you account for the folks here having to take it on the chin so many times since I came? A stroke of bad luck and nothing more? Am I a pawn in some kind of big-stake game? He dismissed this line of thinking right away: You vain, megalomaniac bastard! If that were the case, why the heck people in other villages, and in the counties and provinces beyond, are having it just as bad, too? Perhaps we are all pawns in some game, of cosmic proportions? If that were the case, who are the players? What is at stake?

The loudspeaker in the corner came on toward the evening. The theme song buzzed like a mosquito that hadn't had a chance to sting a human or water buffalo for days. The young girl broadcaster Yingzi had envied didn't sound a bit better: "Good evening, members of the People's Commune. Today is April 1, 1960. . . the natural disaster is temporary, unexpected, and under control. We are confident that under the correct leadership of the Central Government, we will overcome the difficulties and prevail. . . I'm excited to report that relief is on the way. . . ."

Would relief be fast enough to save the lives of people in this village, save the lives of Fuli, Yangyang, Ah Bao, Yingzi, Old Ma, and people who were dear to him?

They went to bed early. There was no need to light the lamp. It would be a complete waste of oil. Shanmeng lay in bed, listening to the quiet breathing of his wife, his son, and his own. As Shanmeng turned and drowsed, he dreamed of two players getting into a brawl over an idiotic game, himself being the dice tossed around on the board. The still lucid part of his consciousness felt it weird and wanted to yell and tell them to quit it, but no sound came out of his mouth. He was being tossed into the air again and before he landed, he was wakened by a loud knock on the front door.

He sat up and listened. Darkness still reigned everywhere, in and outside his home. Who could it be, at this ungodly hour?

"Comrade Shanmeng, open the door," a young man's voice. "Comrade Shanmeng, are you there?"

"Yes, coming!" Shanmeng replied and slid out of bed, his heart flailing nervously.

When he pulled back the bolts, two young men, both in uniforms, armed, were at the door, their faces caked with sweat and dust. Behind them was a wheeled cart; on it were a sack and two small boxes.

"These are for you."

"What? For me? All of this? From whom?"

"We don't' know," one of the soldiers said. "Our instructions were to deliver them to you directly. We were told that you should know."

Yes, Shanmeng nodded, his eyes misting, I should know.

That same night Shanmeng went to a house which he knew so well and could find even blindfolded. Except for a few lone stars flickering in the sky, the world was chilly and deadly quiet although it was already spring. Everything seemed only a step away from death anyway because whatever people were eating, if they ate anything at all, was not fit for humans and barely had enough fuel to keep the fire of life alive.

He knocked on the door. No response. He knocked again and

waited. In the pale light of the night he noticed, under the eaves, several small mounts of roots—chunks and slices mixed together—apparently having been tossed there after being cooked for their dark brown medicinal juice.

"Yingzi? Ah Bao? It's me. Shanmeng."

He heard faint sounds, and then slippers shuffling on the dirt floor. The door opened.

"Brother Shanmeng?" Yingzi asked; the little woman of the house since her mother died rubbed her sleepy eyes. "What time is it? Anything happened? My sis and--"

"No, they're fine," he said and showed the girl the basket in his hand. "Some rice and other little things for you, Ah Bao, and Pa."

"Who is it?" a hoarse voice grumbled weakly from inside the dark interior of the house.

"It's me, Shanmeng."

"What do you want?" The same unfriendly tone, followed by a fit of cough with thick phlegm.

"Pa is sick, very sick."

Shanmeng stepped in and hurried into Old Ma's bedroom.

In the dusk of night Shanmeng made out a form in a old bed wrapped with panels of carved figures—warriors flourishing swords atop grand horses, dancers weaving out long, billowing sleeves, and tillers urging water buffalos with raised whips—who seemed oblivious to the suffering going on right under their noses. The form struggled to sit up in bed, but gave up the attempt when a fit of cough hit him again.

"Are you all right? Should I get you a doctor?"

"Doctor. What doctor?"

Shanmeng knew that he wasn't making any sense at all. Where the heck could he find a doctor at this time in this ghost-wouldn't-lay-eggs place in deep mountains?

"What's wrong?"

"Pa said he's having a headache, like someone is hammering his temples with a stone pounder or something."

Old Ma glowered at his daughter but didn't say anything.

Shanmeng knew that he knew nothing about bacteria, virus,

and medicine in general. What could he do? He turned to check on Ah Bao. Where his bed used to be in the corner, it was empty now.

"Pa doesn't want Ah Bao to sleep here anymore," Yingzi explained.

Shanmeng understood.

Once out of Old Ma's room, Shanmeng said: "Yingzi, cook some nice congee for Pa. Warm food would do him some good."

The little woman of the house nodded.

Ah Bao was sleeping soundly on a bamboo bed in Yingzi's room, free from all the worries, and the pang of hunger that would bother him if he were awake now. His lips moved, as if chewing something with relish.

Fuli's body responded to food almost instantly. Within days Yangyang suckled contently at her swollen breasts again. But Old Ma's condition didn't improve.

"I have to go and see Pa," Fuli said one evening after feeding Yangyang, "even if he will scream in my face."

When they arrived, Ah Bao was more than thrilled. "Mama, Mama!" he cooed, and tickled his baby brother's little feet.

"Sis, Pa's getting worse. Much worse," Yingzi said, teary-eyed.

Old Ma coughed and groaned weakly in his room.

Shanmeng gave the baby to Yingzi and followed Fuli into the interior room.

"Pa?" He heard Fuli calling when he stepped in.

Old Ma, a skeletal shadow of his former self, looked worse than only a few days ago, his cheekbones more prominent, the eyes in the sunken sockets glowing feverishly.

"How're you, Pa? Where does it hurt?" Fuli reached to feel the old man's forehead. Old Ma jerked his head away, his face grimacing in pain.

The room was oppressively quiet except for Old Ma's tumultuous breathing. Then his cracked lips moved. Nothing audible came out. With difficulty the man lifted his right hand and pointed where his heart was.

Fuli broke into a sob. "Pa, I'm sorry. I haven't been a good, filial daughter . . ."

Old Ma's lips moved again; his voice came through sticky phlegm this time: "You . . . no daughter of mine."

Fuli wept with abandon and left the room.

Yingzi met them at the door with the baby in her arms. She sobbed quietly, too. "Pa, you know. He's stubborn."

Fuli wept some more, trembling, until she finally got hold of herself. They all sat at the Eight Immortals table and stared at each other. Blankly. What could they do? Just sit here and wait for the patriarch of the family to breathe his last?

Yangyang, still in his little auntie's arms, cooed suddenly. "What, hungry again?" Yingzi teased and gave the baby back to his mama.

Fuli unbuttoned her blouse and placed her teat into the baby's mouth. Yangyang suckled noisily.

"Yingzi," Fuli looked up suddenly and said, "get me a bowl, quick!"

"What, sis? You want water, or congee?"

"No," Fuli replied. She stood up and gave the baby to Shanmeng. Yangyang started to whine, as if being cheated. Shanmeng patted him gently to calm him down.

Fuli took over the bowl from Yingzi and went into the room behind the kitchen. A minute later—it seemed like a lifetime—Fuli came out with the bowl in hand and walked directly into her former father-in-law's room.

"Pa, I've got medicine for you." Fuli's voice sounded calm.

"Medicine," mumbled Old Ma. "What medicine?"

"Some secret folksy remedy I've heard people talking about. Thousands of years old folksy remedy."

Old Ma looked like he wanted to say something again, to shout, to scream, to howl, perhaps, but nothing came out of his quivering lips.

"Pa, take it, take it from your daughter!" Fuli begged in a commanding voice.

Without waiting for a reply, she put her left hand under the old man's head to help lift it so his cracked lips could reach the bowl.

Old Ma's head, unkempt and damp with sweat, seemed too heavy for Fuli. Shanmeng gave the baby to Yingzi and hurried over to assist.

Old Ma opened his lips reluctantly and took a small sip. The milk in the bowl looked rich and smelled fragrant.

"What's this?" A shocked look in the old man's eyes.

"The remedy I've brought you, Pa. Thousands of years old folksy remedy."

Old Ma's head suddenly weighed a thousand ton as he insisted on being let down on the pillow again. "This old fool would rather die," he said, his skinny chest heaving visibly, "than take food from his own grandson."

31

Shanmeng was woken by the rooster crowing fiercely from the coop in the main room. It crowed again before the echo of its voice had barely faded into the predawn darkness. When the impromptu choir of chickens, dogs, pigs, and nameless animals and birds and insects finished its serenade, the world buzzed with an uneasy quietness.

Shanmeng turned, wrapped his arm around Fuli's shoulder and reached further. Her breasts felt warm and firm even though she had suckled two, no, three babies.

"Ma," their two-year-old daughter cried in the room behind the kitchen.

"Yangmei?" Fuli called in a sleepy voice. "Want to pee? No? Then get back to sleep."

"Mmmm."

"Ma?" A young boy's voice.

"Yangyang?" Fuli sounded more awake now. "Too early to get up for school yet."

She moved to get up, but Shanmeng's hand cupping her breast and his leg nuzzling hers held her in place.

"Too early to get up yet," he whispered.

She fell back, her body snuggling closer.

This is good. Shanmeng thought vaguely. This was his favorite time of the day, holding Fuli in his arms like this. Spring. Summer. Fall. Winter. Rain. Shine. Moon. Sun. Stars. It didn't matter as long as his wife was with him like this, his son and daughter were safe and warm and healthy and well-fed, and all the people dear to him, Old Ma, Yingzi, and Ah Bao, were safe and healthy and fine.

The world was so peaceful at this time of the day. He could hear Yangyang and Yangmei settling back to sleep in their room. Fuli's breath became even again. He began to drowse, too.

The loudspeaker in the corner buzzed. The theme song of the by now too familiar "Socialism is Good" puttered through the early morning dusk, then, "Good morning, members of the People's Commune, today is March 20, 1965. . . ."

People who had survived the three years of famine had rebounded. In their bodies were coursing the same sap of life, the same zest of hope, and the same trust generously, naively, and, yes, blindly placed.

So many things waited to be done. Spraying pesticide on the blooming trees in the orchard. Fertilizing baby tomato and cucumber and potato seedlings in the garden. Weeding the lush green wheat fields that looked so promising.

Shanmeng removed his hand from Fuli's bosom, turned on his back, and yawned deliciously. He needed to get up and get ready for the new day.

Part V

32

The first big-character poster in the Twin-Sun Production Brigade was not much of a fanfare. It was almost a joke.

It appeared on a wall in the townhall one morning hastily pasted over slogans from an erstwhile era. The brushwork was shaky, as if ghostwritten by a semiliterate. And it was unsigned. Shanmeng, like everyone else in the village, couldn't help laughing when he read it:

Beware The Weasel Among Us

Heart eaten by insatiable greed,
Charges a fortune for his breed;
Old mama pig hide wouldn't share,
Even to save flowers of the future;
Heaven only fair and has sharp eyes,
Lets a bouncy bun on his arm arise;
The weasel in him still alive and well,
We be better served if forever beware.

August 7, 1966

But it was no laughing matter for Old Chao, almost ancient by now. An upper-middle-class farmer who had barely survived Land Reforms, the old man teetered back home with a cane and never left his sick, cold bed again, his wife having died during the Famine. Some old folks sighed profusely that they didn't see tears in Jian'er's eyes when he buried his father a month later: "The world isn't what it used to be. . . ."

A few more of such posters appeared but nobody took them seriously except for, of course, those being targeted.

Soon the walls of the townhall were jammed with posters and the tone began to change. Fuli became concerned. She and Shanmeng went to see Old Ma one evening and found the man puffing away at the dining table. Yingzi, a junior at the normal school in the county town outside the mountain, happened to be visiting.

"Chairman Mao is right," Yingzi said, her eyes glinting with excitement. "Revolution is not a dinner party. We have to deal with class enemies with iron fists!"

Old Ma stared at his daughter, a young woman donning short hair and faded army uniform only God knew where she had obtained and shook his head.

"Sis," Fuli said softly, "don't you see Pa is worried?"

"What does Pa have to worry about? A Long Marcher with the kind of revolutionary credentials all of my comrades-in-arms at school envy to death."

Yingzi left the next morning and a few days later sent a letter home saying that she was gone on a Long March of her own with a group of kindred spirits to spread the revolutionary prairie fire all over the country.

One day, scanning the posters in the village townhall, Shanmeng was alarmed by one freshly pasted:

What Revolutionary Credentials?

Written in the same shaky brushwork, and signed: A Diehard Proletarian Fighter, the poster questioned Old Ma's faith in Revolution because he had returned to the village after a minor wound in the leg.

The poster attracted the attention of the whole village, literate and illiterate alike. Shanmeng saw Fuli talking earnestly to Jian'er outside the townhall. Jian'er, still single, listened, and shook his head.

"What is it?" he asked Fuli when they were alone on their way home.

"Nothing," his wife mumbled absent-mindedly, "just wanted to know if Jian'er knew something."

The tone of the posters became meaner, more vicious each day:

Tear off the Sheepskin to Expose the Wolf!
Down with Ma: A Chicken-Hearted Traitor!

Then, one evening in late November, the darkening sky over this part of the Twin-Sun River shuddered with the sound of the school bell—that piece of old, gnarled bomb shell—being tolled overzealously.

It was the first denunciation rally against the village chief. The townhall was so packed that late arrivals had to be content with listening from outside. For a while, no matter how Huifa, Commander of the Red Sun Corps of Toward-Sun ("Twin-Sun" had been dropped as taboo because Mao should be revered as the only Sun) Production Brigade, tried to stir things up, no one came forward to the podium—a school desk placed in front of the anxious crowd.

"As our great leader Chairman Mao said: Revolution is not a dinner party," Huifa shrieked, his face twitching with the glory of the moment. Just over 40, the man's shoulders already hunched noticeably. "There's no middle ground to stand on. All of you here today, you're either with us revolutionaries, or with him!" he turned to point an index finger at Old Ma, who was standing next to the desk, his head being forced to bend in repentance, "A reactionary, a class enemy, a traitor. . . . and we won't call it quits today until we have won a thorough victory! "

Finally, an old man stood up and waddled to the podium, a live pipe in hand.

"Let me fire the first shot," the old man's voice dribbled through the few blackened teeth remaining in his mouth, "and see if it hits the target all right. Mmmm. I should call you Gouzai if I may indulge in being old and befuddled for the moment. I saw you growing up with my own eyes, when you were still a kid running around with bare butt, bare feet, fooling in the river and trying to catch fish and what not. I saw you and my kid brother off—still remember Six-Fingered?—when you went to join the Red Army. Remember all that, Gouzai?"

The village chief looked up and nodded.

"I've meant to tell you for some time now, Gouzai, but haven't had a chance," the old man pointed at Ma with his pipe, its live content falling out, the audience bursting into uneasy laugh. "I was so disappointed when you came back with that limp of yours. Why did you come back that way? Were you scared? Afraid of dying for the Revolution? Six-Fingered never came back. Even his ghost may not have a place to call home, not to say his body."

The old man paused to take a drag at the pipe, found it empty, shook his head in disbelief. "But you did good by the village. I've never, even once, seen you taking one stick of firewood from the collective. . . ."

Huifa's face twitched more visibly.

"However, you did become cocky. You wouldn't listen to me. You had to dig the soil so deep and wanted to launch the stupid satellites. See, how many good folks died during the Famine? Why couldn't you save lives? More people died during the three years than all the deaths I had seen my entire life! How could you sleep-_"

The old man was interrupted by an uproar of nervous laugh. He turned to a livid, fuming Commander Huifa with confusion in his eyes, and then sighed, dabbed away saliva dripping from the corner of his mouth, and waddled back to where he sat before.

Two or three other villagers stammered through their incoherent denunciations before the rally was over.

The bombshell for Shanmeng came a few weeks later in the form of a poster, signed by Jian'er Chao; its title read:

Beware of the Enemy Sleeping By Our Side

Ma's True Colors: Red-Haired with Secret Overseas Ties

It accused the village chief of being a spy for Taiwan and American Imperialists because that was where his son, Heshen, had fled. It also accused Old Ma of spying for the Soviet Revisionists because he had been sheltering a red-haired Russian spy in disguise as a Uyghur.

A red-haired Russian spy?! Shanmeng's head buzzed when he saw the poster. He pushed his way out of the crowd and ran, like when he was ambushed in the first and only battle he saw in Korea.

Lt. Tim Baker, the platoon leader, led them crouching and half crawling through leafless trees and dead bushes toward a village on the other side of the enemy line, hoping to snatch a gook or two for intelligence. The air was cold as fire and seared their face even though it was only October. Under the ghastly moonlight they could make out the village, no more than a dozen or so low thatched mudhouses, all shrouded in deep sleep.

Around midnight, they had covered a small house near the entrance of the village. Pfc James Chafee, a tall Texan, nudged the door open. It screaked. Inside was dizzyingly dark and quiet. Squad Leader Mark Cuming, Charlie Johnson, and Simon Mackenzie went in, their fingers on the trigger of their M-1s and carbines.

Simon could hear his heart hammering the anvil of the night as he crept into an inner room. Suddenly a shadow charged toward him from the pitch-black interior, screaming, brandishing something in hand; someone pulled the trigger—although the order had been not to shoot. More shadows darted out from nowhere, screaming, their hands flourishing in the air as if entranced in a folksy dance. Crazed firing from all around.

Simon's carbine spat fire, too, bouncing in his hands like hell. The shadows froze for a second when bullets hit and then dropped down, and sagged, moaning in pain. One of them fell close to Simon's feet. He recoiled, bent closer to check, and thought he saw a young woman's face, her eyes still open, her long hair, messy, coiling in shiny wetness.

Simon turned and dashed out, almost tripping over bodies on the ground, and was met with earth-shaking firing and explosions and cry from all around. He and his comrades attempted to shoot a bloody path out of the ambush, but one by one they fell.

Simon ran through a stubbly field while firing blindly into the shadows moving toward him and tripped. Before he could struggle to get up, dark barrels of rifles were pointed at him.

As Shanmeng ran home, Colonel Ryan's words came back to haunt him again, like vengeful ghosts that had never gone away: "If you choose the side of our enemy, choose Red China, it'd mean you choose to turn your backs on your country, on your people, on your parents, brothers and sisters, and you'd live to regret!"

Fuli and the kids were not at home. No light was on even though the sun had already set. They must be at the Ma's, comforting the old man. Shanmeng cussed and kicked at the dining table and the stools. He ran into the bedroom and wrapped the quilt around his head. Damn them! Damn the Chinese! Why do they have to do this? I won't give a damn if they all die! Can anyone tell me what the fuck is going on? Hello? Anyone out there can tell me? What the fuck is going on!

He unwrapped the quilt from his head and bolted out of the bedroom and searched. The Little Red Book—three copies of them—had fallen off the table when he kicked. Even he, a Uyghur, a red-haired Russian spy, whatever he was, could stumble through the whole book without the aid of a dictionary now. He could even sing some of the Quotations. He used to marvel at the mind that had uttered those profound thoughts. Look at his forehead, he used to say to himself as he gazed at Mao's portrait on the wall of the main room, it's so big and prominent. Now he felt that on every one of those 270 pages was written the same word: ge ming, revolution, which in Chinese meant, literally, cutting lives. How many lives would have to be cut before it was over?

The books on Fuli's desk and in her box wouldn't give him a

clue either. He had been working on Dream of Red Mansions, Journey to the West, and Romance of Three Kingdoms for several years but hadn't been able to forge beyond the first five chapters of each. Their pages were full of "fantastic talk" all right.

What about the scroll in that unearthed vat long forgotten in the corner of the kitchen? Well, he hadn't taken another look at them for years. It would probably remain a forbidden book to him forever. Damn the lucky hermit who had the foresight to run and never return!

The loudspeaker was blasting the same melodies and the same "Red flags flapping across the five continents and four seas" crap and nothing else as it had been doing these days.

He stepped outside. The ginkgo tree loomed large and tall under a sky lit by a smudged moon and a few solitary stars. He stood there, dazed, dead like.

Suddenly, as if struck by lightning, he came alive again. He turned and dashed home. He stepped on a stool and yanked loose the loudspeaker from the corner; its gibbering stopped instantly. Then he dashed to the orchard and cut the clothesline (a long string of wire left over from when they set up the loudspeaker) between trees, dashed back inside, and connected one end of the wire to the "ear" of a wok and the other end to the loudspeaker.

The trunk of the ginkgo tree proved too thick for him to hold on to. He dashed back to the house, grabbed a bench and a stool, put the stool on the bench, and climbed up on the bench, then the stool. The wok banged against the tree as he hoisted himself up. It sounded like thunderclap, but nobody seemed to have heard. He worked his way up, heavenward, one branch at a time, and stopped when he couldn't go higher anymore.

The dark sheen of Twin-Sun River to his right looked as massive and imposing as ever under the pale moonlight. Beyond the river murky shadows of hills meandered into disquieting unknown. The moon and the stars remained as far out of his reach as ever. To his left were patches of treetops underneath which was the village he had come to know so well, and vast fields of baby wheat readying itself for the onslaught of winter. Shrouded in the evening mist were homes in which folks must be busy preparing supper, feeding chickens and pigs, mulling over the events of the day, conniving how to hurt people more, nursing new wounds on old scars that had barely had time to heal. Somewhere—he knew exactly where—in the petrifying darkness were his wife, his son, his daughter, and other people he loved dearly. What pain they had suffered and what more ordeal they had to go through!

He tied the wok to the topmost segment of the branch he was holding on to. It was a sudden, whimsical idea that came to him out of sheer despair. He had built a most basic radio of some sort while in high school with little more than a magnet, a piece of thin metal cut from a juice can, and some wire. Would this one work?

Once on the ground again, he picked up the loudspeaker and put it against his ear. There was no sound—no human sound—except for the muffled vibration of wind whistling through space, unbounded, infinite space.

Fuck! He let the loudspeaker fall to the ground and sat there, his back against the tree. Then he bolted up again, hauled himself back to the top of the tree, and adjusted the wok by about 90 degrees. Once back on the ground he picked up the loudspeaker and pressed his ear against it again.

The same muffled sound of wind whistling through space.

And then, burring and droning and whizzing in the mix of wind, gradually asserting itself, was a cacophony of human voices.

The clearest, most distinguishable among these was a coy female voice in Chinese which kept repeating the code name of someone inside the mainland and giving him coded instructions, along with the key embedded in the pages of a classic novel.

Shanmeng dropped the loudspeaker on the ground. He was stunned. If this is not spy work, what it is then? He stole a look around. He was still alone in a world buried in deadening shadows.

He picked up the loudspeaker again with the desperation of one long adrift on a dark sea. He wanted to know. He was dying to know what the fuck was really going on.

In the cacophony were five, six other voices, male and female, that sounded arcane, each pulsing with a unique modulation and cadence.

Then in the swirl and bumble of sound he picked up another voice, weaker than an emaciated mosquito on a summer night, that flickered through from long past and from far, faraway. He hadn't heard that tongue, or anything like it, since Peide had left him in the mountain village years ago:

". . . You're listening to the Voice of America, I'm your host, John Chancellor, my guest is Harvard University professor Dr. Henry Kissinger, our topic today is the war in Indochina. . . ."

He pressed his ear against the loudspeaker harder and listened, hanging on to the utterance of each and every syllable.

33

Greta came out of the bathroom with a towel in hand. Her face flushed from the long shower, her eyes glistened, her hair, still damp, cascaded down her bare shoulders.

"Jie," she said, "can you do me a favor? Their blow dryer plug doesn't fit."

"Sure," Ding said and took over the towel gallantly.

Her hair felt effusive and silky as he wrapped the towel around it and twirled and rubbed and massaged rigorously. The nape of the long neck bent in front of him led his vision down the curve of her back only partially covered by a loose-fitting T-shirt. The mild perfume she had on dizzied the air he breathed. Something luscious, tense, and ridiculous, swept over him. He turned his eyes slightly away and tried to focus on the task at hand.

When he was done, she straightened, gathered her lustrous hair with both hands appreciatively, and tossed it to the back over her shoulders. She continued to smooth her hair, grasped it in one thick ponytail, and let it loose again. She stood so close, her eyes, shiny with something more her usual warmth, gazing into his.

Suddenly she moved her face closer and kissed him on the cheek.

"Jie," the clarinet voice lowered to a murmur, her face blushing.

Ding dropped the towel, cupped her head in his quivering hands, and kissed her on the lips.

"Oh, Jie!" Greta mumbled from deep inside, nuzzled against him, and kissed back, "I thought you would never—"

Ding responded by covering her lips again with his own, seeking, demanding, giving, with an urgency he hadn't known for so long, his hands exploring her hair, the nape of her long neck, the curve of her back, dying to know all the mystery of the beautiful girl in his arms although he had felt he knew so much about her already. A tidal wave of nervous, fuddling excitement washed over and sent him somersaulting back to a world he thought he had left behind many, many years ago.

A bundle of change clothes in hand, Jie had sneaked to the backyard of the school where his father, the principal, was being confined in a small dark room to confess his crimes against the Party and the People. His heart lit up at the sight of the dim light filtered through the windowpane.

Seeing a figure coming in his direction, Jie stole behind a wall and watched.

The figure stopped outside his father's room, looked to the left and the right and around, and knocked. The door opened ajar, and a hesitant second later, the figure went in.

Who can that be? Jie was puzzled. Someone wants to hurt dad?

He stole out from behind the wall, and, seeing no one else coming this direction, tiptoed toward father's confinement room.

The lower portion of the windowpane was blocked by dark red paint. Holding his breath, light as a cat, Jie hoisted himself on to the sill, and peeked through an unpainted strip near the top of the window.

A woman was talking to his father. It was Teacher Pan, Jie recognized, a language teacher in her early 30s, a lively woman who had a pleasant, fluty voice. Principal Ding nodded, coughed, and through the weak light of 15 Watts bulb Jie could see the pain and despondence in his eyes.

Father pulled up his shirt. On his chest and around his back were marks, dark red, blue marks, patches of them.

Pan touched the bruised skin with her soft fingertips, as if trying to caress away the marks and the pain deep underneath. Father flinched.

The woman stopped, looked into father's eyes, and reached to feel his face, murmuring something. Then she turned to go. Father grabbed her hand and held it. She froze—surprised?—and then turned back, and put her arms around father's neck. They kissed fiercely, the last kiss, it seemed, that would ready the man for the firing squad tomorrow.

In his entire nine years of being in this world Jie had never seen anything like this between his father and mother; now, he had the misfortune of stumbling upon this scene, with all its infuriating insanity, enacted by his father and a woman other than his mother, completely unaware of the pair of eyes separated only by a thin layer of windowpane.

His head swirling in torpor, Jie jumped off the windowsill, fell, picked himself up, and ran.

When the school had another denunciation rally against his father a few days later, Jie's homeroom teacher pressured him again that he had to draw a clear line between him and his evil father. Jie had resisted the pressure. He had tried to run away and been caught and dragged back by the bullies of his class. But this time, he walked on to the platform without being pushed, the Little Red Book in hand.

"True," the 9-year-old mumbled, tears streaking his cheeks, "my father is a hypocrite, a corrupt bourgeois bad egg."

Father, both knees on shards of broken glass, a heavy wooden board hanging from his neck, turned his head slightly so he could see his son. Their eyes met.

"Great! Comrade Jie Ding!" Du, commander of the school's Red Rebels Corps, cheered, and then urged. "Be specific. In what ways is your father a corrupt bourgeois bad egg?"

"He—"

Father's eyes still on him.

Jie darted his teary eyes away to the crowd down there, and spotted Teacher Pan. She lowered her head and shrank visibly. Bad woman! He hated her, too!

"He. He had a bike, a watch, and used to wear leather shoes, too!" Jie heard himself crying out. "How many workers and peasants can wear watches—"

"Oh," Commander Du groaned disappointedly, "Good, but let's get to the real meat, the really juicy stuff!"

"He—"

Father turned his eyes away, his head hanging even lower.

> *"Down with...!"*
> *"Deep fry...!"*
> *"Annihilate the enemy if he...!"*

The whole place exploded with crazed shouts to cheer Jie on.

The boy felt choked with an urge, an impulse. He fought it, and fought it hard, with whatever oxygen still left in him to hang on to a ray of clarity in his confused mind. He was dying. He tore away from the podium and bolted. He wanted to flee. He wanted to flee from a world cartwheeling with raised fists and distorted faces and deafening, hysterical screams. He wanted to disappear in a world where he could breathe again. He jumped and flew into empty space at the edge of the platform.

Darkness swashed over.

"Are you all right?" Greta gasped between kisses. "Protection? I have one in the bag—"

"No," he mumbled breathily.

Her hands pulling his T-shirt stopped; her body disengaged; her bosom, perky—but not outrageously bountiful like those he had caught glimpses of in magazines and on the Internet more times than he cared to admit—crowned with rosy, erect nipples, heaved with erratic breathing; below her belly button was a tattoo, the size of a gold coin, in the form of a Chinese character: 夢, meng, dream.

"Greta. . ." He stiffened; he could hear quaver in his voice. "I'm so sorry."

Her eyes still aflame with the intensity of the moment, she looked as if she had just been hit by something heavy.

"Fuck!" she said, trembling, and then, getting hold of herself, she smoothed her hair and turned away. "I understand, Jie." She picked up the T-shirt on the floor and pulled it over her head.

Damn! Ding cussed inwardly as he reached for his tank top. What an asshole!

A knock on the door. Not very loud, but assertive enough.

Ding turned to see if Greta had heard the knock; she returned the look with a question mark in her eyes. They hadn't ordered any room service or anything, had they?

"Who is it" Ding asked.

"The office of the Military Archives."

Oh. Ding was pleasantly surprised. They have certainly improved the quality of service here. "Just a sec," he said and opened the door when both he and Greta had put on their clothes and looked smooth and proper again.

The visitors were two men, one tall, in his late 20s, with pimples on his nose, and one short, in his early 40s, like a schoolteacher. They were neatly dressed, polite, their eyes alert.

"Sorry to interrupt, Dr. Ding?" the older man said, taking a quick glance around the room.

Ding nodded. "You're—?"

"I'm from Director Jiang, who you visited today. You're—" he turned to Greta.

"Greta," Greta moved a step closer, ready to shake hands, but changed her mind.

"Director Jiang said he has found the info you were looking for."

"Great!" enthused Ding, yet somehow, he didn't sound very enthusiastic to his own ears. He wondered why. "We'll go and check it out first thing tomorrow."

"Director Jiang would like you to come tonight. Now." There was unmistakable authority in the same flat, monotonous tone.

Ding felt something rushing to his head, his hands shaking despite a voice inside telling him to be calm. He turned to Greta to see if she had registered what was going on.

"Now?" she asked. She looked calm, but her voice betrayed nervousness too.

"Yes. Now. Take all your things with you, too," the man instructed.

"Everything will be all right, Greta," Ding said, in English, and walked to gather things on his bed, "I promise you."

Both visitors flashed Ding a dirty look.

"No talk from now on, not one word!" the younger man said. In English. His accent was thick but was clear enough.

34

He felt a hand on his arm. A soft, womanly hand he knew so well.

"Shanmeng?" There was alarm in the voice. "What are you doing here? Are you all right? What's that thing in your hand?"

She took it from him, put it against her ear, and listened, and listened.

The loudspeaker slid out of her hand; her face turned ghastlier than the pale moonlight.

"Fuli? Are you all right?"

His wife didn't reply. She didn't seem to be breathing.

"Fuli?" He grasped her hand. It was icy cold, shivering.

As if waking up suddenly, Fuli freed her hand from his, bolted up, and ran. He jumped to his feet to run after her, but she had already vanished into the darkness.

He dragged himself home. It felt so dark and empty inside. He kicked at whatever happened to be in his path, left and right, dining table, stools, books, buckets, dustpan, and broom. He needed something to quench the fury aflame inside him. No, he wanted to pour fuel on the fire so that it would burn higher and fiercer and burn the entire goddamn world down. He opened the cupboard in the kitchen and searched, smashing onto the ground bowls and plates and bottles of soybean oil and soy sauce while doing so, and found a bottle on the cupboard's top rung—the bottle he had not touched for years. He pulled out its cork and stuffed its long beak into his mouth. Oh, it felt so goddamn good when a current of liquid fire gushed down his throat, his entire being ablaze with something icy instantly. He kept sucking and gulping down its bubbly content as if his life depended on it. Damn Fuli! Damn the Chinese! Damn Peide! Damn Captain Chen! Damn Shanmeng! Damn Simon Mackenzie! Oh, this feels so goddamn good!

"Pa?" A feeble, frightened voice drifted through the volcanic smoke in his head.

He kept sucking at the bottle.

"Pa? Are you all right?"

He paused, let the latest mouthful hang at his throat and turned his head slightly. Against the pale light from outside the front door he could make out the silhouette of Yangyang, his seven-year-old son, his cheeks smirched with tears. Next to the boy was Yangmei, his two-year-old daughter, sniffling quietly.

Stupefied, he let the beak of the half-empty bottle slip out of his mouth, unsure what to do with the liquid already in his mouth.

Nobody in the family and in the entire village had been able to tell exactly which of the boy's features were his, which Fuli's. Everyone was absolutely positive, though, that being a crossbreed, the boy was unusually smart and handsome. So, it was with Yangmei. Her eyes seemed bigger than those of her peers; her hair even had a hint of auburn luster to it, which made it all the richer. She was dabbing away the running nose with sleeves.

He spat out whatever was still in his mouth, let the bottle in his hand drop to the ground, and smiled. Amazing how fast kids grow. He thought foggily. It was only yesterday that he washed the diapers for Yangyang and Yangmei in the river, diapers made of old shirts and towels, all Fuli's ingenuity, and needlework, of course. When he shook a soiled diaper in the clean, greenish water, fish, itsy-bitsy and chopstick length alike, would swarm over and charge at lightning speed, their mouths open, and vanish just as fast when they had caught a decent morsel; even shrimps, their hairy legs and whiskers quivering from cracks between rocks, would sneak out to partake of the feast.

The first time he witnessed the unintended festival by the riverside Shanmeng felt disgusted. "That's real shit, man!" He wanted to scream at the fish, but couldn't help but find it amazing, too. He remembered, years ago, seeing Sportie waiting, impatiently, for Ah Bao to finish poop so it could have its turn. One time, when Sportie overzealously offered to lick clean the boy's butt, Ah Bao, frightened, and strangely tickled, cried, and bolted without pulling up his pants.

Shanmeng eyed the mess he had created all around him and smiled again, apologetically. "Dad's all right," he mumbled. His speech sounded slurred even to his own ears. "Dad was a bit thirsty, that's all. Don't worry."

"Really?" Yangmei stopped sobbing.

Damn the Chinese! He cussed again in his head. Why are they so gung-ho about doing revolution, ge ming? Why can't they leave folks alone to themselves! How idiotic I am, I have been! How idiotic it all is!

The kids had lingered behind at their grandpa's, but their mother, worried about her husband, had hurried home ahead of them.

"Where's mom?" Yangyang asked.

"Yes, your mother," he said, looking around. "I'll go and find her. Don't you worry."

He found her on the big rock at the old campsite, a lone, frozen figure silhouetted against the cold moonlit sky.

"Fuli?" he called out in a soft, hushed voice.

No reply.

"Fuli?" he whispered again when he was only steps away from her.

"Stay where you are!" his wife said through chattering teeth.

He halted. She was so close that he could almost touch her, but they had never been so far apart. Her wan face and the coldness in her voice made him tremble.

"Are you a spy?" she asked, without turning her head.

"What?"

"Are you a Russian spy?"

"No!"

"Liar!" Fuli turned and locked him with piercing eyes. "Everything makes sense now," she continued, "Why you couldn't speak good Chinese—even though for a Russian your Chinese was good enough. Hahaha!" Her laugh sounded sinister, mean, lethal. "And those parcels coming from nowhere. Oh, don't forget the midnight visit of the two soldiers with food during the Famine!"

"No!" Shanmeng wanted to scream, but somehow couldn't find his voice. "You've got it all messed up. I'm not a Russian spy. I don't know anything about Russia. I don't even speak Russian!"

"What else? Mmm, your big nose, your blue eyes, your red hair, and Xinjiang! Why you knew so little about Xinjiang? Can you dance a Xinjiang dance for me? Eh?"

Shanmeng moved a step closer to explain, but how, and where would he start?

"Don't!" Fuli commanded and moved further away. In her hand was a sharp-edged rock. She turned her eyes to the dark sheen of the massive river and the hills crouching in the misty distance.

"Oh, why me?" she mumbled weakly, as if talking to someome who had all the answers. When she turned to face him again, he saw a long string of teardrops trickling down her cheeks.

Damn the secrecy for all these years. Damn the lies. Time for the goddamn truth.

"Fuli," he heard himself saying in a calm voice. "I should have told you long time ago. I'm not a Russian. I'm not from Xinjiang."

She looked blank. There were no sparks of understanding in her eyes.

"I'm no Russian or Uyghur," he repeated, now nervously.

"Then, what are you?" Her voice seemed from a dream whose amorphous threads were badly woven together. "A ghost from nowhere?"

"I'm an American," he heard himself saying again. A mountain, no less than the Five-Fingered Mountain on the back of the Monkey King for five hundred years—Peide, fuck you, I now know who that stinky monkey is!—had finally been lifted. But he didn't feel one *jin* relieved.

The same blankness in her eyes. What he had said didn't seem to have registered. He hadn't said it loud enough for her to hear?

"I'm an American. My name, my real name, is Simon Mackenzie."

She glanced at the rock in her hand, as if hesitant, and flung it into the bushes.

"Then, you're an American spy?" The same tenuous murmur.

"No!" There was panic in his voice now. "That's not what I'm trying to say!"

"Is this some fantastic talk 'cause you've had a drop too much to drink?"

"No."

"Then, you are an American spy. And that's just as bad, worse, you know that."

"Ask your dad, I mean, pa, Old Ma. Ask Peide, that Captain Chen. Remember him? They all knew. And know."

She winced, or squinted, as if wanting to see something more clearly in the distance.

He began to tell his story, the story of his life being truthfully told for the first time for the last 14 some years, his voice a mere monotonous bumble, all the while conscious of the trees whirring on the hilltops behind them, and the dark shine of the mighty river creased under the cold moonlight.

"Say something in your real mother tongue, then, Red Hair," she said, when he finally wound down to the end of his story, a mocking smile on her face.

"I. . . I love you," he tried in a tongue that he was born into but hadn't used for so many years. It sounded foreign and hollow to his own ears.

The mocking smile in her face faded. In its place was something he couldn't fathom at the moment.

They sat on the rock like two travelers too dog tired from their long journey through perilous terrain to speak anymore. The night deepened. The moon rose higher in the sky. The air felt chillier. A faint frost was descending fast on the world, the hills, the trees, and the vast river.

"Ah," he heard a voice murmuring next to him, as if it were drifting in from a faraway place. "I never thought a river could be this beautiful."

35

The room was not bigger than the jail cell he had seen in Hollywood movies. A small single bed with a reed sheet took up much of the space. The pale light slanted in through the narrow window near the ceiling gave a vague sense of the world outside the cement walls.

Ding remembered himself being escorted to a Chevy minivan parked outside their hotel and Greta to a shiny Lexus SUV. Several plainclothes stepped out of the vehicles to assist. Even if he were foolish enough to throw a punch here and deliver a jump kick there, he would be sent to kiss the cement pavement—as had happened to Rob, his student—and subdued in no time.

As they neared the minivan, Ding could barely make out its interior through its tinted windows. He suddenly turned and walked toward Greta, who was already at the SUV's door. She turned toward him; her eyes lit up with wonder.

He put his arms around her—oh, it feels so damn good—and whispered: "*Je t'aime bien!*" The little French he had learnt to fulfill the second foreign language requirement for his master's degree came in handy.

"No talking!" Someone barked. "Separate them!" A heavy hand was placed on his shoulder but didn't tackle or do anything to create a scene.

Greta held him tight, then looked him in the eye, and kissed him full on the mouth. "Je t'adore!" she murmured and let him go.

He knew he was ready to lay down his life right there, to face anything, any ordeal in the world from then on. He kept hearing it--"Je t'adore!" uttered with such hearty warmth from such a beautiful girl—in his head as they blindfolded him in the minivan. The girl had probably said it on the spur of the moment. But what did it matter?

He heard the muffled sound of Greta protesting in the SUV behind. "I want to see, damn it!"

"It's for your own good, Miss," one of the men said.

"My own good. My ass!"

Good Greta! Ding chuckled to himself.

That was the last he had heard and "seen" of Greta.

It was a long ride, with so many turns that he soon lost track. He wasn't good at directions anyway. But he did remember the sound of tires grinding on rugged surface in the last twenty minutes before they stopped.

"Where's this place?" He had demanded when being led out of the vehicle, still blindfolded. "I want to know. And where's the girl? Where's she? Let her contact the American embassy!"

"Shut up!" Someone hollered and shoved him harshly from behind.

He remembered the flights of steps they climbed, echoes of the heels of leather shoes hammering the cement floor in the hallways, five up and three down, and he lost track again.

He had had ample time to sit there and listen to himself breathing in the hot, damp room, to feel his sweat oozing out of his pores and trickling down his skin, to monitor his thoughts, dark, bright, crimson, about all the people he knew, from childhood all the way to this very moment as they flashed across his mind.

He had had time to relive, frame by frame, the time he had spent with Greta, from the moment they met over two months ago to the most dizzying moment in the hotel room, before the knock on the door by the two unexpected visitors, to their last embrace, and the whispered confession of feelings for each other:

"Je t'aime bien!" he said it aloud again, for his own ears. It had a strange, metallic echo between the cement walls. *"Je t'adore!"*

The guard's eyes appeared at the peek hole. Ding smiled. The eyes disappeared again. He must think I'm mad, Ding thought. Yes, I am mad!

"My own good. My ass!" He shouted and laughed. The cell shook with his voice.

And, of course, he had had time to imagine possible sequels for the scene in the hotel room if it had not been interrupted, mostly variations of the same theme. One time while replaying a favorite sequel in his head he succumbed to the urge and did something he hadn't done since college days when quilts aired outside dormitories on sunny days were a shameless display of maps of outlandish sizes and shapes, greasy, and irascibly ingrained; unmistakable evidence of a measure many young men resorted to against the admonitions of health experts on the peril of sexual dysfunctions in matrimony (oh, from a condemned sin of defiling oneself to a healthy way to self-pleasure recommended by no less than a President Clinton nominee for Surgeon General, civilization had certainly come a long way!). He did so while invoking a familiar name desperately. Disgusted with having to wear the same underwear already soiled by days of sweat, and guilt-stricken toward the girl he had, idiotically, fallen in love with, and strangely, toward Julie, Ding vowed never to stoop that low again: "You're the most ridiculous 42-year-old jerk in the entire universe!"

He had thought of the revolutionary martyrs he had read when a young boy, Liu Hulang, Sister Jiang, and many more, and fancied what was going through their minds when sharp, pointed bamboo pieces were being hammered into their fingernails. He found such comparisons preposterous and blushed. He hadn't been tortured. Nobody had really laid a finger on him yet. All his life so far he had worked like a tireless horse all right but he didn't have any ideal to fight for, a cause to be dedicated to, and a faith to lay down his life for. He had been a drifter in life for so many years. And the trouble he was in now came from a chance meeting, and a commitment he made on the spur of the moment. No more and no less. There was nothing noble about it.

He didn't know how long he would have to stay in the cell. He didn't want to sit there idle, wasting away. He tried pushups with his feet set on the bed frame. It gave his muscles, his lungs, and his will the challenge they badly needed. It made him feel good when sweat trickled down his body and dripped onto the sticky cement floor as he pushed on.

36

A denunciation rally against Old Ma and Shanmeng was being held at the Red Valley Middle School on the other side of the river. The arena was nothing but a makeshift earth stage on the school playground. On this stage were placed a few tables manned by local Red Guards and Red Guards from the province capital, who were here to spread the prairie fire of Revolution. Around the school were hillsides enveloped in the misty gray of mid-January 1967. Old Ma had a heavy board hanging from his neck. On the board was his name in black ink condemned by a bloody red cross. Shanmeng had on a cone-shaped hat at least two feet high, on which were written:

Red-Haired Ghost: Russian Spy

The loudspeakers on the poles blared as Huifa, Commander of the Red Sun Corps, shrieked on:

"Gouzai Ma, you cunning dog! Now we've finally sharpened

our eyes and seen you through for what you are! But you haven't confessed your sky-flooding crimes yet. Let me remind you one last time of our Party's policy—"

"You're no Party member, and have no right to say 'our Party'—" Old Ma mumbled in a voice only those close by could hear.

"You foul-mouthed running dog of the Soviet Revisionists!" Huifa swaggered over and hit Old Ma in the face.

Commander-in-Chief Nina Chen of the Red Guards from the province capital, a young college student who looked like a twin sister of Yingzi's, shouted: "If the enemy refuses to surrender, annihilate him!" The shout was picked up zealously by the Red Guards on the stage and half-heartedly by the hundreds of simple country folks sitting on the dirt ground.

"Is he," Huifa shrieked again, pointing at Shanmeng, "a Russian spy?"

No answer from Old Ma. Huifa tightened his grip on Ma's collars and hit him in the face again.

Commander-in-Chief Nina Chen led the slogan-shouting again:

> "If the enemy refuses to surrender, annihilate him!"
> "Down with the running dog of Soviet Revisionists!"
> "Revolution is no Crime. Rebellion is just!"

Echoes of crazed human voices rumbled in the valley.

Jian'er, now a man in his mid-30s, came on the stage. He seemed a bit unnerved at first by the sea of eyes on him, but soon got hold of himself and launched an attack on Old Ma as a spy with overseas ties.

"Hey, Jian'er," an old man interrupted, "Isn't it true that you'd have died if Old Ma hadn't found you outside the village and taken you home?"

"Yes," an old woman said. "Didn't Old Ma's wife, bless her soul, nurse you like you were her own son?"

Jian'er looked lost, and started to stammer: "Why did you have to bring up those old, stale grains? I'm a Revolutionary, and a veteran, not supposed to be chicken-hearted. Besides, he's not my father anyway. He gave me to the stinky Old Chao! I was an orphan, and I'm still an orphan today, a stark poor proletarian. . . ."

He turned to Shanmeng abruptly, his eyes burning with a passion that must have consumed him for a long time: "You, Red Hair, confess your crimes as a Soviet Spy!"

"I'm not a Soviet spy," Shanmeng said. "That's God's truth."

"What did you just say? God's truth?" Jian'er heehawed. "See, you've confessed even before we give your nerves and bones a good loosening up! What evil God were you talking about, ehhh?"

Damn! Shanmeng cursed himself. How did I let that slip out of my tongue? He hadn't thought of God for so long, the God he had been preached about so much as a boy sitting in the first pew with. . . .

He didn't have time to complete the thought. Jian'er had grabbed his collar and slapped him hard in the face.

"Confess, why did the Soviet Revisionists send you to this valley?!"

Another slap in the face.

Shanmeng's cheeks burned like hell. Something saltish oozed in his swollen mouth.

"No, he's not a Soviet spy!" Old Ma struggled and shouted. "He is from Xinjiang, a revolutionary veteran—"

"From Xinjiang?" Commander Huifa cut him short. "I never bought that horse shit from you, Gouzai Ma! The first time I saw him, I knew, I sensed, that he was some bad egg up to no good here!"

"Red Hair, you a Uygur?" Jian'er yelped again. "Then, give us a fart in Uygur!"

"And show us a Xinjiang dance!" shouted Commander Huifa, with a sinister laugh.

Shanmeng knew he was caught. He had heard Uygur singers on the radio—the loudspeaker at home—so many times that he could probably hum a tune or two but had never seen their dances.

Could he bluff by faking? Not a chance, with the presence of the Red Guards from the province capital.

"Sing us a Uygur song! Show us a Xinjiang dance!"

The crowd clapped and demanded frenziedly, but Shanmeng was not going to oblige.

"I knew this Soviet spy can't give us a Uygur fart!" Jian'er screamed, blue veins in his temple wriggling visibly. "Soviet. Uygur. What difference anyway?!"

"Hey, Comrade Jian'er Chao," Commander-in-Chief Nina Chen corrected him. "A big difference. Xinjiang is like Tibet, Inner Mongolia. It's part of our motherland. The Uygurs are our minority comrades-in-arms in this Revolution. The Soviet Revisionists are a completely different—"

"Oh, I'm sorry, I—" Jian'er looked confused again, but recovered quickly. He knocked the tall hat off Shanmeng's head and shouted, "Confess, you stinky Soviet spy. Why are you here? What's your mission?"

Fists landed on Shanmeng, fists of Jian'er, Huifa, and a few other Red Guards.

"Stop! Stop beating him! He's not a Soviet spy!" It was a familiar voice, a voice whose pitch and tone and timbre had resonated with that of his own for so long and given him so much comfort and joy.

"He, not a Soviet spy?" Commander Huifa asked when two bully Red Guards shoved a woman onto the stage. "What is he then? If anybody knows, you should know, in broad daylight or under the cover of darkness!"

A few in the audience laughed. Then silence fell over everyone as the whole world waited for her answer.

"He's not a Soviet spy. He—"

"Fuli!" Old Ma cried out angrily.

Someone hit Old Ma from behind and forced his head even lower.

"What is he, you bitch," Commander Huifa pressed on, "if not a Soviet spy?!"

It was too late to stop her now. There was no way to stop her anyway. Let the world know the goddamn truth then. Shanmeng thought. It can't get any worse than this.

"An American," Fuli blurted out, her face ashen.

"An American? An American spy?" Commander Huifa repeated incredulously.

"An American?" Jian'er mumbled, stunned, as comprehension came to him slowly. "No wonder! I've always thought you looked so familiar the first time I—"

He turned to Fuli and snarled: "You bitch! First, you married a traitor who turned his back on his motherland, and then this Soviet Spy, no, this American spy! You bitch! This Yankee, this red-haired, big-nosed Yankee, can give you a better fuck, is that it?" He spat into her face and raised his hand.

"Hit her! Hit the bitch!" Some men and women from the audience cheered.

Somehow Jian'er couldn't let his hand land on Fuli.

"Revolutionary comrades-in-arms and all," Commander Huifa hollered, "we have solid evidence that Fuli's parents were anti-revolutionary capitalists executed in the spring of 1950. . . ."

Shanmeng was astounded. Her parents executed by the government! No wonder Fuli had never mentioned her parents, never wanted to talk about them... Poor Fuli! Oh, so much secrecy in the people around him and in his own life, imposed upon or chosen voluntarily, no matter, all of which could be traced back to his decision to disappear from the face of the earth to pursue some outlandish dream of his own.

37

"You've really decided, Simon?" Captain Chen had asked, handing back the exercise book he had corrected. "You can join the others who have made the same decision."

"Not exactly the same, all I want—" he said.

Once again came Colonel Ryan's hoarse voice calling on the non-repatriates to reconsider their decision and to return to the "free world;" the good colonel was standing in a military jeep moving to and fro slowly on the other side of the wired fence, shouting into a bullhorn, his voice all but being drowned by jeers and catcalls from zealous "Progressives," and by shrill chirping of cicadas from the few trees still standing on hillsides not too far away.

Simon didn't want any publicity. He didn't want to be used for propaganda despite the choice he had made. He wanted to stay as far away from the madding world as possible so he could build his own Walden somewhere, his own cabin of clean, quiet life.

"Your own Walden," repeated Captain Chen, his eyes on the American in front of him, "there are many Waldens in the heartland of China, that I can assure you."

Two and a half years of mulish effort to acquire a new language, one character at a time, was not a lot of time. But he had been fascinated by how it sounded, how it looked, and how it was written: 人, man—as simple as a left stroke and a right stroke joined together; 大, big—man being the biggest being in the world when he stretches out the arms, birdlike; 天, sky—a man standing tall and proud under the sky; 明, bright—sun and moon together bringing light to the world. All so simple, and so poetic! Okay, there was the ultimate challenge of tonal control. The same sound "ma" could mean mother (level tone), hemp (rising tone), horse (falling tone followed by rising tone), curse (falling tone). So confusing and yet so infinitely amazing.

He had made good use of every minute of the free time to force his tongue to get used to articulating the new sound, his fingers and wrist to drawing—yes, it was more drawing than writing in the beginning—the strokes that formed the simplest words. He sought out the Camp instructors, whenever he could, not to confess his war crimes, to write and sign on documents protesting the unconscionable use of germ warfare by the UN forces, or to inform on the "troublemakers" among his fellow POWs, but to learn and practice the language of his captors. His "good behavior" had earned him better treatment from his captors. He could stay in the "study room" late in the evening when everybody else had to return to their "dorms." The odd behavior of this mostly reticent auburn-haired POW had raised eyebrows among his compatriots but soon they dismissed him as a harmless eccentric, laughed at whatever ambitions he might have harbored secretly, and left him alone to his pursuits.

He was a fast learner and within the year he could converse with his instructors and Captain Chen in Mandarin. Sometimes he wondered why he hadn't discovered his gift for language sooner.

And he had refused to accept letters from home.

"If you don't write your folks," Captain Chen had said in one of their earliest conversations, pointing at the bundle of mail on the desk with Simon's name on the envelopes, "you should at least read their letters."

"I'd prefer not to," Simon had said, getting up to leave. "It must be a mistake. I don't have a family anymore."

"I've talked to General Ye," Captain Chen said the next day, turning to glance outside the small, sandbag-framed window as if to capture a glimpse of Colonel Ryan whose hoarse voice kept drifting in and out of the sweaty summer air. "It is a pity that you don't want to be more actively involved in our cause of denouncing Imperialist aggressions and promoting world peace, but General Ye says he respects your decision and promises that he'll help make arrangements. In fact, he says he already has a place in mind, a Walden-like place. But once again, you don't have to go that route. You can attend any college or university of your choice—"

"That won't be necessary," Simon said. "A clean, quiet life is all I want."

Captain Chen nodded thoughtfully. "By the way, it just occurred to me that you'll need a new name, a Chinese name, to start your new life in China. Any idea?"

Simon shook his head. He should have thought about that. A new name to start a new life with.

"You know, 培德, Peide, is a transliteration of Peter. It means

Tempering Virtue. I like it that way. Simon. Mmm, what would be a good transliteration of Simon in Chinese? Let me see. You want to build a cabin somewhere, so you won't be bothered, like a hermit. . . mmm, I've got it. How about 山夢, Shanmeng, Mountain Dream. Close to 'Simon' in sound and to what you want in sense? See that 夢, meng, dream? It has lots of grass atop, and underneath. . . ."

"Shanmeng," Simon turned it over in his mouth a few times and liked how it sounded to his ear.

38

On the evening of his fifth day in the cell, the door opened and in stepped the young man with the pimpled nose and an assistant. Ding was blindfolded again and led through hallways and flights of steps. As he trudged along, he heard hurried steps, subdued laughs, nervous murmurs, and muffled groans all around him and in the very air he breathed in. What's going to happen? He wondered. What're they going to do with me?

They stopped. Someone removed the blindfold. Ding blinked and squinted and found himself in a room flooded with bright florescent light.

Like a painting by minimalist artists such as Mark Rothko, the room was bare, having been designed strictly with its utilitarian functions in mind, perhaps, except for a table and a few chairs, all looking old and overused. He wondered what kind of cityscape— or rural landscape?—was churning outside the walls at this hour of the day.

He heard steps coming in.

An important looking man, followed by the "schoolteacher" he had seen before, marched in and sat down in a centrally positioned chair behind the table.

The man looked ruddy (benefit of alcoholic stimulant today?)

and acutely conscious of the thinning top of his hair, which was slick, and all puffed up. The leather briefcase he had just placed on the table gave him an authoritative, almost distinguished air.

For a few excruciatingly long seconds Puffed Head, School Teacher, and Pimple sat behind the table without saying a word, all like live human models in a postmodern art exhibition, as if to give Ding adequate time to appreciate the weight of the moment, to anticipate the severity of what would happen next.

"Please sit down," Puffed Head nodded to a chair in the middle of the room. His voice was thin, somewhat scratchy, like when you scrubbed the mirror in the bathroom a bit too strenuously.

"Your name?" he asked, off-handedly when Ding had assumed the seat.

"Jie Ding."

"Age?"

"42."

"Residence?"

He gave his address in Princetown.

"Princeton? Like Princeton University?" Pimple, the note-taker, asked in English, with a deferential look to Puffed Head, who kept his eyes on Ding, his face giving no clue whether he was annoyed by the curiosity of his subordinate.

"No," Ding corrected and spelled it out for Pimple. A sense of superiority, of control, arose inside him, but he checked it right away.

"Citizenship?"

"People's Republic of China."

"But you hold an American green card."

"Like thousands of thousands of other Chinese who work and live in the US."

A mocking smile curled around Puffed Head' lips.

"Your profession?"

"College Professor. Professor of humanities."

"Professor of humanities?" Pimple interjected again.

These people, Ding mused, they think all Chinese professionals in the US are in business, engineering, science, and nothing else.

"I'm one of those oddballs, you know," Ding said after explaining what a professor of humanities would teach, "who didn't defect to more lucrative fields and fortunately did find exit at the end of an apparent dead end."

They, the interrogators and the interrogatee, shared a chuckle together, a moment of light-heartedness.

"Hope you've been equally loyal in more important matters," Puffed Head said, the smile on his face waning, "and will be wise enough to turn when you see dead end ahead." He paused, apparently pleased with his own quick wit. "Mmmm, let's pick up where we'd left off a moment ago. "Where did you work before you left for—"

"Where's the American girl now?" Ding cut him short. "Where have you placed her?"

Puffed Head was not pleased with the interruption. The muscles in his face twitched as he stared at Ding. "That, mmm, is not your business."

"She was with me and that makes her my business."

"Hear, hear," Puffed Head sneered. "Who says chivalry is dead, eh? Your American girlfriend, she is fine. She's an American citizen and will be dealt with accordingly. Worry about yourself, my hero."

"What does 'will be dealt with accordingly' mean?" Ding kept his eyes on Puffed Head to pressure for an answer.

"It means what it means. That's all I can tell you." Puffed Head didn't blink for a second either. "Now, Professor Ding, you know why we've invited you over here today?"

A hell of an invitation.

"What, you don't know?" Puffed Head sounded incredulous, disappointed. He sat back in the chair and studied his fingertips. "You look like an intelligent person. A college Professor, with a PhD. So, you should know our policies."

"Yes, I do, but where I am coming from, I believe in innocence until proven guilty, and as far as I am concerned, I don't know what law I—"

"Do I need to remind you that you are still a citizen of the People's Republic?" Puffed Head's voice suddenly rose in pitch. It sounded like broken glass. "And if you were an American citizen, like that girlfriend of yours, it'd have been a different ball game. Even then, you'd still need to abide by our laws . . ."

What would Julie and Emily say when I tell them this later? Ding wondered. "Serve you right, Da Jiao Shou," Julie might say. "Told you apply, but you wanted be sentimental about motherland."

"We know everything about you, and your American girl——"

"Then, why both——" Ding said, "Why the hell are you wasting my time here!?"

Puffed Head stood up: "We want to see whether you're still a worthy, loyal Chinese. This time around, whether there will be exit at the end of the dead end, hahaha, it all depends on--"

"Your attitude," Ding finished the sentence for him.

"Yes, you're an intelligent man, as I said."

Upon returning to his room, Ding found his carryon bag near the door. In it were his clothing and everything else, wrinkled, balled, having been tampered with; inside his wallet he found the same stack of brand new RMB notes and hunter green US dollars. The only thing missing was the large vanilla envelope from Tom, copies of important entries from Peide's diaries, and his passport.

Someone looked in through the peek hole. The same guard, a man in his late 40s.

Ding hurried to the door and looked the man in the eye. He saw no hatred, no sympathy, no nothing.

"Please do me a favor, a big favor!" He implored in a hushed tone, and, without waiting for the man to answer, he fumbled in his bag. He found a pen, tore off a sheet from a notebook, and scribbled. "Call this number for me, please!" he passed the note through the peek hole, trembling, not knowing how the man would respond.

The guard kept staring at him blankly as if he hadn't heard the request. Then he took the note and disappeared.

39

Two Red Guards shoved Fuli to Shanmeng's side and forced her on her knees, her beautiful hair a big, tangled mess.

"Hit her! Hit the bitch!" The mob continued to shout.

She hunched down as spitting, cussing, kicking landed on her.

Something hot erupted inside Shanmeng. "Leave her alone!" He roared like a lion. "Hit me instead. She didn't know! She didn't know anything. Hit me ten times over!"

Fists and feet landed on him instead, his face swelling into a ridiculous, gooey blur instantly, yet he had never felt so good. He deserved it for the pain he had caused Fuli, Old Ma, Ah Bao, Yangyang and Yangmei, and everyone else in the family. Damn the Chinese! Damn Peide, Captain Chen! Damn Shanmeng, Simon Mackenzie! I am ready to die, here and now, and die without any cowardly regrets. . . .

"Hey, Comrade Jian'er Chao," a by now familiar voice came through the blinding haze. It was Commander-in-Chief Nina Chen. The rain blows on Shanmeng stopped. "You said this American spy looked familiar the first time you saw him, right? How did you know?"

Silence.

Awkward, ominous silence.

"Yes, Jian'er," demanded another Red Guard from the province capital. "Tell us, how did you know? And how did you know this woman's first husband turned his back on our motherland?"

"I—"

"He was—" Fuli mumbled through her swollen, cracked lips, without lifting her head.

"Fuli!" Old Ma cried out angrily, but it was too late.

"Taken prisoner, too, by. . . ."

"What?" Commander-in-Chief Nina Chen sounded incredulous and pleased with herself. "No wonder you knew! You're a traitor to your motherland, too!"

"Jian'er!" Huifa fumed with apparent indignation. "I thought you were a Revolutionary veteran, but you're a stinky traitor, too! You must also be an American spy, being sent back to sabotage. . . ."

"I am a diehard Revolutionary—" Jian'er struggled as he was being shoved next to Old Ma.

A loud slap in his face from Huifa: "No more!"

"Today's denunciation rally is a huge success," Huifa turned to address the crowd above the commotion, "we've uncovered a nest of evil birds, a cell of American spies in the heartland of our dear motherland. . . ."

Shanmeng turned to glance at Fuli by his side with a big "why" in his eyes.

"Serve him right," she murmured.

He nodded vaguely. "Yes, serve him right. And serve me right, too."

Then, she said, a note of pride in her hushed voice: "I've burned it."

"What?"

"That scroll in the vat. I've burned it. . . just in case."

Oh, that goddamn scroll with all the coded messages, how could I have forgotten!

He nodded approvingly and smiled.

40

He had had two more days to reflect, to replay the scenes, prequels, possible sequels, to get soaked in sweat doing pushups, sit-ups, headstands, when he was led to the interrogation room again. An unexamined life was not worth living. Who said it? But an over-examined life? Would excessive scrupulous introspection pale the ability to act, as in the case of Hamlet? Ding mused as he shuffled along the hallway and the flights of steps through the maze of the building. Should he ask for legal representation—"I want my lawyer!"—as in so Hollywood films he had seen? So far in his life he hadn't encountered a situation that would need serious legal representation other than when closing the purchase of his home. Home. Julie. Emily. Did they already know what was going on here? What would Julie say when she found out that he had been arrested—detained—on route to this curious place with a rather attractive young American woman called Greta? Could he explain things to Julie? He did have mushy, dizzying feelings for Greta--"Je t'aime bien!" "Je t'adore!"—and had connected with her at a level far beyond he had ever had with Julie. Had he sinned? Had he lusted? Theirs—his with Greta—could be characterized as emotional rather than full-blown sexual affair? And how he longed to see Greta again. He wanted to know that she was fine.

"So, you've had time to think things through?" asked Puffed Head behind the table, his hair impeccably groomed.

"About what?"

"The crimes you've committed."

"What crimes?"

"You know."

"I don't."

"Betraying your motherland, and spying against her?"

Ding wanted to laugh, like the heroes he had seen in movies, but couldn't really. How would he respond to Julie when she accused him of having betrayed her? Should he react angrily? Should he laugh it off? Should he play dumb? Whichever way he would react, would he be convincing? He felt that even the most innocent soul in the world could have a guilty-as-charged look on the face when being thus confronted, because all humanity, even the noblest amongst them, were not above sin, whether in thoughts or in deeds.

"This is the most absurd thing I've ever heard," he said in a monotone, as if the one being charged was not him.

"Why did you try to pry into our national secrets?"

"What national secrets?"

Puffed Head gave School Teacher a nod, who pulled out a computer paper box from under the table. On top of the file in the box was a large vanilla envelope.

"So, let's cut to the chase. Why did you lie about the purpose of your visit to the National Museum of Modern Wars?" Puffed Head asked, watching him closely while smoothing the top of his thinning hair gingerly.

"I didn't lie. I was just trying to make it easier for the people there."

"What information, and documents, did you take from the Museum?"

"You already know," Ding said with a nod in the direction of the box. "No classified information."

"You're in no position to judge what's classified and what is not."

"The Korean War has been over for fifty years now. What secrets could there be? I was only helping an American family to find their kid brother, who must be in his early 70s now."

This is as good as the oral defense of the PhD dissertation, Ding caught himself thinking.

"Why did you fly to Beijing to visit the widow of Commissar Chen?"

"For the same reason. You wouldn't believe that Commissar Chen was an American spy, would you?"

"How I think of the late Commissar Chen is none of your business. And I have to remind you that you are the one under interrogation, not me."

Ding shrugged, and let his eyes wander to the bare walls. If I stay here any longer, I could become a geometric form in a minimalist painting of this room, too.

Puffed Head coughed. "We've been following you. We know your every move. We even know everything you said and did in the US."

Ding turned to face his inquisitors again. So they have done their homework, he thought.

Pimple picked up a sheet from a folder in front of him and began to read:

". . . Ten Years is nothing but a ripple in the long river of history, yet it should be long enough for the Chinese government to face the facts, to own up its errors, and to start the healing process. The albatross on its neck would not. . . ."

Somehow Ding didn't feel flattered while listening to Pimple reading aloud the column he had written to commemorate the tenth anniversary of Tiananmen Square. Someone on this side of the Pacific had been keeping a file on him, too.

"Why did you write rubbish like that?" Puffed Head interrupted Pimple and asked.

Ding didn't bother to reply.

"Who was behind it?"

Still no reply from Ding.

"Who are the members of your organization?"

Ding shifted in the seat and asked, slowly, and encouragingly, as if inviting a student of his to contribute to class discussions, "Why don't you read from the other piece I wrote?"

"Which piece?" Puffed Head was taken aback.

"The one about the spy plane?"

Pimple searched in the folder, found something, looked to Puffed Head deferentially, and began to read:

". . . The United States and China are being entangled in a multi-partner geopolitical tango, making it impossible for them not to step on each other's toes now and then. . . A single spark from an unexpected spot may start a hellish fire, from which neither could escape unscorched. . . ."

As Pimple struggled on, Puffed Head listened attentively and appeared to be following, and comprehending, as far as Ding could tell.

"Would I write that if I were a spy for anyone? Would any other Chinese stick his neck out to write something like that so that FBI or CIA could have a file on him, like the one you have?"

If Puffed Head was caught off guard by the logic of Ding's argument, his face didn't show it.

"Then tell us about this American girlfriend of yours," he asked.

"What do you want to know?"

"Everything."

"Didn't you say you already knew. . . everything?"

"Your attitude."

Even if his attitude was "right," Ding thought, there wasn't much information he could give about Greta. That was the strangest thing about their relationship. He had felt he knew Greta so much, so well. They had spent so much time together. They had talked about so many things and had connected at such a deep level. Yet, when it came down to it, he couldn't give more than one complete sentence of useful information about her. He didn't even have her phone number or address.

"Nothing beyond what you already know."

"Trying to be a hero? She has already confessed everything."

"What everything? Ask her to come in and compare notes."

"Hahaha, playing a trick on me so you get to see her again? I can see that in your eyes!"

Ding kept a straight face, like the heroes he admired in movies.

"Your attitude is bad," Puffed Head shook his head. "So far. You don't need me to remind you what this could mean to you, your family, here and elsewhere. Your life will be a dead end if you don't cooperate with us."

In that scratchy voice of apparent sincerity, concern, and threat Ding detected a note of the nervousness of someone close to the end of his wit.

What next? Ding pictured chili juice being forced into his nose, pointed bamboo pieces knocked into his fingernails, electric shockwaves cramping throughout his body, and a slow death by a thousand cuts.

But he was being spared the pain, and glory, perhaps, of being a hero. Slowly Puffed Head stood up from his chair. He looked tired, and disappointed.

"Why do you have to poke your nose into things other than music, architecture, whatever, if I understand that's what you do?"

"I'm a professor of humanities."

"Professor of humanities!" Puffed Head sneered. "Let me ask you this: Which side would you choose if, I mean if, China, your motherland, and America, go to war? Ehhh, my professor?"

Someone else had asked Ding the same question before. It was Rob, the pale, long-haired kid who had got hurt protesting WTO, when they chitchatted in his office one day after class.

"I'll choose Humanity's side," Ding had replied. "I'll get involved with International Red Cross, some UN peace-making effort, I guess, if I don't get sent to some internment camp."

Rob had smiled but appeared unconvinced. He must have thought Ding's answer a cop-out.

"Some choice you'd have to make!" Puffed Head grunted through his nose. "For now, though, if you want to rot in that cell of yours, it's your free choice, too!"

41

The cacophony of angry shouts, hushed whispers, and cracked loudspeakers droning in the distance quieted down. In its place was cold wind buzzing through the leaky roof of a dingy warehouse.

Old Ma, sprawled on the ground, breathed laboriously; his messy hair and sideburns quivered with each breath. Jian'er Chao huddled in a corner; his head buried between arched knees. He hadn't uttered one word since the sudden reversal of his fortune two days ago. Shanmeng's head still rang with blinding echoes, his face bruised and swollen. His lips hurt whenever he tried to chew the cold bun and sip from the bowl.

Old Ma stirred as if he wanted to sit up, the big-character posters Shanmeng had torn from the wall and placed underneath him brattled. At the noise, Jian'er looked up. Even in the darkness Shanmeng could see a mix of things in that pair of eyes: fear, shame, anger, suspicion. They looked familiar. He had seen that kind of eyes before, at the Camp, and elsewhere, when people, feeling trapped, were ready to jump, and attack viciously, regardless of who they would hurt, including themselves.

"Jian'er, let me ask you something," Old Ma said, gasping. "Why biting people like a mad dog?"

Jian'er hid his head between the legs again.

"Why?"

"You want to know why?" Jian'er said, lifting his head slowly. "Have you ever been a prisoner for three years? Three years! Every day you have to fight for every scrap of food and space. You have to watch your own shadows all the time and still get stabbed in the back. And you have no idea what the American devils do to you. They tempt you with food, candy, chocolate, and talk about freedom, God, and the crap every day. Then, they bring in these Taiwan and South Korean agents from nowhere. These damn agents smile and talk to you about freedom, God, too, and poke between your legs, behind your ass with pointed clubs at the same time, and toy with your fingers, your nose, your ears with sharp knives, if you don't agree with them, if you don't want to go places they want you to go. Heshen and I--"

"Don't mention my son!" Old Ma roared and coughed.

But Jian'er had to finish what he had probably wanted to say for many years. "Then Heshen and a few others just disappeared one night. . . I don't know what happened, where they went. . ."

Old Ma moaned, his chest heaving. "When I found you under the tree, a pitiable thing, this tiny, a little rat—"

"You should have left me alone," Jian'er whimpered, "or poured a gourd of water over my mouth."

Old Ma sighed and turned to Shanmeng. "Why are you in this mess?"

Lately Shanmeng had been wondering about that question too. And there seemed no simple, easy answer.

Growing up in a small town in the middle of nowhere, he was full of innocent fun and curiosity, sometimes too curious for his own good.

"Six days? How could God create the universe in only six days?"

"Why did God have to destroy his own children with flood? Why couldn't he save them from their evil ways if he is so powerful?"

"Why did God have to test Abraham's love by asking him to slaughter his own son for sacrifice? Shouldn't God know already?"

"Why did God divide people into rich and poor, healthy and sick, good and bad? Why not make everybody rich, healthy, good, and happy? "

"Why. . . ."

At first, when he asked such questions from the first pew, Pastor Higgins, a small man whose bald scalp glowed under the candlelight from the altar, would smile and explain in as kind and patient a voice as he could muster, his large Adam's apple wiggling strenuously, but little Simon knew that the pastor was annoyed because he would avoid calling Simon again whenever there was another raised hand.

His parents were a bit uneasy about their young son, too, but the smile on their faces betrayed no real worry at first. They thought it was a phase, and soon their son would channel his curiosity to things more reasonable and more practical.

Being nerdy—he had too many questions in the classroom, too—Simon wasn't the most popular among his classmates, either, but he was, generally, a happy lad with a sunny temperament. When did he change? When did he start to brood and become restless, and bitter?

When a new student came to his high school spring of his junior year, and sat next to him in algebra, social studies, and English classes. She was shy, always walking with lowered chin in the hallway, a few books hugged in the chest, dark, luxuriant hair cascading to the small of the back. Her features—light brown skin, vivid mouth, large, thoughtful, no, broody eyes—made her stand out among the usual blonds, redheads, hazels. She rarely spoke up in class unless called upon by the teacher.

What really caught Simon's attention was a poem she read in class, about the anguish of her father and mother who, when young, were forced to give up their native culture, language, and customs to become truly American:

> *Those good people who say that these schools*
> *Are stomachs that turn*
> *Indians into Americans*
> *Like a lion that eats an ox*
> *turns the ox into a lion,*
> *those good people*
> *are deaf to*
> *the anguished cry of the ox*
> *when being ambushed,*
> *when being torn to death*
> *one bloody piece at a time;*
> *those good people*
> *are blind to*
> *the ox that has vanished*
> *leaving in its wake*
> *a soul-less, bare-bone skeleton.*

They began to talk. He sought her out after class, of course. And they met now and then during the summer. He visited Marie's home once. Her father, Andrew Johnson, a water engineering mechanic, and her mother, Gail, a seamstress, both soft-spoken to a fault, treated Simon politely.

"Aren't they, your parents, a sort of living proof of the success of those schools?" Simon asked one day as they sat under a tall black cherry by Lake Prince. He picked up a fallen cherry and put it in his mouth. It tasted acidic and he spat it out right away. Nearby a squirrel and a gang of goldfinches, busy feasting themselves on the fruit, didn't seem to mind the acidity at all.

"At what price?" Marie said, slowly chewing the cherry in her mouth.

She wasn't much of a swimmer, and had to be coaxed into changing into shorts—"No, no swimsuits!"—and wading into the translucent water. At first she could only float and swim the doggie style, but soon her breaststroke was as good as anybody else her long arms and legs weaving in the water gracefully.

She was something to see on the ice, however, when the lake had frozen deep and solid. Her long hair tied back with a red handkerchief, she would float past skaters and spin and jump whenever she fancied, a dream in motion, and in bloom. And holding his hand she'd guide a clumsy Simon as he learnt to "walk" all over again. He did eventually manage to skate solo; whenever he tripped and fell, she would "fly" toward him from nowhere and give him her soft, warm hand.

They talked about many things, school, movies, books they were reading on their own. She loved Twain, Melville, Emerson, Chekhov, Ibsen, but was not particularly fond of James Feminore Cooper.

"Savage heroism versus civilized heroism?" she said, her eyebrows tightening. "So it is civilized to go and kill and grab somebody else's land and savage to defend it? What kind of logic is that?"

They both were fascinated by Henry Thoreau's Walden and wondered what it would be like to "disappear" from human society and live life in the raw for a while.

"I'd love to borrow my dad's car one day and we go see Walden and the cabin for ourselves. Wouldn't that be fun?" He wondered aloud.

"Sure, I'd love that, too," she said. "If we all go and see it like that, though, it wouldn't be Thoreau's Walden anymore, right? I mean we can, we should perhaps, seek and build our Walden, our own cabin, inside ourselves. Does that make sense at all?"

And their first kiss, the first real kiss Simon had with a girl, was initiated by Marie. He wasn't expecting it when he gave her a card and a small box of Hershey chocolate for her birthday, nothing poetic or extravagant. But she was so touched, her voice sparkling with joy, like it was the most precious gift she had ever received.

Simon's parents didn't take it seriously until one day they read Simon's diaries, and the letters they wrote each other. They knew that their son was drifting away from them toward a future they didn't know, and they couldn't accept. They began to drop hints about how they felt, a word here, and there, and through the tone of their voices and facial expressions whenever the girl's name came up. To no avail. Nothing changed with Simon coming home late and leaving right after dinner, except that his parents had no access to his diaries and letters anymore. Before long things escalated into direct confrontations, and a shouting match at the Thanksgiving dinner table.

"I don't want no Sitting Bull, Dancing Wolf's offspring to be my daughter-in-law, period!" his father announced finally, throwing the shiny brass fork and knife back on his plate when Simon refused to quit seeing Marie. Sally, startled, growled from underneath the dining table.

"For your information, her family name is not Sitting Bull, Dancing Wolf, Wandering Cloud," Simon mumbled after blowing his nose into the holiday-themed napkin. "It's the good old Johnson."

"That don't make a shade of difference to me!"

Tommy, home for the holiday, who was completing college on the GI Bill, intervened by picking up where they had left talking about how the Cleveland Indians' defeat of the Boston Red Sox had ruined a possible all-Boston World Series that year.

His father, not in the mood to talk sports anymore, went to the living room, followed by his mother. An argument, in subdued tones, ensued there.

"Do you have to be that harsh on the boy?" Simon heard his mother whispering. "I don't want my grandchildren to be some cross, half-breeds, either, but. . . ."

"Why can't the damn kid date someone like Dora? Why can't he be like Tommy, or Jimmy! What does he see in that girl, that kind of people that don't even get mentioned in the good old book.
"

"Can't let it happen. Have to do something. . . ."

When spring semester began, Marie didn't show up in class. Worried, he dashed to her home after school and was met with a For Sale sign in the yard and the silent darkness inside the locked door.

Simon was devastated. The beautiful dreams he had woven for his life, for their future together, had suddenly vanished without leaving behind a trace, or a slip of paper.

It was not until weeks later that he succeeded in prying from his mother an answer to the sudden disappearance of Marie's family. His parents had paid a visit to the Johnson's soon after Thanksgiving.

A part of him—his heart—went dead. He didn't make a scene at home. He never fought his father or mother again from then on despite a burning urge to scream in their faces: "How could you, of all people, do this? Your own parents felt so humiliated at the Ellis Island, and you yourselves so insulted whenever people dismiss you as drunken, lazy good-for-nothings?!" He drifted through the last year of high school like a zombie, stupefied by bouts of drinking, by indifference to himself, to his family, and to the world around him.

Sometimes he would go and lie down under the tall black cherry alone and try not to think or feel anything. As the cool, damp grass seeped through his skin and sunlight danced amongst leafy branches above, the scene of the last time he and Marie were together would pop up in his mind again.

It was the day before New Year's, unseasonably warm. They could hear snow melting crisply in the woods on the hillsides. Grass, having been refreshed by snow, was showing a hint of tender, moist green. The water in the lake was a bluish sheen under the dizzying sunshine. Yet there were no birds. Not a single goldfinch, pigeon, or blue jay on the bare black cherry. Because there was no fruit or seed or anything else for them to feast on?

"The birds," Marie said, her chin cupped in her hand propped on her knee. "I wonder if they still remember the tree, our tree, once they are gone."

"Or," Simon said, "if the tree will still remember the birds when they are back, if they do come back to the same tree."

"That's an interesting way to put it," Marie looked deep into Simon's eyes and smiled. "Let's hope they both will never forget."

They remained quiet most of the time that day, the quietness accented by the murmur of snow melting and the echo of an occasional Ford Model T, a truck, a tractor sputtering by, a lone hiker testing the capacity of his lungs, some nondescript noise, all being carried over from the town on the other side of the hill—their buffer from the town, a temporary one at the best.

As they kissed goodbye that day, the longest, most lingering kiss of theirs, Simon noticed Marie's eyes moistening, her hands caressing his hair and his neck urgently, as if trying to collect something, an irascible imprint, perhaps, for her consciousness. At the time he was touched and thought it was love, joy, and the intensity of both. Now he knew there was something else, too.

When the Korean War broke out he was the first in town to sign up. He could now leave and never look back again.

"If you want to fuck up your future with this girl," his father had blared up a few days after the Thanksgiving dinner, "that's fine, but just don't call yourself Mackenzie anymore!"

Now, a lifetime later and half a globe away, languishing in a filthy warehouse like a prisoner again, he, Shanmeng, Simon Mackenzie, no matter—hadn't he failed in running away from who he was? Who and what the heck he was anyway?

42

"If I hadn't left," Old Ma was saying, "I might have made a division commander, as that Captain Chen said, Remember? But I might have been dead ten times over, too, and my bones being scattered, and rotting God knows where."

Shanmeng stared into the deepened night as he listened to Old Ma's story. Jian'er stirred in his corner and soon snored.

Winter 1941. Gouzai Ma and a small detachment he was commanding fell into an ambush by the enemy many times their size and had to fight for days to break through. Those who made it, a dozen out of the original 51, ran out of food soon. They ate everything and anything they could find, leather belts, tree barks, dead animals found in the wild.

One night it snowed, snowflakes big as pine leaves. In the blink of the eye the world was buried in knee-deep white. Ma and his men, cold, hungry, and tired after a day of fleeing on empty bellies, huddled together in a shallow cave and drowsed. Close to daybreak, they were startled by a whirlwind of motion near the cave's mouth. The dozen men sat up, their weapons drawn, ready for the worst. Ma, bent double, crawled next to Baby Face, the young lad who was sentinel for the night.

"What is it?" he whispered, eyes wide-open, searching, finger on the trigger of the revolver. No reply from Baby Face, who seemed mesmerized by the view outside.

The snow had stopped during the night. The world outside the cave was sickeningly bright under a clear sky. There was nothing out of the ordinary, ominous, as far as eye could see.

Except for a pair of swans. Less than twenty steps from the cave's mouth. Tall, elegant, graceful, their snow-white body would have been invisible if it hadn't been for their long red beaks.

Ma was mesmerized, too, but for only a moment, because his men hadn't had any real food for days. He aimed and pulled the trigger. The deafening report rocked the sleepy hillside and was followed by a heart-piecing cry flitting into the sky.

He darted out, like a hound, and found a tall swan toppled in the snow, its white feathers soaked in dark red, its eyes still glinting with fading life. Overhead, a white phantom hovered, crying in mournful tones.

He grabbed the dead swan and dragged it into the cave. Ma

and his men had a feast that morning. They would have swallowed all the feathers if they could have cooked them. But from that day on, the bereaved swan's haunting cry followed them like a shadow everywhere they went, day and night. Not too far behind the swan were sporadic gunshots from the pursuing troops.

One day, when the lone swan caught up with them again and sang its woeful song on the roof of a mudhouse where they had stopped to give their sore feet a break, Ma pulled the trigger again. To put the bird out of its misery. And to throw the enemy off their scent. He didn't touch a morsel of the delicacy his men cooked that day. When he was wounded again in a battle the following spring—he almost lost his leg—he had a good excuse to leave and return home.

"Did I chicken out?" Old Ma said, shifting, the wrinkled big-character posters brattled underneath him. "I don't know. I just felt that I had seen enough killing of lives. I'd killed so many that I lost count. I didn't want to be a 'butcher' anymore. I'm not a bookman, but I know we've had too many wars already. Dynasties rise and fall, emperors come and go, like change of seasons, but it's always the common folks who suffer, who have to do the fighting and dying, who have to bear it all, losing sons, losing husbands, losing brothers, and watching womenfolk being raped right in front of your eyes without being able to do a damn thing about it. So, I quit. I didn't want to have anything to do with wars anymore. Oh, what a moron I was! How can I really quit? 'Cause war has never and will never quit me."

43

He woke up with a start when the door cracked ajar, and a chipped plate and a bowl was being pushed in. Old Ma coughed and breathed even again. Jian'er, head wrapped in both hands, elbows propped on knees, seemed still fast asleep. He was about to fall back to sleep again when Jian'er bolted up and made a dash to the door. "I want to speak to someone," he demanded shrilly, "Commander Huifa . . . any Red Guard from the province! I've important information to report!" He was led out of the room.

"Mountains can be moved, but. . . ." Old Ma sighed.

In a few minutes a gang of Red Guards rushed in, several armed with sticks and old M-1 rifles. They tied Old Ma and Shanmeng up, had them strung together with a rope, and led them outside. A solemn procession marched out of the village, being watched by curious, anxious, frightened eyes from behind doors.

About halfway up the long slope of the tall hill outside the village, the young Red Guards were beginning to show signs of boredom and fatigue, but they marched on, sipping water from grass-green flasks and biting steam buns from their bags embroidered with "Serve The People."

The sky and the trees and bushes rippling into the nebulous distance looked the same as the last time he was here, with Peide, over ten years ago, yet so much had changed. The trail, paved with cedar and pebbles, was now wide enough for a truck. He was being marched in the opposite direction of home to only God knows where, to an unknown minefield of future, fear and despair droning inside him like the waterfall crashing down somewhere in the distance. Thinking thus, and thinking that he would never see Fuli, Yangyang, Yangmei, and Ah Bao—where the heck is Yingzi now?—again, Shanmeng felt his legs weakening, his body churning with fits of feverish sweat.

"Are you all right?" Old Ma turned and asked with his eyes. And in those eyes Shanmeng saw the same hearty laugh he had seen on a dark night many years ago: "This old horse can still race anyone. Want to try me? Hahaha!" Shanmeng nodded and hastened to keep up.

When they stopped for meal after sunset, the young Red Guards dropped to the ground like sandbags and complained about stiffened ankles and blisters.

Commander-in-Chief Nina Chen, sitting on a rock, hair messy with sweat, removed the sneakers to take a look at her feet, eyebrows knit in pain.

"Anybody knows how to get rid of blisters?"

No one replied. No one seemed to know what to do.

Old Ma hesitated, and then limped over.

The girl looked up, vigilance in her eyes: "What do you want?"

"You asked about the blisters."

"Okay?"

"You've got a needle?"

44

He refused to sit on his butt and rot into the gooey, fetid cement. He sang every song he had learnt when he was a child. There were not too many and they were all from the Eight Model Peking Operas, pet projects of Madame Mao, Mao's poems that had been turned into songs, hymns celebrating the Long March and other Revolution milestones. He thought he had long forgotten them. He thought the wind and rain of time had ground away whatever those fiery days had sculpted in his consciousness. He thought Beethoven, Mozart, Picasso, Shakespeare, Sophocles, Faulkner, Hardy, Freud, Derrida, had had enough time to elbow away a few things in the finite, precious space of his mind. But he was wrong. These revolutionary melodies and lyrics had seeped so deep into his being that he could never shed them like skin. He could still let them gush out of his lips shamelessly, acutely conscious of the irony that they were from a time that had scarred him irreparably.

When he had sung his voice hoarse, Ding would become quiet and let his mind wander back to the scenes of his life and replay their sequels, real, imagined, while lying on the tiny metal wire bed, sitting cross-legged, doing push-ups, sit-ups, or headstands against the wall.

One morning, minutes into a headstand, blood coursing in his temples forcefully, as if ready to burst, the door opened. Instead of the usual cold buns and congee and pickled vegetables, he saw a pair of leather shoes, newly shined, sharply creased pants, well starched shirt, and meticulously groomed thin hair, benefit of generous use of mousse.

Puffed Head stood at the door and watched and waited patiently for Ding to come down from the wall and stand on his feet again.

"Professor Ding," he moved closer and grasped Ding's hand warmly, "why the heck didn't you tell me the real purpose of your visit in the first place? We could have avoided so much misunderstanding. Hahaha."

The real purpose of my visit? Ding was perplexed by the sudden warmth from an unexpected source. Hadn't he told them a thousand times already?

"We would have appreciated the significance of your effort to help the American family find their brother lost during the Korean War. As you well know, Sino-American relations are not in the best shape since the spy plane incident. This, I mean what you're doing, could help repair. . . okay, you know all this already, I figure, being a professor of humanities. I'm embarrassed for showing off my poor skills in front of a master carpenter. . . ."

Puffed Head's two associates, School Teacher and Pimple, were waiting outside, a smile lurking underneath their otherwise expressionless faces.

"Based on the information you've provided us," Puffed Head continued, "I believe we've found someone, a likely match to what you're looking for. When you are finished cleaning up and packing, we can arrange for a car to—"

"Oh, that won't be necessary," Ding tried to sound calm even though his head reeled giddily. "Just give me the address, the contact info, and I'll be fine."

A few minutes later Ding gave his cell one last glance and stepped out. Passing the old guard, he stopped and grasped his

hand. "Thank you for taking good care of me for so long!" he said.
"No sweat," the old guard grinned.

45

Shanmeng had stared at the pad of paper and pen for three days without putting one word down. He knew that the best way to protect oneself under such circumstances was to say and speak the least one could.

The room felt smaller than the one he and fellow POWs had crammed in at the Camp. It was damp and smelled of urine and odors left behind by its previous occupants. The town, however, seemed larger than when he and Peide had stayed overnight many years ago, with wider streets, more buildings. Everything looked dusty, gray, so wreathed in red—red armbands, red slogans, red flags, Little Red Books, red posters . . . a sea of loud, flustering red.

"Write down your confessions!" He was told again and again. What was there to confess, really? Was he a spy? A Russian spy? A spy for the country he had long left behind? What was there to spy on? Mountains, rivers, trees, shrubs, sunrise, sunset, rain, snow, flood, drought, simple good-heartedness of folks who tilled the soil their ancestors had tilled and drunk the water that had irrigated and deluged the same farmland generations after generations? Who would be interested in the intelligence? Who would be paying for it? None, perhaps. The land he had chosen over his native land, the land where he had thought he could disappear and live unassumingly, the land that claimed to be blessed with a splendid civilization of at least four thousand years—why was there this much madness, this much stupidity that pit neighbors against each other, forced wife to condemn husband, son father, children their parents, students their teachers?

"What? Not a single word?" his jailers—Shanmeng couldn't

tell they were police officers or Red Guards—looked upset whenever they came to check on him. "Your attitude is bad and this doesn't bode well for you."

Shanmeng, sitting on the dreadful floor, mulled it drowsily and often the same old question presented itself again: Have I made a wrong choice?

He didn't have an answer for that. He had been so messily entangled in the life of his choice that the question had become irrelevant.

Would he languish here? What would happen to Fuli, Yangyang, and Yangmei if he wouldn't see them again? And Ah Bao? That was the hardest part of it all: The life of the Ma's would have followed its own trajectory if he—Simon, Shanmeng, Red Hair—hadn't bumped in them and thrown everything off balance. But he couldn't really say that, could he? That wouldn't be fair to himself, would it? Because when it came down to it, human society was no more than the crisscrossing—involuntary, forced, deliberate, no matter—of the lives of its members, which would produce warm smiles, angry glares, faster heartbeats, happy unions, tragic collisions, burning, flattened villages and towns and bodies falling by the wayside. He couldn't have helped whatever choice he had made.

He was aroused by the muffled sound of a familiar voice down the hallway: "Go ask General Ye. Ask Captain Chen. That's all I'm going to say."

Someone sneered: "Take a pee and see who you are. Wanting to see some General Ye, Captain Chen! You'll sit here and watch your stinky ass rot until you've come clean!"

Old Ma laughed hoarsely, a the-world-can-go-to-hell kind of laugh.

Shanmeng himself was visited twice a day, one in the morning and one in the evening, for food (congee, steam bun, pickled vegetables) and for confessions. Otherwise he was left alone. Where he was, he was safe, ironically, compared to Fuli and the kids, who were left to fend for themselves. What kind of husband, and father, was he? When could he see them all again? And Old

Ma, only a few cells down the hallway?

An eternity had thus crept by when one day, close to noon, there came a commotion from the other end of the hallway. Voices talking in excited tones and heavy footsteps. A long minute later the commotion moved in his direction, toward his cell. A key was inserted into the lock. The rust-molded door swung open.

Standing akimbo in the doorway, silhouetted against the light through a window in the hallway, was a man in wool army uniform. Although the face was in the shadow, the eyes behind the wire-rimmed glasses glinted with acute consciousness of his status and the situation at hand. Behind him were two young soldiers, armed.

So, the moment has come? The thought flitted across his mind. They were here to take him out to face a firing squad? Was he ready? Did he have any final remarks to make? What would he say anyway?

"Simon," the man said in English—perfect American accent—and stepped in. The voice of a ghost from the past.

Shanmeng was flabbergasted.

"Shanmeng, oh, yes, Red Hair! Hahaha, what a name!" The man burst out laughing, the voice echoing metallically between ceiling, floor, and walls. "It's me. Peter. Peide. Captain Chen."

"Peter?" The two syllables sounded rusty, awkward even to his own ears.

Of course, it was Peter. The man in front of him looked all but identical to the young intelligence officer who had helped get him where he was today, only that this was a somewhat older, more distinguished copy. The eyes behind the glasses blinked with the same simian playfulness.

Something else had not changed: Peter, the captor, Simon, the captive. Sort of.

Peter, no, Commissar Chen, grasped his hand, shook it vigorously, and patted him in the back: "You're liberated, Red Hair!" He turned and nodded to someone outside the door. "So is Comrade Ma."

Old Ma shuffled in. Hairy, stinky, his eyes glowing with a

crazed smile.

Commissar Chen had been sent down by the Cultural Revolutionary Committee of the Central Government, headed by no less than Madame Mao herself, to inspect how well the prairie fire of Revolution had spread from Beijing, since the first shot was fired by Mao himself with his "Down With the Capitalist Headquarters!" big-character poster.

"When Nina, my daughter, told me a bizarre story of this red-haired American, possibly an American spy, she and her comrades-in-arms had encountered in the middle of nowhere, I thought it had to be you!" Commissar Chen said as they walked toward a black Volga outside the county jail.

Who else could it be, really? Shanmeng thought, grinning.

"I'd love to go with you and visit Twin-Sun River again," Commissar Chen said, opening the door of the car for Shanmeng and Old Ma. "But so many things are rivaling for my attention. Oh, Red Hair, I love this new name of yours, take good care, and try not to get into anymore trouble. I may not be able to come and literate you again."

"I'll have to liberate myself then," Shanmeng grinned heartily.

46

Ding found a phone booth outside a shopping plaza not far from Judge Bao Park—the building where he had spent the last two weeks was actually only a ten-minute walk away.

"Jesus, Jie, what a mess you've got yourself into!" Professor Zhu marveled at the other end. "You're lucky that I'm your father-in-law and know a few people high up there. Otherwise--"

"That's exactly why I married your daughter!" was on the tip of his tongue, as a joke, but he held it back. He knew that was true at least partially true. And on account of the old man alone, if nothing else, he would have to make his marriage with Julie work. Not to mention Emily.

"Your university has been very anxious about you. The president, dean of your school, department chair, your colleagues and students—they wrote and called the Chinese embassy, the American Consulate in Shanghai, anyone they could reach. They vouched for you. Tom, and Dora, they called every day. Your school started, let me see, Aug. 27, four days into the fall semester already, but the department chair, Dr. Evans, said to tell you not to worry. Your classes are covered."

"What about Julie and Emily?" Ding shifted the phone to his right ear. Busy shoppers and casual pedestrians passed by. One man stopped at about two meters away from him, waited, and then changed his mind.

"They've worried themselves to death. They wanted to come back to help you. I told them not to 'cause it would only complicate things. Besides, I'm still alive and can still pull some strings. Oh, they had their citizenship ceremony last Friday. Julie and Emily sounded thrilled. Your local paper had a big story about them, and you. Mmmm, what else? Okay, I almost forgot. The two are in New York City now, as guests of Tom, Dora, and their grandson, something like that. They are visiting and waiting to welcome you home, red carpet, at JFK."

Ding could picture what his family reunion would be like. And smiled.

"Shall I book the flight for you, Jie? Yes? Good. How about giving you a week to tie up the loose ends there?"

"That'd fantastic, Dad." Somehow that term of endearment didn't come out right to his ear even though the old man had been nothing but kind to him.

"And Greta, that accomplice of yours," Professor Zhu said, an afterthought, perhaps, "she came back to school quietly, didn't talk to anyone, and then disappeared. Nobody knows where she's gone. Amazing young woman. Jie, if I were you, I—"

"I understand," Ding interrupted. His heart ached dully. Greta, a born adventurer. Could she have been sent over for some clandestine operation? Pooo! He dismissed the idea right away. For what? To gather intelligence of Chinese art history? Where's Greta in the world now? He wondered.

The next call he made was to his mother, who picked up the phone after four long rings. A young woman, who had been waiting for the pay phone five to six steps away, shot him an angry glare and left.

"Jie, I thought you. . . ." mother sniffled.

"I'm all right now, Ma," he said, a lump in his throat.

"When I couldn't find a word about you, your whereabouts, from anyone, I felt the world sinking in darkness again like 30 years ago. You still remember those days, Jie?"

"Yes, but everything is all right now, Ma."

"And I blamed myself for having not told you what I should have a long time ago. What if . . . and I didn't have a chance to tell you at all?"

What now? Ding's heart clinched. Some dark family secret? Someone in the family diagnosed with terminal illness?

"My fault, Ma, but now you have a chance to. . . ." The mouthpiece shook in his hand.

"Oh, nothing much, really," Mother said. "It's just that whatever bothered you about your father, you know what I'm talking about? he told me himself. Everything. Soon after he was liberated. And I said to him that it didn't matter as long as he was all right, that he had come out alive."

That dark night so long ago, everything he had seen that dark night while propped on the windowsill, the ensuing denunciation rallies, himself marching to the podium— surfaced in his mind again like an old nightmare being played from a beat-up projector.

"Jie, are you still there?"

"Mmmm."

"Your father was so proud of you and couldn't quit talking about you when you left for America. It was his dying wish that I tell you this. I mean, Jie, if I can understand him, and forgive him, why can't you? The old man. . . ."

Ding's eyes misted, and leaked, dousing the memory of a tortured time in his life.

47

The same tall walnut tree stood guarding the entrance when the Volga pulled into the village by early evening, but it seemed uncannily quiet. Later they were told that a dog in a neighboring village had gone mad and bit a man who in turn chased and bit people like a mad dog. So all the dogs in the river valley had been killed to prevent rabies from becoming a pandemic outbreak.

Knowing Commissar Chen, they didn't insist that the soldier driver stay overnight before heading back. Besides, what could they have to treat the young man anyway?

No light was on in his home. The door was locked. Shanmeng pushed and through the crack saw only darkness inside. And deadly silence.

"Perhaps they are all at my place?" Old Ma suggested.

They hurried along the familiar trail leading to the Ma residence. He could make out the bleary outline of the house in the thickening dusk even from a distance.

The front door was open. Astride the threshold was a figure, a young man, actually, with a long stick in hand, like a sentinel. He bolted up at the sight of the approaching shadows and made some threatening noise, the long stick at the ready.

"Ah Bao," Old Ma cried out. "It's grandpa! And Uncle Red Hair!"

Two smaller figures came rushing out, Yangyang and Yangmei. Ah Bao whimpered excitedly: "Grandpa back. Red Hair back. Told you so!"

"Where's your ma?" Shanmeng asked as they all went inside;

on the old Eight Immortals Table were bowls and unfinished supper.

Ah Bao whimpered again. This time, it was the sound of unutterable pain.

"Mama, no more," Yangmei said between choking sobs, her hands tight around his strong neck. "Mama is gone."

"What happened?! What happened?!" The sky crashed on Shanmeng's head.

Between Ah Bao and the two younger children, Shanmeng and Old Ma got a gist of what had happened.

Fuli had been so distraught after Shanmeng and Old Ma were taken away that she would sit at the door and mumble the same thing over and again: "I've killed him! I've killed them!" She still cooked and washed for the kids, but when they talked to her, she sounded like she wasn't there anymore.

"Ah Bao," she said one day at the dining table. "Ma may have to go away, for a long, long time. Will you take care of your brother and sister?"

Ah Bao nodded even though he didn't understand why his mother was saying this.

"You will be a good brother to your sister, and Ah Bao, too?" She turned to Yangyang and asked. The boy had a vague feeling that something was not right but was too young to be alarmed by what was going on.

"Where're you going, Ma?" Yangyang asked. "To see pa and grandpa?"

"Maybe, don't really know," their mother said blankly, then turned to Yangmei. "Sis, you'll listen to your brothers, right?"

"Mmm," the little girl promised readily.

One evening Fuli went to the riverside to wash things and didn't return. Two days later, a woman's body was found downstream, bloated, face torn to shreds by fish.

Shanmeng dropped Yangmei down on her feet and bolted out of the door. Fuli! Fuli! He hollered with his whole being, but no sound came out of his mouth. He ran to the riverside, to the washing station he had set up many years ago, and jumped.

The water, icy cold, poured bubbly into his pockets and seeped through to his skin. It burnt like fire, but he didn't give a damn. He struck forward, water splashing nearby and rippling into endless darkness. Fuli, I'm coming!

Epilogue

Ding had tried to imagine what he would look like today ever since he saw the picture in Tom's basement over three months ago. Grizzled and wrinkled. Bald at the top. Hunchbacked with a cane. Cataractous if not semi-blind. Hard of hearing, for sure. All possible older versions of the young man with deep-set eyes grinning happily to the camera. But meeting the man in person— the needle he had been looking for in a big sea, so to speak—in the deep mountains was not exactly what Ding had been prepared for.

Simon Mackenzie, aka Shanmeng, Red Hair, didn't look crushed by the 48 years of life in his adopted country. A bit taller than his elder brother, Simon ("Call me Shanmeng!") was upright in posture, brisk in movement, and still had a firm handshake, the roughened hands of a life-time farmer. His hair had thinned to less than half his more youthful self, but far from becoming bald.

In place of the restlessness simmering underneath the deep-set eyes was calm, not necessarily resignation or indifference, let alone cynicism, but an attitude, a philosophy, Ding was ready to call it, a kind of humor only people who had weathered it all and had come to peace with themselves (and with the rest of the world?) could have achieved.

There was something in his vocal quality, pitch, cadence, timbre, enunciation, all of these together, that reminded Ding of Tom, and the teary old man in the aged videotape. His speech was somewhat slow, tinged with a noticeable slur, and he switched easily between Chinese, with flawless local accent, and English, but Ding detected a bit of stiffness, a passé, another era kind of flavor in his English idioms. He tried but couldn't put his finger on it. If only Greta—who had drifted through his life like a cloud—were here.

Shanmeng remained composed as he sat in the sofa and turned the pages of the album which had traveled a long, tortuous way before reaching his hands. He stared at the young man in the picture taken half a century ago as if he couldn't believe that he had been that young once, or it was actually a younger version of himself at all.

"Simon," he looked up from the album and murmured, for the benefit of his own ears, and for everyone else in the room. "Shanmeng. They do sound alike, don't they?"

Ding gave the old man a reassuring smile. All the signs and billboards on the road map, undrawn—though Captain Peter Chen did sketch something in his diaries—and haphazardly followed, had led him to Tom's long lost kid brother.

They couldn't play the videotape because Shanmeng didn't own a VCR and because the VCRs of his neighbors used a different system than that in America. I should have thought of that, Ding regretted.

Shanmeng's wife, a vibrant woman in her mid-50s, marveled and sighed as each new page in the album was turned.

So did a middle-aged man sitting on the other side of Shanmeng, his eyes wide-open in wonder: "Uncle Red Hair, look! Their noses!"

"Their noses, mmm, not bigger than mine, right, Ah Bao?"

"No. The same!" Ah Bao cried out happily, like a child.

A farm dog, with black and white spots, crouched near the door watching the coming and going on the cedar-padded road outside, its ears twitching alertly.

"It all seemed like a long-forgotten dream," the old man murmured as he closed the album finally.

Then it was time to see the host family's albums. Shanmeng's wife came to where Ding was sitting and narrated. The old man himself remained in the sofa; his eyes narrowed in an apparent effort to put back the missing pieces in the puzzle of his life.

"No," Shanmeng's wife sighed. "There are no pictures of Ah Bao's grandma, my mother. I don't remember a photographer ever coming to our village back then. Ah Bao still remembers her, though, and gets excited when we talk about Grandma."

There were several yellowed pictures of a young woman in school uniform: white blouse, black skirt, short hair, a bit reserved, but full of esprit, alone or with friends.

"Ah Bao's mother, my sister-in-law, when she was a student at County High in the late '40s. Isn't she a beauty?" She took a glance at her husband, who was still gazing outside with the same lost look in his eyes.

One album was filled with pictures of a young woman in faded army uniform, armband on the left arm, the Little Red Book hugged close to heart, brimming with youth, verve, and zeal, alone, together with comrades-in-arms, in front of Mao's old residence in Changsha, at the summit of Mount Jinggang, on the Tiananmen Square, and atop the Heavenly Peace Rostrum—pictures from the same era that had seared a young boy named Jie badly.

"Those," the hostess dismissed with a smile, "were from my wild days."

There was a Happy Family picture dated spring 1977 taken under the tall ginkgo tree with their house in the background, the first such picture of the family.

Sitting on a bench in the middle was Grandpa, grayed, lank, as if having just recovered from a long bout of illness, but in good spirits, flanked by Shanmeng, a man who had just passed his prime, but by no means old yet, and his wife, a more matronly, tamed copy of the vivacious young Red Guard in the earlier pictures; behind them stood Ah Bao, grinning, carefree, and two other children, a young man about 18 or 19 years old, and a girl a few years younger, both looking strikingly handsome and intelligent.

"My father," Ding's hostess murmured, pointing at the old man in the picture. "Ah Bao's grandpa. He passed away not long after that picture was taken. . . . The youngest two? That's Yangyang and Yangmei, my sister-in-law's kids. Aren't they adorable?"

The dog whimpered vigilantly when a faint burr appeared in the distance, which soon crescendoed into a truck carrying a bulldozer that seemed too large and heavy for it to handle. As the truck rumbled past, the very ground shaking, the dog charged out, growling furiously, followed by a laughing Ah Bao trying to rein it back.

Shanmeng turned his gaze back inside his home, an irritated look on his face: "Twin-Sun River Shangri-La, that's what they're building here. What a pretentious name."

Ding and his hostess returned their attention to a new album which featured pictures of Yangyang and Yangmei, their college days, weddings, and families.

"Where are they now?" Ding asked when he had advanced to the last page.

"Oh, they're not too interested in this ghost-wouldn't-lay-eggs place, Shangri-La or not," the hostess said as she organized the albums on the coffee table. "Visiting? Yes. Staying forever? No."

"C'mon, Yingzi," Shanmeng was back to the conversation again. "You really want them to live here?"

"And you?" Yingzi retorted, smiling.

The old man shrugged.

Yangyang, a brilliant computer engineer, had been too busy running a high-tech consulting firm in Shenzhen to visit more than once a year. The main theme of Yangmei's life, a graduate of Shanghai Institute of International Trade, was flying across time zones to hammer out deals with transnational conglomerates.

And the grandchildren?

"Marianne," Shanmeng said, shaking his head, "has just started high school, but she's already dreaming of going to college in the States and earning a MBA, MD, something like that. . . . Ray, that little devil, is too young to think that far yet. He is really into music, watercolor, Chinese ink brush, cartoons, whatever catches his fancy. Kids nowadays."

Shanmeng himself had turned down invitations to teach English at a major university in the province capital, and at the county normal school, Fuli and Yingzi's alma mater, in the early

1980s.

"I told the schools' representatives," Shanmeng chuckled. "I'm not going anywhere. I belong here. And I'm teaching English any way."

By then the village school, led by Principal Yingzi Ma, had expanded into a full-fledged school with a junior high division. Theirs was the first in the county to offer English beginning from fifth grade. Shanmeng developed most of the material for the English lessons he taught, from basic to advanced.

Since his retirement (Yingzi still had a couple more years to go before calling it quits) Shanmeng had lived a quiet but busy life, reading, writing, and taking care of the vegetable garden and the orchard. Half of their house, actually a two-story building with a balcony, looked like a more recent addition, the other half, lower, much smaller, seemed as ancient as the gingko tree.

"I wouldn't want to hear about it," Shanmeng grinned, "but Yangyang and Yangmei would have raised hell if we hadn't agreed to their modernization and expansion scheme."

"When I came back from Beijing that winter," Yingzi interjected, "it was hell here." She went to their study and came back with a shoe box.

"Yingzi?" Shanmeng looked into his wife's face. "I thought that was for you, and for ourselves, exclusively."

"I'm the coauthor," Yingzi smiled, "and own half of the story, as you've always said. So I—"

"What is it?" Ding asked, his interest piqued. "I don't mean to—"

"Nothing," Shanmeng murmured, "but 'Pages full of fantastic talk, /Penned with heart-rending tears'—" The old man let the verse hang in midair, a pained, faraway look surfacing in his deep-set eyes.

"So that the world doesn't call the author mad," Ding improvised. "His soul it has to hear."

"Exactly, Professor Ding," Yingzi gave her husband a reproachful look. "That's what I've been telling him." With that she handed Ding the box which contained a big stack of manuscripts.

Ding turned to Shanmeng. "May I?"

"She's my boss, you know," Shanmeng feigned resignation. "Principal Ma both at home and at school. You know what I mean, Jie?"

"I feel your pain, Simon, I mean, Shanmeng," Ding flashed him a knowing smile and picked up the first sheet from the stack.

It was in English. The handwriting was a neat, graceful cursive that Ding rarely saw among his students today. It was penmanship he would love to have mastered himself.

Ah Bao came back breathily, followed by the dog wagging its tail. "Dog chase, auntie. Long way!" he reported, took a cup from Yingzi, and drank noisily. Chubby and slow in movement, he could have been a rather handsome man if his eyes glinted with just a bit more intelligence.

"There's a good boy, Ah Bao," Yingzi reassured, her eyes following Ah Bao as he went and sat next to Shanmeng in the sofa. The old man rubbed Ah Bao's gray-streaked hair feelingly.

"More tea, Professor Ding?" Yingzi asked as her eyes moved away from her nephew to the guest.

"I'm fine, really."

Suddenly Ding felt an overwhelming urge to ask the question that had been on the tip of his tongue since he stepped into their home. He sat up straight in the chair, looked Shanmeng in the eye, and asked in as calm a voice as he could muster: "Shanmeng, I'm curious why you didn't try to reconnect with your family all these years?"

"My family?" Shanmeng seemed taken aback by the question. "My family is here. We're already as connected as can be, right, hon?" He turned to Yingzi for confirmation.

"He means your parents and siblings in the US, Red Hair!" Yingzi said half-seriously and came to sit by her husband, holding his hand in hers.

She and the kids, Yingzi said, Yangyang, Yangmei, and the grandchildren, had been nagging him about it for years, but Shanmeng sat there and listened and wouldn't do anything. One day when the nagging became too much for him to bear, he flared:

"Will you all just quit? Will you leave it be? You won't be happy until you have gone around and upset everybody's life, including mine?"

"They, whoever they are," said Yangyang, who was about to graduate from college then, "must have been looking for you all these years. Just imagine what they must have been through."

"And it'd be selfish just to think of your own feelings, dad," Yangmei said, without daring to look her father in the eye. She had just received the results of her college entrance exams.

"Shhhh!" Yingzi intervened when she saw the cornered look in her husband's eyes. She remembered being terrified by the same look winter 1976 when two men from Beijing came in a jeep to talk to Shanmeng and her father about a Peide Chen. Her father, a frail old man then, stood at the door and admonished the visitors: "Take it from a Long Marcher who can still breathe today: Captain Chen is a good man. I know a good man when I see one!" And sent the visitors on their way back to where they came from.

"Why didn't you shut the door on me?" Ding couldn't resist.

"Oh, you," Shanmeng chuckled. "You looked harmless enough. To quote Pa, I know a good man when I see one. But don't push it, young man. I won't allow any intruder or imposter in my 世外桃源, Peach Orchard Outside the World, you know."

"You mean your Walden?"

"Walden?" Shanmeng looked puzzled. "That rings a bell, a very distant bell."

"An American version of the Peach Orchard Outside the World."

"Oh." The puzzle lingered in the old man's eyes.

Ding hadn't been too impressed when he visited Walden Pond a few summers ago. The pond itself wasn't big enough to have an imposing presence. What really ruined the impression for him was tourists like himself, swarms of them, taking snapshots, bringing with them beach towels and lounges, and endless streams of sputtering cars. . . . He wondered what Thoreau himself would have to say if he saw the curious multitudes hurrying through his erstwhile refuge from human society: The same old mass of men lead lives of quiet desperation? Real Waldens, real Peach Orchards Outside the World, Ding thought, must be few and far between in today's world. Probably nonexistent.

The dog barked suddenly and charged out again. "Back!" Ah Bao hollered and went after the dog. The same truck, now free of its load, roared past again.

Shanmeng frowned and hurried out to check on Ah Bao and the dog.

"Tell you something," Yingzi whispered, "the old man's been more receptive to the idea, you know, recently, since the stroke he had last year. Oh, the feverish delirium he was in when I returned after, you know, my wild Red Guard days. The poor man couldn't even recognize me. . . ."

Ding read deep into the night in bed in a guest room upstairs. He was captivated from the very first page: In a thatched hut on a river in the deep mountains, the eccentric, reclusive first-person narrator is bent over the scroll entrusted to him by an ancient traveler who came from a faraway place. . . . .

About 50 pages later Ding glanced at his watch and reached to turn off the light. Something to read on the flight home for sure.

If the story is inspired by the experience of Simon Mackenzie, aka Shanmeng, Red Hair, at all, Ding mused in the darkness, so far there is not the faintest allusion to his earlier life. The fever that Yingzi, Principal Ma, mentioned must have burnt holes in his memory. The things Tom has prepared should help. And there's so much I can tell him about Princetown, and Princetown West High. Oh, yes, wait till the brothers meet again after half a century.

The Boeing 747 he was on board was caught in thunderous lightning and almost crashed. At the airport Julie and Emily ran toward him with flowers. Between hugging and cupping Julie's face in his quivering hands, he heard himself declaring: "*Je t'aime bien! Non, Je t'adore!*" "What?" Julie's face, lined with confusion, jerked away. "What did you say?" Before he could explain, the glass ceiling of the airport had collapsed into a small dimly lit room where Greta, stripped to the waist, was guiding his hand to the tattoo below her belly button. A sudden, gentle tap from the window startled him. He turned and saw a young face pressed against the pane from outside, the eyes popped with astonishment. Emily's eyes. No, the eyes of the 9-year-old Jie. No, the eyes of Julie. He broke away from Greta and ran after the shadow that had leapt off the windowsill. The shadow, having morphed into a dried red leaf, being cheered on by a gusty wind, kept bouncing away from his grasp, and just when he finally caught it in his hand he tripped, and plunged into the grinning mouth of a teary old man whose face looked so familiar. . . .

Ding woke up in a puddle of sweat; his legs, stiff and sore, as if having run a marathon, dangled over the bedside. What a dream, he thought, slowly pulling his legs back on the gossamer bamboo mat. Some subconscious way for the mind to sort things out, perhaps; a sign that time for reckoning has come—A rooster crowed from somewhere downstairs. Its fierce note held so long as if the rooster wouldn't quit serenading the dawn until its throat bled. In its wake arose a choir of roosters near and far, a choir of dogs, frogs, toads, eels, snakes, nameless insects along the river under the moon-lit summer-autumn sky—and time to get up, for sure, and go with Shanmeng to the top of the hill to witness a ball of fire, of gold ablaze, rising, melting heaven and earth and river in its splendor.

Acknowledgements

Heart-felt thanks go to the many people who have helped shape this book in so many ways:

— Arthur Ford and Patricia Dickinson for reading the complete manuscript and offering numerous constructive comments;

— Louisa Burns-Bisogno, Pam McDaniel, Ellen Muir, Ma-Yi Theatre Company, the National Academy of Television Arts and Sciences (New York Chapter), and the many talented members of Actors Equity Association, who presented an impressive stage reading of a screenplay I wrote based on the story on March 24, 2008;

— Tong Ruimin of Shanghai Theater Academy and his many talented colleagues and friends for a well-received stage production of a play I wrote based on the story on April 24-28, 2009;

— Merrilee Warholak, Chris Robyn, Andy Thibault, John Briggs, Lionel Bascom, Dorothy Aufiero, Mark Byers, Ji Wang, Frank Xiao, Joan Chen, Jiangchao Wang, and many more for their friendship, encouragement, and assistance;

I am deeply grateful to Connecticut State University for a grant which made it possible for me to travel to China to conduct research for the book.

Finally, I owe so much to my father and mother as well as my brother Shouxing and sister Yumei for their love and to Xiaohong, my wife, Frank, and Crystal for being the first readers of the story and for their unfaltering faith, love, and support.

About the Author

A native of Nanjing, China, Shouhua Qi came to the United States for his doctoral studies in 1989. He is the author of *Purple Mountain: A Story of the Rape of Nanking* (2010; entitled *When the Purple Mountain Burns: A Novel*, when first published in 2005), *Red Guard Fantasies and Other Stories* (2007), *Bridging the Pacific: Searching for Cross-Cultural Understanding Between the United States and China* (2000), and the editor and translator of *Pearl Jacket and Other Stories: Flash Fiction from Contemporary China* (2008).

His most recent novel, *Becoming Monkey King: The Untold Story* (2025), is a fantasy/mystery/adventure, the 16th century Chinese classic *Journey to the West* reimagined for readers in the twenty-first century and told for the first time in Monkey's own witty, whimsical, and (self)righteous voice.

Among his many other books are *Culture, History, and the Reception of Tennessee Williams in China* (Palgrave Macmillan, 2022), *Adapting Western Classics for the Chinese Stage* (Routledge, 2018), *The Brontë Sisters in Other Wor(l)ds* (Palgrave Macmillan, 2014), and *Western Literature in China and the Translation of a Nation* (Palgrave Macmillan, 2012)

Qi is a professor emeritus of English at Western Connecticut State University and adjunct professor of English and Comparative Literature at San Diego State University.

Webpage: https://sites.wcsu.edu/qis/

www.ingramcontent.com/pod-product-compliance
Lightning Source LLC
Chambersburg PA
CBHW031313170626
46807CB00001B/406